"LUCY, WE HAVE TO TALK ..."

Jeff gave her a beseeching look. "We've shared too much. I have to know...is there any future for us?"

"Jeff, don't," she whispered. "Don't ask me now." Why couldn't he just leave things as they were?

"When then? When this is all over and you're back with Roy?" he asked sharply. "Can you honestly say you love him?"

"I..." she began, but her voice faltered, and moisture glistened in her eyes.

Jeff touched her cheek. He felt like a heel, but he had to know.

"I don't know how to answer you," she finally mumbled, turning away from him. But her heart knew the truth. Roy was a cowardly excuse. Lucy was afraid of her feelings for Jeff, afraid of being hurt once again....

ABOUT THE AUTHOR

Shadow on the Sun is set in sunny, romantic
Mexico, a favorite vacation spot for the Colorado-
based writing team of Lynn Erickson. Carla
Peltonen and Molly Swanton have both been there
several times with their families. Molly never did
find any money in her hotel room, but Carla had
a few tense moments on a small plane like the
heroine's. Both writers swear they saw the real
Jeff Zanicek. Fans of this delightful twosome
should watch for their next book, a thriller set in
western Canada.

Books by Lynn Erickson

HARLEQUIN SUPERROMANCE

132–SNOWBIRD
157–THE FACES OF DAWN
184–A CHANCE WORTH TAKING
199–STORMSWEPT
231–A DANGEROUS SENTIMENT
255–TANGLED DREAMS
276–A PERFECT GEM
298–FOOL'S GOLD
320–FIRECLOUD

HARLEQUIN INTRIGUE

42–ARENA OF FEAR

Lynn Erickson

SHADOW ON THE SUN

Harlequin Books

TORONTO • NEW YORK • LONDON
AMSTERDAM • PARIS • SYDNEY • HAMBURG
STOCKHOLM • ATHENS • TOKYO • MILAN

Published March 1989

First printing January 1989

ISBN 0-373-70347-3

This book is dedicated
to Lucy Hibberd who
answered every question I had about flying.

CHAPTER ONE

JEFF ZANICEK STOOD in the middle of his living room and massaged the back of his neck as he surveyed the damage. No wonder he couldn't keep a cleaning lady. Of course, last night had been exceptionally rowdy, what with six of the guys over to watch the Edmonton Oilers slaughter the Philadelphia Flyers. But, if truth were told, a before snapshot of the living room would have been indistinguishable from an after.

Washing down two aspirin with a flat Coke, he kicked at a beer can; it landed in an open pizza box next to the TV set. Maybe he ought to spend the morning straightening up the place. He'd been planning on driving up to Copper Mountain ski area for the day, but, what the hay, his poor old battered knees could use a rest. Then, too, there was the skyrocketing price of lift tickets in Colorado.

"Cleaning it is," he said firmly. And he would even drag the trash cans out of the garage for the garbage truck. "Won't *they* be surprised."

It had been a helluva year—almost a year—since Jeff had retired from the Denver Gents National Hockey League team. Since then he'd been bored, even a little depressed most of the time. He'd found odd jobs, but nothing lucrative since that ad he'd done six months ago for the nationally known underwear manufacturer. The TV commercial had been a tremendous success—everyone in the U.S. sure recognized him; at least in a pair of jockey shorts they did. But now those residuals were drying up, and he wasn't about to accept the latest offer he'd had: putting on a pair of panty hose for the cameras. Let the football superjocks do that one. Jeff, "Zany" to his fellow hockey players, wasn't *that* desperate.

It wasn't until Jeff was out of the shower and the phone rang that he realized he had a hangover. What was he stooping to? He hadn't had a hangover in years. "Yeah, hello," he said, cradling the receiver on his shoulder, half stumbling while he tugged on his pants.

"Jeff? That you?"

"Yeah, it's me."

"Doesn't sound like you," Roy Letterman said.

"I'm a little under the weather, pal. Too much beer."

"No kidding? That's not like you."

"Um, well. I'm not going to make a career of it, Roy, so spare me a lecture, please."

"You're a big boy, Jeff. I figure you can take care of yourself."

"I wish you'd tell my sister that."

Roy laughed. "Hey, you're over thirty. *You* tell her."

"Sure . . . What's up? Need some tickets to tonight's Gents game? I got a couple . . ."

"No," Roy said, "I'm stuck in meetings for the next few days. In fact—" Roy cleared his throat "—I was hoping you could do me a little favor."

"Oh?"

"Tell you what. If you could drop by the office at say . . . eleven, I'll fill you in."

"Let me check my calendar," Jeff said sarcastically.

"I really appreciate this," Roy replied. "See you then. Thanks, Zany."

"I haven't said yes yet, buddy."

Jeff did spend an hour straightening up the living room and kitchen, but he barely made a dent in the clutter. Nance, on the other hand, would have had the place spotless by now. But Nance was gone. For over a year, in fact. She just hadn't been able to take his constant traveling with the team, or his rowdy friends, or his refusal to consider the future.

At least there hadn't been a divorce; Nance, a career girl in fashion design, had not yet been interested in marriage. So they had parted friends. She'd even left him the house they'd bought together, the house in Lakewood, Colorado, suburbia U.S.A.

"All I want is my half of the down payment," she'd said. "You can keep your motorcycle and Windsurfer and skis, not to mention your golf clubs and tennis rackets and set of weights...."

"I get the picture," he'd said glumly. "I need a garage more than you." He'd brightened then. "Sure you don't want to stay? Get hitched? Have a few kids?"

"No, thanks, Zany. I'd say I've *had* a few kids around here already. You and the boys."

"My teammates? *The guys?*"

In retrospect, Jeff couldn't really blame her for leaving. His career had just about been over, a combination of bad knees and that final clincher—the scandal.

Life's not over, Jeff told himself as he warmed up his mortgaged-to-the-hilt red Corvette. It was a raw January day. *Thirty-four isn't so old.*

In truth, save for his bum knees, Jeff hadn't lost an ounce of his athletic ability or the sex appeal that the ladies loved. His manner was still laid back and friendly; there was not an intense bone in his body—off the ice. At five foot eleven, Jeff's physique was perfectly proportioned, well muscled and kept in shape as a matter of habit, even though he was no longer a professional athlete. His knees were crisscrossed with scars from various major and minor operations—battle scars, the guys called them—but with modern surgical technique and lots of physical therapy, Jeff still had a few good years left. Well, maybe not with the Gents....

His green eyes were still clear, his dark blond hair still thick, his smile still endearingly guileless. It was that tilt of his head and his smile that came across so well in the jockey shorts ad. Or so the women told him.

Backing his beloved Corvette out of the driveway, Jeff thought about the next car payment coming due and wondered whether he should take that panty hose job. After all, every woman in America had seem him practically naked, anyway. Just last week he'd been at the supermarket and two women with kids in their carts had approached him blushing and giggling and asked him to sign the waistbands on some underwear they were buying.

He took the Sixth Avenue Freeway into downtown Denver and found a spot in a parking lot just off the Sixteenth Street Mall. Roy Letterman's office was in one of the new glass-and-steel skyscrapers that had visibly altered Denver's skyline in recent years. Forty-six floors up, Jeff's lifelong friend certainly held a lofty position in the business world. From his office window you could see Pike's Peak, sixty miles to the south. Talk about a room with a view.... Roy, as vice president of operations for one of the country's largest hotel chains, had it made. The trouble was, Jeff so often mused, his pal was heading for burnout. Roy was the epitome of the Type A executive who craves constant challenge and somehow is never busy enough. He and Roy were opposites, no denying that. Opposites, but as close as they come.

Jeff supposed it had always been that way. Their moms had gone to college together in Boulder, and after marriage they had lived only two blocks apart. Jeff and Roy had played together for almost eighteen years, until Roy headed East to hotel and restaurant management school and Jeff had stayed in Colorado, attending Denver University—which had a great ice hockey program. Then, after graduation, Roy had landed a good job with the hotel chain, and Jeff, star of his college team, had signed with the Denver-based Gents. The rest was history. Twelve great whirlwind years of affluence and national recognition, and now obscurity.

The elevator rose quickly and silently, and the only telltale sign of its ascent was the pressure Jeff felt in his ears. He held his nose with his fingers and blew, as the people on the elevator looked at him with distaste. Soon the doors swished open to reveal a plush reception area done in shiny black marble and gleaming steel. Even the receptionist's paper clips were as black as her dress.

"Hello, Mr. Zanicek," she said, smiling, "so nice to see you again. I'll just find out if Mr. Letterman is free." Her ruby-red fingernails glistened as she pressed a button. "He'll see you now, Mr. Zanicek. You know the way."

Jeff always felt out of place in the sweeping office complex. Eight hundred dollar suits were not his thing—even if he could have afforded them. Rather, Jeff lived in natty sweaters and frayed shirts. Dressing up meant putting on his once-good camel-hair sport coat. He owned slacks, even had them dry-cleaned, but he preferred jeans or baggy, comfortable cords.

He knew the way to Roy's office, although it had been months since he'd been there. Some of the office personnel looked vaguely familiar; others were strangers, busy and disinterested. Roy wouldn't have had anyone working for him who *didn't* look preoccupied and tense, a little paranoid.

He passed a desk where two women were bent over a pile of papers, and one looked up, then nudged the other. "That's...that's the guy in the underwear!" he heard the taller one whisper, and they both tittered behind their manicures.

Well, thought Jeff, at least he hadn't faded into total obscurity yet, and he blushed.

Roy greeted him at his door. "Come on in. Right on time. Amazing."

"What else have I got to do?" Jeff shook Roy's hand and sat comfortably in the cushiony, revolving chair. Glancing around the room, he whistled through his teeth. "Changed things some in here, haven't you?"

Roy smiled. "Some."

"Boy, this place is . . . it's, ah, flashy."

"You mean glitzy."

"Yeah, better word. Who's the designer? Mr. Art Nouveau himself?"

"Very amusing."

Jeff swiveled idly in his seat and took in the decor, making comments here and there, doing an ace job of ribbing his friend. "Nice Louis Quinze floor, Roy," he said, eyeing the shining parquet that seemed straight out of the palace of Versailles. "Oh, and I just *love* the new paintings. What, ah, are they?" He cocked his head, closing one eye at an oil rendering of colorful cubes, with something faintly resembling a sun in the middle. "Is that earth? And our sun?"

"Hardly." Roy kept up with the game. "It's called Alleyway and Flashlight. Those are discarded boxes."

"I knew that."

"Um."

But it was Roy's new desk that provided Jeff with his best lines. "Someone have a kidney operation?"

"Gosh, you're a riot today, Jeff," Roy said.

"No, I'm serious. Tell me this thing—" he touched the glossy, lacquered surface of the desk "—doesn't look like someone's insides."

"Okay. Enough. I give in. To be honest, I'm not wild about the decor myself. And if I told you what it cost, you'd flip."

"I just bet I would."

Roy finally sat down behind his oddly shaped desk and smiled. He was an extremely attractive man, his brown hair receding a bit at the temples but his body still lean and fit. Jeff had always thought he looked a little like a young Gregory Peck, but taller and straighter. "Glad you could make it," Roy was saying. "By the way, any word yet on that coaching job over at D.U.?" He was referring to the head coaching position that had come up that fall at Jeff's alma mater.

Jeff shrugged and picked up an ultramodern paperweight, turning it in his hands. "I keep bugging them for an answer, but...I doubt I'll get one until this business with the Gents is cleared up."

Roy swore softly. "I can't believe it. Accusing you, of all people."

"Yeah, well, when my knees got bad last season, I guess it looked like I was throwing those games."

"But anyone who knows you, Jeff..."

"I'm trying to clear it up."

"How? I mean, look, it's none of my business, buddy, but until the hockey commissioner has someone's head on his desk, the fingers are still going to be pointed in your direction. Seems to me you need to get off your duff and—"

"You don't have to tell *me* that," Jeff interrupted, putting the paperweight back on the desk.

"And you can't expect to nail down that coaching job, either, until you're cleared."

"Look," Jeff said, "if I could get a handle on who really threw those games, I'd do something about it."

"Hire a private detective. Someone got paid pretty good, and it has to show up somewhere. I could lend you..."

Jeff shook his head. "Thanks, but it's just something I'm going to have to work out on my own. I've been going to all the games, Roy, and I think I might know who took some money."

"It's happening again this season?"

"Maybe. I can't tell too much yet."

Roy pressed the intercom on his desk. "Linda, would you bring in two cups of coffee, please? Black."

"So," Jeff said, "what's up? You mentioned a favor?"

Roy frowned and stood, going to the glass wall that overlooked Lincoln Street. "I've got myself in a jam."

"You?"

"We're all entitled to a few."

"So shoot."

"I'm supposed to fly down to Cozumel, Mexico—"

"I know where it is."

"Tomorrow. I'd planned on a week's vacation. But this hotel project in Telluride has run into a few snags."

"Can't it wait?"

"No. That's the trouble. The Telluride city council is calling a special meeting tonight to take a vote on the project. There's a problem with the number of hotel rooms versus parking spaces and employee housing."

"The city won't hold up a forty-million-dollar project for that, Roy."

Roy laughed grimly. "Yes, they will. In fact, they might scrub the whole thing. Three years of planning and eight million dollars, down the old proverbial drain."

"Phew. That's amazing."

"So is the city council there," Roy replied.

"Okay," Jeff said, "but *you* need a vacation. Send someone else to Telluride."

"I don't dare. Besides, the chairman of the board is flying in from Chicago. I *have* to be there."

"Then delay your trip a day or two."

"That's just what I was planning." Roy turned around and faced Jeff. "Now comes the favor part."

"I can't imagine . . ." Jeff began.

"It's Lucy."

"Lucy?"

"Hammond. You know . . ."

"Of the railroad Hammonds? The family in the society pages? Charity events, all that?"

"That's Lucy, do-gooder of the year, a real sweetheart. We've been dating for a few months, and this was to be our first real time together alone."

"Look," Jeff said, sipping on his coffee, wishing he had another couple of aspirin, "I'm not following the plan here. Just call this Lucy and tell her you have to put the trip off. Seems simple enough, pal."

"Um," Roy mumbled, "it would be, except I can't call her."

"They don't have phones at the Hammond place?" Jeff grinned his lopsided grin.

"Very funny. No, Lucy's somewhere in Mexico already, some jungle village...you know, her charity work with kids."

"Her folks don't know how to get in touch with her?" Jeff was beginning to get an inkling of this favor.

Roy shook his head. "Lucy is very independent. She flies her own plane, and I haven't the faintest idea where she is."

"You haven't *any* idea what village?"

"Not the slightest. She does so much volunteer work... She may have mentioned it last week..." Roy shrugged.

"Listen," Jeff said, "I don't think I like the sound of this."

"She's very special to me, Jeff. Very. And I can't leave her standing out on that tarmac for two days while I'm hung up in business meetings."

"Bag the business, like I said. If she's that special..."

"You know I can't."

"I know you're so stressed out and tied up in your work you can't see daylight, buddy."

"It's my nature. I'm sorry, but I can't change."

"You could. Don't give me that bull."

"Okay, then let's say I don't *want* to change."

A weighty silence fell between them for a minute. Jeff wished there were a way of persuading his friend to let loose for once, but what could he say that he hadn't already said a dozen times?

"Look," Roy began again, "you could take my ticket, Jeff, and be there tomorrow. Meet Lucy, tell her how sorry I am."

"Leave a message for her at the Cozumel airport," Jeff suggested quickly.

But Roy shook his dark head. "That's no way to handle it. You don't know Lucy. Like I said, she's special. She'd never leave *me* waiting."

"Ah, hell," Jeff muttered, "I'm not an escort service. What would I do with her for two whole days? No way."

"Get a tan. Go diving. *Eat.*"

"I can't."

"You can. She'll adore you, pal. All the women do. And she's really easy to get along with."

"Good personality," Jeff said under his breath, "wonderful." He sighed. "Send someone else, Roy. This just isn't my thing."

"Who else can I trust?"

He had Jeff there.

"Please. I know it's a big favor, but I'm caught between a rock and a hard spot. I don't want to blow this hotel deal, and I sure don't want to blow this thing with Lucy. Come on," Roy said as he strode to his desk and opened a drawer, "take the plane ticket. I'll have Linda change the name."

"Damn it," Jeff grumbled, "I'm not going to do this for you."

But in the end he stepped back onto the elevator, frowning, cursing under his breath, the ticket and a thousand dollars in cash safely stuffed in his pocket.

Zany's escort service, he thought in disgust.

By the time Jeff was home in his three-bedroom, two-bath disaster area, he'd decided to call the whole thing off. It wasn't the trip; it wasn't Cozumel. What bugged him was the reception he'd get from Ms Lucy Hammond, rich philanthropist. No way was this woman going to appreciate Roy's gesture. Heck, she'd probably be as mad as blazes—not that he'd blame her—and take it out on him.

He tossed his car keys on the coffee table, nudged aside his ski poles, which lay on the couch, and dialed Roy's office.

"Oh, I'm sorry, Mr. Zanicek, but Mr. Letterman just left for Telluride."

"Can I leave a message?"

"Well, now, Mr. Letterman will be out of reach of the office for some time...."

"Never mind." Jeff hung up in frustration.

He wasn't going to do it. If this woman was so darn special, then Roy should be going! Besides, Jeff thought, he hadn't the slightest idea what to pack. Slacks? Shorts? A summer suit? God forbid a suit! Did the tourists wear dinner jackets?

Damn it, Roy!

His bag, as yet still empty, laid out on the unmade bed, Jeff headed over to McNicol's Sports Arena, where the Gents would be warming up for the game that night. It had started to spit snow, the gray clouds amassing to the west over the foothills of the Rockies. He turned on his headlights and wipers and frowned. Snow was great up in the ski areas, but here in the city it piled up in dirty, depressing mounds along the side of the road and was nothing more than a nuisance. Of course, it never snowed on the sunny isle of Cozumel....

Jeff still had his parking pass at the arena, one of those lifetime perks the owners of the Gents gave away freely to the ex-players. And he had two season passes, as well—for life. He missed the rink, the camaraderie, the pushing and shoving and stinging towel snapping in the locker room. He missed the travel, and he missed being in the limelight. What he could do without was the recent notoriety.

Who *had* thrown those games last year? He had a couple of ideas, but what he needed was proof.

Jeff walked down the familiar gray cement corridor. God, how many times had he walked this way, his mouth dry, his pulse quick, his adrenaline flowing, as he readied himself mentally for a game? How he loved that feeling, the thrill of anticipation, the knowledge that soon he'd be on the ice doing what he loved best, pushing himself to his limits, striving for that perfection of timing and movement and teamwork that won games.

He pushed open the door to the locker room and breathed in the aroma, the familiar beloved stink of sweat and grungy clothes and well-used equipment. As always, the place was humid, messy and crowded with milling players, scarred benches and gray metal lockers. A crumbled jockstrap lay in one corner. Home. As comfortable and secure as the womb.

God, he loved this place.

Jeff was greeted warmly. There wasn't a man on the team who thought for a minute that he had taken money to make sure the Gents had lost those games.

The trust didn't do him much good, though, because the Denver press had gotten on his case, made insinuating statements, and the hockey commissioner had listened. The truth was, Jeff thought, the Gents *should* have won those games and everyone, the players and fans and reporters, knew it. The witch hunt had started, and because his knees had hurt like hell and his playing had been lousy, he'd been blamed.

"Hey, Zany, my man," Scooter Hansen called from where he sat on a bench, getting dressed, "what gives?" Scooter adjusted his protective cup and fastened the garter belt that held up his long socks.

Jeff sauntered over, reached out a finger, hooked a garter strap and snapped it. "Not much. You guys up to the Rangers tonight? I hear their goalie's been hot lately."

Scooter pulled his padded pants up and adjusted the straps over his shoulders, getting bigger with every layer. "I'll take his head off, Zany, if he gets cute with me." He shrugged the red-and-blue jersey over his head. Denver Gents was printed on the front, his name and number on the back. He reached for his skates as Jeff stood, hands on hips, grinning at him.

"Sure you will," Jeff said. Scooter spent as much time in the penalty box as any player. He batted Scooter's helmet and moved along the ranks of lockers until he found Marty Cerros, one of his closest friends on the team.

"Zany, good to see ya. Staying for the game tonight? We're gonna draw blood, my man."

"You're too old to draw blood," Jeff said lightly.

"Yeah, I guess I'll hang around. Nothing else to do." *Except pack.*

"The pressure let up on you yet about that bribe business?"

"You gotta be kidding," Jeff replied, and stuffed his hands in his pockets. "They keep putting me off over at D.U. about that coaching job."

"It'll pass."

"Doubt it," Jeff said. "People never forget. The only way out is to clear myself."

"How you gonna do that?" Marty faked a check to Jeff's chest with his shoulder, and Jeff saw that his friend was missing another tooth.

"Don't know, exactly. I suppose I'll have to find out who really threw the games."

"No small task, that. We all have our bad days, you know."

"I've been thinking of looking over the video tapes of those games."

"The commissioner's done that already," Marty pointed out.

"Yeah, but he doesn't know a hockey stick from a puck."

"This is true, my man."

The Gents demolished the Rangers that night, seven to two. While Jeff sat in the screaming, bloodthirsty throng, he watched the individual players carefully, their moves, their penalties, their passes, their checks to the boards. Todd played terribly, even though it was a big win, and so did Larry. But what did that mean? Because of the frantic speed of the play in hockey, it was darn near impossible to catch an intentional screwup. Maybe he *would* get those tapes and study them, in slow motion, and he might just spot something.

By the time Jeff got home it was past midnight. Of course, he'd stopped at Molly's Sports Center with the team, and he'd shot six games of pool, forgoing the beer for Cokes. He looked at the clock and sighed. The flight to Cozumel was scheduled to leave at 10:05 in the morning. If he was going to be on it, he'd better pack. On the other hand, he could try to get hold of Roy in Telluride, tell his buddy the trip was off. He could...

Lucy Hammond. The *railroad* Hammonds. A woman with so much money she spent it all on charity—impoverished kids. Maybe this Lucy didn't care about children at all and used the charity work as a tax dodge. That way she could fly her little plane to isolated Mexican villages and write the whole works off.

Idly Jeff wondered if she was pretty. With her kind of money she could be *made* pretty—plastic surgery, tucks, clothes, all the expensive stuff. And Roy, as preoccupied with business as he was, would never even notice.

Now Jeff, on the other hand, liked the more natural type of woman. The glitzy ones made him nervous. No, for him it was a girl who looked you square in the eye and told the truth. It was hamburgers and pizzas and tacos.

He switched on the TV in the bedroom for company and eyed his closet. What would he take to Cozumel—if he went, that was? Casual stuff. Swimming trunks, that pair of white slacks Nance had bought him, maybe one dress shirt. His shaving kit. And there was that silly red-flowered Hawaiian shirt the guys had given him for his thirtieth birthday.

God, he'd have to eat meals with Ms Hammond, swim with her, all that fun stuff. And he bet she would get bored easily. Would she find his hockey stories funny? Probably she liked Roy's tales of how to turn big money into bigger money.

He could tell her about his bank account. Let's see, he had fifteen hundred dollars in it at last count, and monthly mortgage was due soon. If he gave up eating he might make it for two more months. What a joke, Jeff thought, accused of taking bribes! So where was all the money?

Yeah, he could cry on Lucy Hammond's shoulder, and by the time Roy arrived, she'd be so darned glad to see the last of him that Roy, no doubt, would never ask another favor of Jeffrey Zanicek again.

He sat on the edge of his bed and pulled off his sweater, letting it fall to the floor inside out. He sighed, feeling melancholy and lonely. It sure would have been nice to come home to someone, someone he could really talk to, who would have rolled over in bed, looked at the clock and said, "Where have you been, you jerk?" And then there were those two empty bedrooms. What would it be like to have a couple of kids sleeping in them—boys, of course—future ice hockey stars? Oh, his sister, Claire, lived only a few miles away, and she had a boy, twelve now, but the kid had inherited his father's genes and was a klutz on the ice. Claire's daughter, at ten years old, was a far better skater.

Feeling more and more down by the minute, Jeff halfheartedly tossed a few things in his bag. Outside the snow was getting heavier, and the falling barometer wasn't doing a thing for his mood, not to mention his aching knees. Maybe this Hammond woman would tear his eyes out when he told her he'd come in Roy's stead, but at least he could heal on a sunny beach. Or just maybe she'd be a sweetheart as Roy had said, and they could lie on the sand, sipping tall, cool fruit drinks, and laugh a little.

It all began to sound wonderful in Jeff's mind until he snapped off his light, curled up in bed and realized that he'd forgotten to get a description of Lucy Hammond from Roy.

Oh, great.

CHAPTER TWO

THE GREEN JUNGLE CANOPY of Cozumel Island rolled into view at 3:12 as Lucy Hammond corrected her approach heading. *An emerald isle in turquoise water,* she thought, turning on her radio. "Cozumel tower, this is Bonanza two-two-six-Lima-Hotel, ten miles west." "Lima Hotel" was the international code for her plane's call letters, *LH*, understood by all air traffic controllers. She could have spoken Spanish, but the men in the tower were used to English, so it didn't matter.

A controller answered, echoing in her headset: "Bonanza two-two-six-Lima-Hotel. What is your point of departure and altitude?"

"Point of departure Merida, altitude thirty-two hundred feet."

She was right on time. The weather had been perfect, the flight from Merida uneventful, but she was hot and rumpled, sweaty and eaten alive from insect bites after her stay in Yaxcaba and that morning's long jouncing jeep ride to the airport.

"What is your intention in Cozumel?" inquired the tower, following routine.

"Bonanza two-two-six-Lima-Hotel landing Cozumel."

"Report again when five miles west," said the tower.

Her trip to Yaxcaba had been successful. The Hammond Foundation would donate money for an orphanage; all the red tape was taken care of, permissions granted, small, customary bribes given to oil the machine. Construction would start after the rainy season, and a good foreman was available to oversee the job. Satisfaction soothed Lucy's mosquito bites to an extent, but she wished desperately that she could get into a shower, a long, hot shower, and wash off the week's grime before meeting Roy.

Roy Letterman. Her heart beat with anticipation, then dismay. Here she was, dirty and not exactly smelling like a rose. In her wrinkled khaki slacks, bush jacket and desert boots, she was a living advertisement for Banana Republic Travel Clothing Company.

She was dying to see Roy, and she would soon. He was due in at 3:35 p.m. on a Continental flight—in seven minutes, to be exact—and she had no time for a shower. Oh, well, he wouldn't care, he'd be so glad to see her.

Or would he? Oh, he'd be glad to *see* her, but Lucy had a nagging feeling that Roy, who was always perfectly groomed, smelling of Chaps after-shave, manicured, razor cut and dressed to the teeth, wouldn't appreciate her untidy appearance, even as a function of her great haste to meet him on time.

Did true love depend on how well you were dressed? She smiled. No. Roy wasn't *that* shallow.

Lucy circled into the wind on the correct course. Cozumel, tropical resort island of the Caribbean. She'd never been there, but she was going to love it—and so was Roy. They were going to spend time together alone, that so-called quality time, beyond the reach of their responsibilities. They would lie on the beach, eat *mar-*

iscos, seafood, until they burst, swim and snorkel in the transparent blue water, maybe fly to some of the Mayan ruins on the mainland. An idyll.

She was several miles from the airport over the narrow channel between the Yucatán peninsula and the island. She checked her instruments automatically—everything was normal.

She loved Roy Letterman. Lucy corrected herself: she *thought* she loved Roy. She needed time to be sure, and the languid tropical pace of this island would provide that time. They hadn't talked marriage yet, although it was understood that was the next step—sort of understood, anyway. And she knew, beyond a doubt, that Roy Letterman was the perfect mate for her. First and foremost, he had lots of money of his own, so he wasn't after hers. That, as crass as it sounded, was important. Lucy had been burned too many times by fortune hunters to tempt fate again.

And Roy saw her better qualities. He didn't mind that she wasn't the most glamorous woman on earth. It was true he had suggested that she replace her glasses with contact lenses, but she knew she should do that, anyway. Even her mother told her so. She could wear more makeup, buy expensive designer clothes, but Roy never pushed her to do that. He appreciated her brains, her ideals, her hard work for the Hammond Foundation, her plain, average looks, her nice face. Didn't they say that really gorgeous men, like Roy, were attracted to, well, quieter-looking women?

She'd been trying to convince Roy to take some time off for weeks. She admired and respected his driving ambition, but she was afraid he didn't know how to relax. Lucy got the feeling that Roy's career came first, even before her, and she understood and accepted that to a point. But he needed to show her that he really did care, that he really could respond to her needs.

So, Cozumel was a kind of test. For both of them, Lucy suspected.

It was 3:37 p.m. and the Cozumel airport was clearly visible five miles ahead of her, the hot tarmac of the runways radiating heat waves up at her. "Cozumel tower, Bonanza two-two-six-Lima-Hotel five miles west," she said.

"Clear to land. Active runway twenty-six, right traffic. Look for a Cessna on half mile final. Wind is two-eighty at eight knots," the tower replied.

The runway was rushing up at her, her wheels were touching, squealing, bouncing, then rolling swiftly and smoothly along, and she was down.

The Continental jet floated in on the heavy air only a few minutes later. Lucy saw it as she was talking to the young Mexican boy who'd appeared as if by magic, arranging for him to watch her plane for a few pesos and gathering her documents to get stamped by the *comondante* in the tower.

"Roy," she whispered, her mouth turning up into a smile. He was on that plane. She forgot all about the boy as she grabbed her bag, ran her fingers through her short, upswept brown hair, pulled her jacket straight and took her glasses off, stuffing them in one of the many pockets. The jet immediately turned into a silver blur.

"Damn," she mumbled, hurrying toward the terminal, wanting to be there when Roy walked down the steps, wanting to see him smile his dazzling smile and hold out his arms to her.

It seemed to take forever before the plane was stationary in front of the terminal, before the stairs were

wheeled out and the doors unlatched. First class de-
planed immediately, and Roy would, of course, fly first
class. She stood near the bottom of the aluminum
stairs, ignoring the baggage carts and handlers, the
mechanics and other workers, close enough to recognize Roy without her glasses. She wiped perspiration
from her forehead with her wrist, not realizing that she
had left behind a grimy smear.

Finally. A blond American woman came down the
stairs, a gray-haired man, another couple, a Mexican
businessman, three blue-haired older ladies, nervous
and tentative. A family from Texas—she could hear
their accents. A man, Roy's age. Was it him? She
squinted, trying to focus—no, his hair was lighter, he
was shorter than Roy and his shirttail was hanging out
on one side. He was cute, though.... Her eyes swiftly
passed on. A very fat Mexican lady with lots of diamonds.

Then the coach passengers started deplaning. Teen-
agers, mothers with babies, young families, Mexicans,
natives of Cozumel.

No Roy.

She waited until every person had climbed down
from the plane, including the flight attendants and the
cockpit crew. But Roy wasn't there.

Her heart fell; disappointment flooded her. She felt
like a child deprived of a treat. The same awful, frus-
trated feeling of abandonment and betrayal swept her.
The yawning abyss, the chasm, the *lack*.

Tears stung her eyes. Automatically she put her
glasses on, as if to hide them. Where was Roy? What
had happened?

Slowly, lethargically, she trudged toward the terminal and entered its modern, air-conditioned neu-

trality, trying to gather her thoughts. Something had come up and he hadn't been able to contact her, that was it. He was taking a later flight. He'd left a message for her at the hotel.

Or she could call his office. Sure, Linda would know where he was. All she had to do was phone.

She reached in her canvas, canteen-style bag and pulled out her address book. Yes, there was Roy's office number—she should know it by heart, shouldn't she? She glanced around for a phone. Over there, by the duty-free shop.

She started toward the phone, then stopped abruptly. A smile curved her lips. Roy had arrived early and was waiting for her at the hotel. The Cozumel Caribe, that was its name. He'd made reservations last week, before she had left for Yaxcaba. That was it, of course.

She strode over to the phone and looked up the Cozumel Caribe's number. She dialed it, listened to the ring, the polite desk clerk's greeting. In fluent Spanish she asked if Señor Roy Letterman had checked in yet.

"Momento, por favor."

She waited, tapping her foot restlessly, impatiently. Oh, just wait till she told him how mean he was not to meet her! And he'd apologize and kiss her, and they'd go out to dinner at a romantic, open-air restaurant. A wine bottle would be cooling in a silver—

"I am very sorry, *señorita*, but Roy Letterman has not arrived yet."

She hung up, uncharacteristically without even saying thank you.

Behind her a man cleared his throat. Thinking he wanted to use the phone, she automatically picked up her bag to move aside. Her mind whirled with questions and disappointment and pain. Where was Roy?

Her heart squeezed with sudden apprehension. Had something happened to him?

The man cleared his throat again. "Excuse me," he said, and it occurred to Lucy that he was talking to her.

"Excuse me," the man repeated.

"Yes?" she replied blankly, finally looking at him. Familiar face, cute, the man she'd thought was Roy earlier. What on earth did he want with her?

He smiled uncertainly, obviously embarrassed. Maybe he needed Mexican coins to put in the pay phone. "I saw you using the phone," he said. "I wondered..."

She stared at him, at a loss. Dark blond hair, features that were rough but attractive.... There was something about his face, the crooked smile, the way he tilted his head...

"Yes?" she repeated.

"Goddamn it," he said, as if to himself, massaging the back of his neck in an unconscious gesture. "Would you be Lucy Hammond?"

She looked at him in astonishment. "Yes," she answered, "but...?"

He grinned at her, relieved, and held out a hand. "Boy, am I glad to see you!"

She looked at his hand, then up at his face again. "But who are you?"

"Oh, sorry." He dropped his hand. "My name is Jeffrey Zanicek, that's Zan-i-check. I'm a friend of Roy's...."

"Roy? Where is Roy?" she asked. "Is he all right?"

A rueful expression crossed Jeff's face. "Oh, sure, he's fine."

"Oh." She felt foolish. What did this man, this Jeffrey Zanicek, want with her?

"Look, I'm sorry," Jeff said. "Let me start at the beginning. I thought you must be Lucy. That is, Roy didn't tell me what you looked like, but he did say you were off in some village and you looked sort of, uh, jungleish, if you know what I mean...."

"Roy told you I'd be here?"

Jeffrey shifted his wrinkled sport coat from one arm to the other and shuffled his feet. "Well, the thing is—" he looked up as if asking for help from heaven "—Roy sent me to meet you."

"*What?*"

He put his hands out placatingly. "Now look, he couldn't make it, some unavoidable meeting. He said he couldn't phone you or anything. He begged me... well, he asked, so that you wouldn't be left here alone."

"Roy sent *you* to meet me?" she repeated, then she gave a short laugh.

"Well, we're old buddies. We go way back. If one of us needs a favor, the other does it." Jeffrey shrugged, and she knew he was not real comfortable with his role as understudy.

"Oh, Roy," she said to herself, "how could you?"

"There was this meeting in Telluride, see, and the chairman of the board was coming, but Roy said he'd be here in two days."

"And you were coming down here, anyway," she finished for him.

"Well—" he hesitated "—not exactly."

"Do you mean Roy *paid* for you to come down here?" she asked, her cheeks growing red.

"Uh." He swallowed. "Sort of."

"Oh, God." Lucy put her face in her hands. "Oh, Roy."

"Hey, don't get upset. He'll be here soon. It's not so bad. You know Roy—he's a busy guy," Jeff said, and she felt him pat her timidly on the back.

Lucy looked up at Jeff. "So he bought me an escort," she said tightly.

"Um . . ." he began.

"Do you do this sort of thing for a living?" she asked sarcastically, taking out her disappointment and humiliation on this stranger.

A dull red flush spread across his face. "No," he said, "I'm doing a favor for a friend, that's all."

Lucy took a deep breath. It wasn't this poor guy's fault. It was Roy's fault. "I'm sorry," she said, "I'm just kind of mad, I guess."

"Hey, I bet you are. I tried to tell Roy not to send me, but, uh, you know him, he's awful busy, and the meeting was important, something about a hotel in Telluride," Jeff said in a rush.

He doesn't want to put down his friend, Lucy thought.

"How about a nice cool drink?" Jeff asked. "We can go in the café there and sit down, maybe talk a little, decide what you want to do. What do you say?"

She stood there studying Jeffrey Zanicek, confused, angry at Roy, wondering what to do, trying not to take it out on Roy's friend. How could Roy have done this to her? "Okay," she said.

Jeff picked up her overnight bag, slung it over his shoulder with his and took her elbow. "Good," he said, "maybe we can both catch our breaths."

The had tall, frosty Pepsis with juicy lemon wedges. Jeff sat with unstudied, casual grace, his legs out in front of him, feet crossed at the ankles. He was an easygoing guy, utterly unlike his old friend Roy.

"So our moms were school friends and we were practically brought up together," he was saying. "Now I know we're not alike and everyone wonders why we're such good buddies, but it works for us. 'Course, Roy's so busy we don't see so much of each other these days, and then I used to be on the road a lot." He stopped suddenly, as if not wanting to pursue that subject.

"What do you do?" Lucy inquired. "You said you traveled a lot . . ."

"I'm a hockey player, Lucy. Can I call you 'Lucy'?" His expression sobered. "I *was* a hockey player. I retired last year."

Lucy leaned forward. "Oh, my goodness, you're *that* Jeff. Roy mentioned you. I remember."

He smiled shyly. "Yeah, Roy's a real Gents fan. The Denver Gents, that's my team. You ever see a game?"

"Well, no, I guess not."

He shook his head. "You're missing a great sport."

She watched him drink his soda in big gulps. His Adam's apple worked when he swallowed. He had a strong neck, muscular, and broad shoulders under the white polo shirt, which had a hole in it at the corner of the front placket. His shirttail still hung out, and he looked easy in his skin, relaxed. As he talked, she kept trying to recall why, if she'd never seen a Gents game, his face seemed familiar.

"Did Roy ever introduce me to you?" she finally asked.

"No, I don't think so. I would have remembered. Why?"

"You look familiar," she said, and he blushed and upended his empty glass, as if to hide behind it.

"I bet I saw your picture in the paper," she said. "The sports page or something."

"Probably." He put down his glass and changed the subject. "So, Lucy, what do you want to do? Go to your hotel? The beach? You hungry?"

"I've got to get a shower. I don't always look like this," she said with chagrin. "I've been washing in cold water for a week and I'm covered with mosquito bites. Maybe I'll go to the hotel and clean up, stay a night, then fly home."

"But . . . but Roy'll be here in two days."

"Oh, I don't know. He's sort of spoiled my vacation, you know. It won't be the same even if he shows up."

"*If?*"

"It's hard to trust Roy now that he's done this," she said sadly.

"Oh, Lucy, hey, I *know* he'll be here. He was practically frantic when he called me. I mean, he didn't know what to do. But he promised . . ."

"He promised to meet me here today, too," Lucy said softly, and noted that Jeff had the sense to keep his mouth shut. An uneasy silence hung between them for a moment, then someone behind the bar dropped a glass, and they both looked at each other and started to talk at the same time.

"I guess we—"

"Do you want—"

He laughed and pushed himself back from the table. "Let's go to the hotel. You take a shower and we'll wing it from there, okay?"

The taxi followed a zigzag path through the city of San Miguel, then turned north along the shoreline. The coast of the Yucatán Peninsula was visible as a blurry line miles across the water. The sun glittered on the tropical blue of the sea on one side; exotic birds called from the dense jungle on the other. Elegant resort hotels lined the shore. Lucy sighed. She was supposed to have shared this with Roy.

The Cozumel Caribe Hotel was a bit funky—a hodge-podge of bungalows and a tall, more modern structure set back off the beach. But the sand was lovely—pinkish—and the grounds were lush and green, flower scented. Their bungalows were next door to each other, the desk clerk told them in accented English, but, he apologized, unfortunately, without the connecting doors Señor Letterman had requested.

"Oh, that's all right," Lucy said quickly, glancing at Jeff.

"Oh, sure, fine," he replied, discomfited, and Lucy got angry at Roy all over again for putting them both in this embarrassing situation. She was beginning to feel sorry for Jeff, who had made this long trip for nothing and who very obviously wished himself anywhere but here, checking into a hotel with a strange, disheveled woman.

They walked in silence down the palm-lined path, checking room numbers. Lucy stopped in front of her bungalow and dropped her bag. "Look, Jeff, you really don't have to worry about me. I think I'll go home tomorrow, but you can stay and have some fun. Wait for Roy, why don't you?"

His face fell. "Boy, Roy would kill me if I let you do that. I promised to, you know..."

"Entertain me? Oh, Jeff, it's not your responsibility."

"Sure it is." He played with his room key, turning it over in his fingers. "At least let's have dinner together. You have to eat, I have to eat, right?"

"Look, don't feel you have to do this out of some perverted sense of duty. I'll be fine on my own. Roy had no right to ask you to baby-sit me."

"Okay, then, leave Roy out of this. *I'm* asking you to dinner."

His eyes locked with hers, serious now. He had nice eyes, green, sincere, their corners slanted down.

Lucy sighed. He was determined to fulfill his duties. She wondered how much money Roy had paid him to do this job, then berated herself. *How did you get to be so cynical, Lucy?* she asked herself. *Easy,* she answered, *by letting men walk all over me.* "Okay," she said, relenting. "How about seven? I'll meet you down in the bar."

"I'll knock," said Jeff, surprisingly sure of himself, "and we'll go down to the bar together."

In her room was a huge arrangement of flowers: birds-of-paradise, lilies and strange, brightly colored tropical blossoms in a burst of vivid hues. A bottle of champagne stood in an ice bucket, and a small white envelope was propped up against it. She opened it. "Forgive me, darling," it read. "The meeting was unavoidable. See you shortly. Love, Roy."

She bit her lip and smiled to herself. Leave it to Roy to make the grand gesture—everything money could buy, except Roy himself. Her heart softened despite her reluctance to forgive him. It was probably her fault, for being in such an unreachable place for the past week. These things happened. He'd be here in two days. She *could* wait. Her plan to get to know him still might work. After all, you had to compromise in any relationship. Perhaps she was just being selfish, a spoiled little rich girl balked in her desires.... What an awful thought!

She put the note down, wiped a drop from the sweating champagne bucket and leaned over to smell the flowers. The exotic jungle blooms had no scent at all.

The shower felt marvelous. She scrubbed her hair twice, shaved her legs, rubbed grime and perspiration off her body. The hot water made her mosquito bites itch, but it felt so good that she stood under it for ages.

Her dress was simple, a white cotton knit that traveled well, basically a long tank top. She shook it out, and a spider fell onto the floor. There *had* been a goodly menagerie of insects in the house in Yaxcaba.... A belt of handwoven Mexican striped fabric and white sandals completed her outfit. Her hair was easy, especially in the humidity of Cozumel, as it had more natural wave to it. Lucy hated to fuss with her hair, and she traveled so much, she needed a simple style. Short, thick and wavy, her hair swept back over her ears from her bangs. All she had to do was comb it.

Mascara. She studied herself in the mirror and took her glasses off. Still something was missing. Earrings. The only ones she had were a pair she'd bought in Merida, silver-and-turquoise dangles, a gift perfect for her feminine mother. She got them out of the tissue they were wrapped in and put them on. They swung prettily when she moved her head, frivolous silver-and-blue flowers, not at all like Lucy. But she left them on, anyway.

What an odd situation she was in. Her initial sharp anger and disappointment had subsided somewhat. She even had to admit that Jeff had helped blunt the edge of her anger, first because her innate sense of fair play and courtesy didn't allow her to show her temper in front of him, and second because Jeff had a knack of making her feel, well, comfortable. Maybe, Lucy mused wryly, Roy wasn't so unwise at all, sending Jeff in his place.

She wondered if she should knock on Jeff's door and ask him to share a glass of champagne with her. But, no, that was presuming a lot, being pushy, and Lucy had a horror of being aggressive. It was the family money and her own trust fund that made her so sensitive, she knew. She was always afraid people would think she was using her money to get what she wanted.

What *did* she want?

She had wanted to spend time—quality time—with Roy. She wanted a man, like Roy, whom she could love and marry, who loved her in return, not for her family's wealth or position, but for Lucy herself, with all her imperfections. She wanted to make a difference in the world, however slight, to help poor children, disadvantaged children. Perhaps there was some truth in the often repeated maxim that the very rich were politically liberal because they felt guilty. Lucy had no argument with that assessment; except that she wasn't guilty, and she'd be damned if she'd apologize for her family's success, but she did feel a duty to share her good fortune.

She stared at herself in the mirror and wondered what Roy was doing right now. Was he thinking of her, or was he up to his ears in tense negotiations? Her silver earrings sent a flash of reflected light into her eyes, and she was pursuing the notion that Roy would much prefer gold-and-diamonds to silver-and-turquoise, when there was a knock on the door.

Jeff had showered, too; his hair was damp, the marks of the comb's teeth still visible in it. He wore a red Hawaiian short-sleeved shirt and a navy blazer. He seemed very young and earnest, a little nervous, a nice guy caught in an awkward spot.

"You look great," he said, openly surprised. "Different."

She smiled. People often said that when she took off her glasses; she suspected they were not even aware of why she looked different. "You'll have to read the menu for me, though."

"Hey, that's okay. As long as it says chili or tacos." He took her elbow, and his fingers were warm and strong.

The restaurant was outside on a stone veranda overlooking the beach. Like so many of the buildings on this sultry island, it consisted of a roof supported by stone columns and open sides, surrounded by palm trees and flowering plants and vines, all verdant and bursting with growth in the heat and humidity. The fragrance of jasmine was heavy on the damp air.

"Nice place," Jeff said as they were seated.

"Lovely," she agreed.

The had fancy rum concoctions in pineapple halves and marvelously fresh gulf shrimp, called *camarones* on the menu. Lucy ordered in fluent Spanish, although the waiter probably spoke English, but she'd always felt that it was polite to speak the language of the country you were in, if you could.

"Wow, you have that lingo down pat," Jeff commented.

"I've spent a lot of time in Mexico and South America. I had to learn it," she explained.

"Yeah, Roy told me you come down here a lot and that you fly your own plane. Is that how you got here today?"

"Yes, I flew in from Merida."

"And you aren't nervous or anything flying around by yourself?"

"Not nervous, careful. I love to fly. Roy's flown with me several times. Did he mention that?"

"No, he didn't."

"As a matter of fact, he'd planned to fly home with me after this week." She frowned. "But now I don't know. I really don't think I'll stay...."

"Come on, don't feel that way. Roy'll be here day after tomorrow. You'll have a terrific time."

"Did he tell you to say that?" she asked lightly.

Jeff looked hurt. "Hey, no way. I just know Roy. He told me you were very special to him. That's why he sent me—so you wouldn't be left in the lurch. He cares, Lucy, really he does."

She played with a silver fork. "That was an eloquent speech, Jeff."

"It's the truth."

An odd situation, Lucy thought once again. Here she was in a romantic restaurant, with the moon-silvered ocean licking at the beach, the palms clicking in the offshore breeze, candlelight and a handsome man across the table from her. Except he was the wrong handsome man.

Jeff had relaxed over dinner and was an exceedingly pleasant companion. He seemed not to have a care in the world, a happy-go-lucky sort. She figured she knew his kind: boyishly mussed sandy hair, charm spilling from sexy green eyes—where *had* she seen those eyes before?—and a manly way of sitting, knees splayed athletically. His profile was blunt, his nose lumpy, probably broken in hockey games, his brow ridge heavy with a square forehead and a long chin. He had nice lines bracketing either side of his mouth, a cocky smile that lit up his face and a way of listening with total attention, as if she were the most important person on earth.

Oh, yes, she knew the type. Roy's choice as a companion for her was ironic in many ways. She'd had some bad experiences when she was younger, falling for sporty ne'er-do-wells like this hockey player. They were always handsome, well built and loaded with charm, but she'd never trust one again. One man she'd been crazy about, Monty, had been a football player. Why did she always go for the athletes, the boys who never grew up? Well, Monty had used her credit card as if it were his own, and when she'd gotten the bills he'd been furious that she questioned him about it. So long, Monty. Then there had been Art, who'd borrowed money for a business scheme. The business had gone under, and he'd never even offered to pay her back. It made a girl wary.

Joel, a race-car driver, had been the worst of the bunch. He'd walked out on her when she'd balked at financing his new Indy 500 Formula One race car, then had the nerve to sue her for breach of contract! That hurt, oh, did that hurt. She really had thought Joel had loved her. Well, he hadn't, and she'd learned, and now she only went out with men who wore three-piece suits, had sound careers and plenty of money of their own.

Unlike Jeffrey Zanicek.

"So," he was saying, "what were you doing in the jungle where Roy couldn't call you?"

She told him all about the orphanage of Yaxcaba.

"Do you build orphanages all over?" he asked.

"Well, not really. It's hard to do in foreign countries. This project just happened to work out. What I really do is run the programs set up by the Hammond Foundation. There's an institution in Denver for disadvantaged children, a kind of foster home for the ones too old to be adopted. And then there are programs in other cities, homes for battered women and so on."

"You're a busy lady. No wonder you have a plane," Jeff said. "So you're an employee of this Hammond Foundation?"

"Well, sort of. My grandfather set it up as a nonprofit organization, a constructive way to dodge taxes, you could say."

"And you run it?"

"There's a board of directors, of course. Family members. But I do a lot of the actual on-the-spot management. My elder sister's married and has kids and isn't interested. My younger brother is studying to be an architect." She shrugged. "So it fell to me. But I love it."

"Commendable," Jeff said, studying her, his head tilted.

"Enough about me. Tell me something about yourself. How have you and Roy stayed friends for so long?" Lucy asked.

"You mean, how come two such radically different people are buddies?" he asked, grinning. "Hey, I know how it looks, but Roy and I are good for each other. I relax him and he inspires me."

"And you're a hockey player," she said, "and Roy loves hockey."

The grin was wiped from Jeff's face. "I *was* a hockey player. I had to quit last year. My knees were getting pretty bad. I've had them operated on so many times they look like a patchwork quilt."

"So you're retired," she said. "What do you do now?"

He looked out over the softly sighing ocean. "Oh, this and that. I've applied for a coaching position at Denver University. That's where I went to school."

"That would be a great job, wouldn't it?" Lucy asked, wondering at the edge to Jeff's voice.

"Yeah, it would be great. *If* I got it," he said.

"Well, wouldn't they want you? I mean, a big-time hockey star like you. You'd be a real asset."

"Oh, sure, I'd be a good coach. Hey, I love those boys. Heck, I was one of them not so long ago. There are a few problems, though," he said evasively.

She wondered what the problems were, but she certainly didn't know Jeff well enough to ask. "The Gents were your team you said, didn't you?"

He brightened. "Well, I played in Buffalo for the Sabers for a couple of years. But I was glad when I got traded back to the Gents. I like being in Denver. I even bought a house. Nance and I…" He hesitated. "Nance was my girl. We almost got married, but you know how it is, I was on the road a lot. It happens."

"Sure, I bet it does."

"It was a great life. We won the Stanley Cup two years ago, you know."

He spoke with a kind of yearning, and Lucy realized that he missed his sport, his team, his old life. A used-up, retired athlete. What a shame.

"I guess I do remember that," she said. "Wasn't there a ticker tape parade downtown when the team got home?"

"There sure was," he replied, his eyes lighting up with remembrance. "What a day."

"The Gents. I guess I have heard more about your team than I thought. I just didn't pay attention," Lucy mused.

"We didn't do so well last year," he continued. "We lost our goalie, Uri, and my knees were getting bad. We had some rookies who needed shaping up, but they should be coming along."

"The Denver Gents," Lucy said pensively. "I do remember reading about the Gents. Last year. Wasn't there something...?"

Jeff averted his eyes. "Yeah, there was."

"Something..." She looked at him closely, questioningly. "I think Roy must have told me, but I didn't really pay attention. There were some games that were thrown, was that it?"

"That's what they say," Jeff replied with that same edge.

"Don't they know who—"

"You may as well hear this," Jeff said, cutting her off. "I was *asked* to retire. Good old Jeffrey Zanicek, scapegoat."

Lucy gazed down at her hands, horribly embarrassed. A long moment of unsettling silence fell like a curtain between them. "You said scapegoat," she began awkwardly. "I take it someone else is guilty. Is that person still playing?"

"Yes."

"Is there anything you can do, you know, to clear your name?"

He laughed bitterly. "Now you sound exactly like Roy," he said. "'Zany, you've got to do something.'"

"'Zany'?"

"My nickname."

Lucy smiled tentatively. "A zany fellow," she mused. "I like it." And in reply she finally got a little smile out of him.

It struck Lucy then—the coaching job at D.U. Naturally, if there was a cloud over Jeff's head, they wouldn't hire him. So that was the problem. Interesting.

A warm, fragrant breeze lifted the corners of the tablecloth. They ordered snifters of sweet Kahlua and sipped slowly.

"Oh, it sure was a good life," Jeff was saying wistfully. "The crowds. There's nothing like a crowd screaming for a goal to fire you up. It's so good when every move is just right. And the guys, they're your best buddies in the world. You're a team. Boy, we had some great guys. There was this crazy Finn, couldn't speak a word of English, but could he play hockey. He just yelled 'shoot' all the time and drank vodka straight all night."

"It must have been fun."

"Fun, oh, that it was. We'd play practical jokes on one another. There were these twins on the team, the Barbeau brothers from New Hampshire. They'd always switch positions and you never knew who you were passing to. 'Frank and Hank,' we called them. Actually their names were François and Henri. They were pieces of work, I'll tell you. They got into more fights than anyone on the team—with each other!"

Lucy laughed. Jeff had a way of telling stories, a good sense of humor, great timing. The Kahlua slipped languidly down her throat, and she felt a sense of peace fill her.

She studied him as he called the waiter over and asked for the bill. *"Por favor,"* he said to the man, then grinned, proud of himself, boyishly proud. It hit her again, the familiarity of that smile, that expression. She'd seen him somewhere . . .

Abruptly the picture flew into her head, complete, clear, a television commercial with Jeff posed—that same exact expression on his face: shy, proud, humorous. But the ad was for men's underwear, and Jeff was posing in nothing but a pair of bright red briefs.

"Oh, for heaven's sake," Lucy said, bursting out laughing. "Now I know where I've seen you! Oh, Jeff, I would have recognized you better without your clothes on," she said without thinking.

"Why, Miss Hammond," Jeff replied, leaning forward and folding his arms on the table, "I think you've got the wrong person." And they both laughed until the heads of the other diners turned.

CHAPTER THREE

IT WAS A WARM NIGHT for January, even in the sub-tropics, and Lucy pulled her knit dress over her head and stretched out on her bed clad in only her underwear. Outside the bungalow, she could hear the palm leaves stirring pleasantly in a gentle night wind and the occasional shuffling of feet along the garden path. Lovers returning to their rooms, their fingers entwined, the balmy air caressing their faces, she thought, fantasizing.

She put the images from her head, but a dull ache remained in the pit of her stomach. Just how important was this meeting of Roy's? More important than she was, obviously. She supposed there were drawbacks to the three-piece-suit executive type. Roy, she knew, had not had a vacation in over two years. In fact, the Cozumel trip had been her idea; at least, she had neatly planted the seeds in his mind, then watched them take hold and sprout. She wished now that the notion had been his in the first place, that he had wanted this trip, dreamed about it, counted the days and hours until they were alone together.

And yet, Lucy mused, she would still marry Roy if he asked her. She'd marry him and put up with his frequent absences, the untimely meetings and sudden out-of-town business trips. She'd marry him because he was a good man, he'd never cheat on her and, of course, she loved him.

But Lucy could just see herself in the big house they would buy. She'd have dinner parties for foundation members and business associates, and Roy would call in the middle of the first course and tell her how sorry he was, but he'd gotten hung up.... And what about children? She was thirty-two, not getting any younger. An image unbidden popped into her mind: she was in the hospital, having a baby, and the nurse came in. *"I'm so sorry, Mrs. Letterman, but your husband's flight from Chicago was delayed...."*

What *would* it be like being married to a busy executive?

It occurred to Lucy to get up and put on her nightgown before she drifted off to sleep. But somehow it was so comfortable to lie there in the dim light, a soft breeze creeping in the partially open window. She felt tired suddenly, mentally done in. It had been a long ten days in Yaxcaba, and before that, she'd been frantically rushing around Denver, trying to raise another twenty thousand dollars for a new wing at the children's shelter on Colfax Avenue. She'd needed a vacation, and the thought of it had kept her going. But now it seemed the only sensible thing to do was to fly home in the morning. Roy's two days were probably going to turn into a week.

Lucy's eyelids were half-closed. Lazily she glanced at the empty closet—why unpack when she was leaving, anyway? She reached for the switch on the bedside lamp, and that was when it caught her eye. On the shelf in the closet was a paper bag. She probably never would have seen it if it hadn't been for the angle of her vision. The last guest must have left it there. Or maybe,

Lucy thought idly, one of the maids had forgotten her lunch bag. A sandwich, fruit . . .

She finally rose and pulled her nightgown out of her case, then walked to the closet. If there was a sandwich in the bag, by morning it might smell to high heaven. On her tiptoes, she reached up and took hold of the bag. It was bulky and surprisingly heavy. She opened it, half expecting a bad odor to assail her, but it was a full ten seconds before her brain registered what the contents actually were.

Lucy blinked, suddenly wide-awake. It couldn't be . . .

She moved back toward the bed and the light from the lamp, put her glasses on to see better, then sat down abruptly. This was ridiculous. It couldn't be . . .

Gingerly, disbelieving, she dumped the contents onto the bedspread. Neatly strapped wads of fifty and one hundred dollar bills tumbled out. For a long moment she could only sit staring at the piles, mesmerized. Then, carefully, as if they might suddenly vanish, Lucy touched the piles one by one. Surely she'd wake up to find this all a silly dream.

But the stacks were real.

Lucy stood and began pacing the room, her finger on her chin. Every so often she spun around sharply, adjusting her glasses, making sure the money was still there.

"Crazy," she kept saying, "this is just too crazy."

It only made sense to count it. Wetting her index finger with her tongue and flipping through the bills, she figured there must be a half a million U.S. dollars lying on her bed—give or take fifty thousand.

"Half a million dollars!" she whispered, stunned. Who on earth would leave so much money stuffed in a brown bag in a hotel room?

Suddenly she felt like laughing. This was really quite impossible, some stupid joke. Roy? Had Roy... But that was absurd. A maid?

Slowly, still dazed, she stuffed the stacks back into the bag, then looked furtively around her room. She'd never be able to sleep with that money in here—just the thought of it would drive her mad. She'd take it to the desk clerk.

Take a half a million dollars to a night clerk? By morning he'd be in Paris!

The police. Of course.

But what would she tell them?

"You see, guys, I found this money...." Mexican police were paranoid these days, what with the big drug deals going on. Lucy, the drug dealer....

She had to think about this carefully. As giddy as she felt, she knew this was no laughing matter. The money hadn't just appeared in that closet; it belonged to someone. And it wasn't the proceeds from somebody's salary check.

Quickly, as if the bag had somehow become tainted, Lucy shoved it under her bed and began to pace the room again. Wherever the money had come from, it had to be illegitimate. No one left that kind of cash lying around.

Suddenly Lucy had to get out of the room. She'd go for a walk on the beach, that was it, a walk on the warm sandy beach to clear her mind, to settle her down. Hurriedly she put on slacks and a camp shirt, then glanced at the bed. Would the money be safe? She giggled out loud, a hysterical bubble welling up in her breast. It would be a blessing to come back to the room and find it gone, a figment of her imagination vanished into thin air!

The Cozumel Caribe Hotel nestled in an inlet whose beach carved a long half-moon into the black sea. Lucy stood at the water's edge, feeling the waves suck at her bare feet, listening to the ebb and flow, seeing the moon's silvered trail glitter across the wave tops.

What was she going to do with that bag of money? What was *safe* to do, what was *right*?

She kicked at the water, her head hanging, trying to make sense of her dilemma.

A couple sat in some high-backed beach chairs behind her, giggling. Mariachi music drifted from the veranda of the hotel, fading in and out with the breeze. She wished fervently that Roy was here with her, that she could dump this problem on him, ask him what to do—

"Lucy?" a voice asked tentatively.

She whirled, startled.

"Sorry," Jeff Zanicek said, "but I thought that was you."

"Oh, I . . ."

"You all right?"

"Oh, yes, I'm fine." She took a deep breath. She *had* to tell someone; she had to get it off her chest. "I'm glad you came along." Oh, this was ridiculous. He'd never believe her. "I, ah, gosh, this is going to sound crazy."

"Hey, do you have a problem?"

She swallowed. "Yes, I have a problem. Will you promise not to laugh?"

"Sure." His head was cocked in that way he had.

"What would you say if I told you I just found a bag of money in my room?" she asked all in a rush.

"Now there's a new one," Jeff said, a corner of his mouth lifting into a smile.

"No, I'm serious. Honest."

His face fell a little. "You sure it isn't the Kahlua?"

"I found a bag, Jeff, stuffed full of money. A half million dollars," she whispered, and gave a little shiver despite the warm breeze.

Jeff stared at her. "This is some kind of a joke," he said, cocking his head again. "Now comes the punch line, right?"

"Wrong," Lucy breathed, then explained exactly what had happened. "I put it under my bed."

"Okay," he said, taking her hand, "this I have to see. Come on."

She let him steer her across the sand and along the path until they were at her door. "I hope it's gone," she said, putting the key in the lock. "I really do. Then you can laugh all you want, and so will I."

Unfortunately the sack was still perfectly safe, hidden in the shadows beneath her bed.

"Too bad," Lucy said when Jeff stood up and dumped the money onto her bed. "I was hoping—"

"You counted this?" he asked, an amazed expression on his face.

Lucy nodded slowly. "It's a half million, give or take loose change." But he wasn't listening. Instead Jeff stood there with his hands on his hips, whistling through his teeth as he stared at the piles and piles of money. "What are we going to do?" Lucy asked anxiously.

"Well," he said finally, "I always wanted a sailboat, and they say the Mediterranean is nice this time of year."

"Be serious. What *are* we going to do?" she repeated. "I can't just leave it here in this bag."

Jeff muttered something, then said, "I need to think about this. Wow."

"*We* need to think," Lucy said firmly. She began to put the money away, while Jeff stood alongside the bed and frowned. "There," she said when it was hidden again. "For now I don't know what else to do."

"Me, neither," He glanced at her and whistled softly again. "Let's get some air. Talk this out."

It was past eleven when they strolled down toward the water's edge again and wandered along the moonlit cove. The gentle waves tickled Lucy's toes and the soft, fine sand squished up around her ankles warmly. This was crazy, she kept thinking; here they were, practically in paradise, walking along a wind-kissed shore in the tropics, a lopsided moon silvering the sea in bright swaths, the aroma of flowers drifting on the breeze. It should have been idyllic. But there was no Roy, and there was that crumpled brown bag in her room.

Jeff was silent as he walked, his trousers rolled up, his hands hidden in his pockets. Yet there was a vitality in him, an easy energy that seeped from his well-muscled body, that was somehow comforting. She felt oddly, intuitively, that she could count on this man. And yet, hadn't she been totally wrong about his type too many times before?

"I keep thinking," he said, "that we ought to call the local police, but if that money is connected to something shady, well..."

"We'll be mixed up in quite a mess," Lucy finished.

He nodded. "I don't care for the two of us locked up in a Mexican jail, either. We might be gray by the time they let us go."

"But why would someone leave a bag of money like that? I mean, *I'd* have to be dead or something to do such a crazy thing," she said.

"We could do some checking," Jeff suggested. "Call the local hospital, look in the newspaper."

They stopped for a moment, and Lucy stared up at him, thinking. There really weren't many choices, she knew. They could keep it, but that was a repugnant notion, and she would never be able to live with herself. Although, she thought fleetingly, Jeff might not think it was such a bad idea. The notion chilled her. She tilted her head, unaware of the length of time she was standing there, contemplating him.

He sure could use that kind of money, she reflected. He'd all but admitted he was without means of support right now.

Lucy shook off the unsettling thought. She was not being fair, only using past experience as an excuse to see him in the worst light.

"I don't think we have a choice," she found herself saying. "We have to turn the money over to the authorities and take our chances that they'll believe our story."

"No one is ever going to claim it, you know," Jeff said. "It's got to be dirty money, Lucy. Only a maniac would walk into a police station and admit it belonged to him. And how would he prove it?"

"I realize that," she said, "but we don't have any other choice."

"I suppose not," Jeff answered, but there was reluctance in his tone.

For a time they kept walking, until a rocky jetty impeded them. Lucy sat down on one of the damp boulders and dug her feet into the sand. "I'm *never* going to be able to sleep tonight," she said, twisting her toes in the grainy water.

"After we see the police," Jeff said, "you can rest all day."

"If we aren't held for questioning."

"There is that." He laughed lightly and skipped a pebble across the calm silvered surface of the water.

"Besides," Lucy said, looking up at his face, "I'm planning on flying out of here in the morning."

"You're still bent on that?"

He sounded disappointed, but, then, he was only thinking of Roy, of course. "It's for the best," she said quietly.

"Look, it's none of my business, but Roy is a special guy. He's worth it, Lucy, honest."

"You don't have to tell me that."

"Then wait for him. Day after tomorrow you'll be glad you did."

"Day after tomorrow," Lucy said darkly, "I'll be in Denver."

Jeff sat beside her, close, a little too close, she thought. "I don't want you to take this wrong or anything," he began, leaning his head toward hers, "because I love Roy like a brother. But sometimes he just doesn't see the trees for the forest."

"The forest for the trees," Lucy said, "I think."

"Whatever. The point is, Roy is too stressed out to realize what he might be throwing away."

"Me?"

"Of course you, Lucy. Who else? But if you could hang in there..."

"Who said I wasn't going to hang in there? I'm only flying back to Denver. It's not the end."

"But it's wrong."

"Oh? And how's that?"

"You know," he said, gazing at her in earnest, "you two won't have this special time together."

Lucy shrugged. "Quality time," she said. "I hate that expression."

"Yeah, I do, too, but there *is* truth to it."

"Um."

"Stay, Lucy. We'll take care of the money and then have a good time. I'm not such a bad fellow."

She glanced at him in surprise, the edge of loneliness in his voice taking her off guard. "You're a very nice person, Jeff," she said.

"There's another great word—*nice*."

"You know what I mean."

"Maybe."

Lucy smiled. "Are you fishing?"

"Me?"

"Yes, Mr. Zanicek—Zany. I think you're fishing for compliments."

"A guy can use all he can get."

"Well, then," she said, "I do think you're funny."

"Thanks," he replied, almost bashfully.

"And you're cute."

"In my jockey shorts."

"Yes," she agreed, looking down at her hands, "although I suspect you know that."

"The trouble is," Jeff said, serious again, "I'm in between opportunities now."

"Well, you just need to get busy and find out who the crook is on your old hockey team."

"Sure."

He *was* easy to talk to, Lucy decided as they sat there, gazing out across the water. He was uncomplicated and, she sensed, lonely. It seemed a shame, a handsome, nice person like Jeff going through this difficult time in his life without someone, a woman, to lean on.

She stole a sidelong glance at him. He was good-looking all right, sexy, youthful, and already she liked the way he cocked his head when he was listening.

"A penny for your thoughts," Jeff said, rousing her.

"Oh, I was thinking about the money."

"And are you thinking about giving Roy a break and staying?"

"Jeff, I already told you—"

"You know," he said abruptly, coming to his feet and pulling her up, too, "now's not the time to make these decisions. Let's talk about it tomorrow. What do you say?"

"I say," Lucy replied, "that you have an awful stubborn streak, Zany." She realized then that he still had hold of her hands and that they were standing there very close, too close. Awkwardly she took her hands from his and looked down at her feet. "I suppose we ought to get back," she mumbled, aware that her heart was beating just a little too rapidly.

It was well past midnight when they walked back into the circle of light from the hotel and headed along the path toward the bungalows. Lucy felt confused. What was she doing enjoying Jeff's company even the tiniest bit? She realized that she'd been acutely aware of him the whole way back and that once, when her arm had brushed his, she'd felt her skin tingle.

It was only disappointment on her part, Lucy convinced herself; plain and simple, she missed Roy.

"Well," he was saying, "would you be more comfortable if I kept that bag in my room?"

"Oh," Lucy said, "I hadn't thought about it. I suppose it would be sensible."

They rounded a bend in the path, Jeff holding aside a palm frond for Lucy, when suddenly she stopped short, adjusting her glasses and stared ahead. It looked like there were two people at her bungalow door—a tall, dark-haired man in a suit and a maid. "Jeff," Lucy said, "isn't that my room?" She pushed at her glasses again with a finger.

"Sure looks like it. Come on." He took her elbow and they picked up the pace, but then the strange man seemed to notice them and did an odd thing; he said something to the maid and hurried away in the opposite direction, disappearing around a corner into the night.

Lucy paused, wondering if she was imagining things.

"Come on," Jeff urged, tugging at her arm.

"But what . . . ?" she started to say, hurrying after him.

The maid—the night housekeeper, actually—was holding a big key ring and babbling away in Spanish. Lucy listened patiently, frowning, until the woman threw up her hands and went trudging on down the path.

"What was that all about?" Jeff asked.

She shook her head, half amused, half perplexed. "That was the night housekeeper. She was just letting some man into his room."

"Into *your* room?"

"No, no. He'd lost his key or something. He got his room number mixed up." She shrugged it off.

"Let me get this straight," Jeff was saying. "The guy needed to be let into *his* room, right?"

"That's what she told me."

"Okay, fine, happens all the time. But tell me this, how come he left?"

"Well, I don't..."

"In fact," Jeff said tightly, "it looked to me like he split in a big hurry when he saw us coming."

Lucy stared at Jeff for a long moment, then suddenly, simultaneously, they both said, "You don't suppose..."

CHAPTER FOUR

"THIS IS JUST GREAT," Jeff said as Lucy unlocked her door. "Just swell."

"You're acting as if it's *my* fault," she said defensively, then caught herself. "Sorry. I guess that man really shook me up."

"And I'm sorry I snapped at you." Jeff walked ahead of her, turning on lights, doing a poor job of covering the fact that he was searching the place—for a possible intruder, Lucy thought grimly. "Check the bag, will you?" Jeff said as he poked his head into her bathroom.

She got down onto her hands and knees and pulled up the bedspread. "Still here." But when she glanced up at him she could see he wasn't really listening. Instead he was staring at the lavish display of flowers and the champagne bucket.

"From Roy," she said, getting to her feet, dusting off her hands.

"Nice gesture." He looked away from the table then and went to the window, closing it, switching on the air-conditioning.

"But I *like* fresh air," Lucy protested. "This is ridiculous. I'm not safe in my own room?"

He let out a breath and shook his head gently. "I know," he said, "it's hard to swallow. But I'd feel better if you kept the window closed."

"I'm calling the front desk," Lucy said decisively, angrily. "Let's just see if some guest really did lose his key." She dialed, then had to wait and wait, and the answers she finally got were unsatisfactory.

"Well?" Jeff asked.

"The clerk said no one asked him about a lost key tonight. He even checked with the housekeeper, but—get *this*—she claims she didn't let anyone into a room."

"She's scared," he said sympathetically.

"Well, so am I," Lucy admitted, and plunked herself down on the bed. "Darn."

"Do you want to call the police?" Jeff asked carefully. But Lucy was still against it, still concerned that the two of them might be getting in over their heads. "You know," Jeff said, "I don't like the idea of your sleeping in here tonight, not one bit."

"Sleep? I'm as wired as a battery. I'll never sleep, anyway," she replied, getting up and turning around in the middle of the room, wishing she could see the humor—if there was any—in the situation. "Oh, hey, let's open the champagne. I think we both need a drink, don't you?" She would have done anything at that moment just so she wouldn't have to think anymore.

"You sure?" He was looking at her oddly.

But Lucy was already pulling the foil and wire off the bottle and tugging at the cork. "Boy, am I sure. This stuff's going to foam all over, though. It's warm."

It did foam, but she held the bottle over the bathroom sink, then poured the two crystal glasses full. "A toast?" she asked, raising her glass.

"To Roy," Jeff said, and met her gaze.

"To Roy, absent but not forgotten, right?" Lucy felt giddy; the whole situation was unreal, a bad movie.

She drank the too-sweet, bubbly champagne and felt it hit her stomach like molten honey. "Wow."

"Look, Lucy, I really don't think you should stay in this room tonight," Jeff said again.

"Why don't we just stay up all night?"

"Bad idea. Listen, there's room in mine. I'd feel better. I mean, for your safety. And I'm sure Roy wouldn't mind."

She turned away, vaguely unsettled, but glad, too. She *really* didn't want to stay alone in her room, and Lord knows she was tired.

Nevertheless, it would be awfully, well, intimate. "Maybe there's a spare room in the hotel," Lucy said quickly. "I'll try the desk clerk."

While she tried the desk once more, Jeff took a drink of the champagne and grimaced, his eyes catching hers. "Thank you, anyway," she said over the phone, then hung up. "Not a spare corner in the place till tomorrow afternoon. It's the height of the season."

"I can stay in here," Jeff suggested. "We'll switch rooms."

"I don't know. I mean, you won't be any safer in here than I would be."

He smiled, putting down his glass with a clink. "I'm trying to be gallant."

"To heck with that," she said firmly, "we'll do fine together." Without thinking, she added, "Wouldn't Roy be surprised?"

"I'm sure he would" was all Jeff said.

She gathered up the essentials, her makeup case, nightgown, even a paperback she'd been carrying around for months. Although, she suspected, tonight she wasn't going to get any reading done. While she collected her things, she couldn't help watching Jeff out of the corner of her eye. He was standing near the table, running a finger thoughtfully across the satin-smooth surface of an orange flower petal, his brow creased deeply. There was something so lonely, so distant about him that her heart squeezed unaccountably. Easy and carefree on the surface, she thought, picking up her toothbrush, but inside something was troubled.

"Well," Lucy announced with false cheer, "all set."

He turned at the sound of her voice. "Guess I better get the money," he said. "In fact, I've got a locked flight bag, and maybe I'd better put it in the hotel safe."

Jeff's room was a mirror-image of hers, but without the flowers and champagne bucket. While she stood in the middle of the floor, holding her things to her chest, he emptied his nylon flight bag and stuffed it with the money.

"Don't forget to lock it," Lucy warned.

"If I can remember the combination." He locked the bag and hefted it as if checking its weight. "Half a million," he mused.

"Spooky," Lucy said.

"Look, I'll take this on down to the desk. Be sure you lock up after me. The chain and all."

"You don't think . . ."

"I don't *think* anything, Lucy. I'm only taking every precaution." Jeff strode to the door, pulled it open and paused. "Listen, make yourself at home, you know." He shot her a reassuring smile. "Oh, and you take the bed. The couch will be fine with me. It pulls out."

"I couldn't," Lucy began.

"Let's argue this later," he said, and disappeared out the door.

Lucy sighed and looked around Jeff's room. Her head was buzzing from the champagne, and weariness sat heavily on her. Maybe she'd sleep, after all. She glanced around once more, noting a wet towel on the armchair by the bed, the open leather travel bag with clothes hanging out—a man's hotel room. A *strange* man's room, she reminded herself, then decided it might be prudent to put on her nightgown—the black lacy thing she'd bought for this trip—and be covered up and on the couch before he got back.

She brushed her teeth hurriedly and folded her clothes, then headed for the couch, feeling ridiculous in the transparent nightgown that was made to reveal rather than cover. Why hadn't she brought along her familiar, safe, oversize T-shirt?

She tossed aside the cushions on the couch and pulled out the sofa bed, seeing the thin coverlet over the sheets. Goose bumps raised on her arms and back as the faint breeze from the air-conditioner brushed her skin. Maybe he'd turn the thing off.

Jeff was back by the time she was drawing the cover over her legs. She had a strong urge to pull it all the way to her chin, but that was even more ridiculous. Besides, Lucy thought, they were both adults; Jeff had seen women in less than this. *He's Roy's friend. He won't care, anyway.*

"I thought you were going to put the chain in place." He tossed the room key onto the dresser with a clatter.

"Oh," Lucy replied, "I never even remembered." She saw his eyes, which had swiveled to her when he'd spoken, shift away quickly. "Sorry," she said, "about the chain."

"Um," he mumbled, and began to take off his sport coat. He was about to toss it on the chair with the towel, when he seemed to catch himself and hung it in the closet. Lucy slid down deeper under the coverlet and wiggled her cold toes, yawning, but feeling too keyed-up to close her eyes. He took off his red shirt when she watched, trying to think of something to say, and then, thankfully, he headed toward the bathroom.

This isn't going to work, Lucy decided. She'd never sleep in this awkward situation. But what choice was there? Go back to her room? Not a chance.

Behind the closed bathroom door the water was running, the toilet flushing. She pretended that none of it was really happening. Tomorrow she'd fly home. Roy would think it was all a great story, a riot. Or would he?

Jeff emerged from the bathroom, softly whistling. She stole a casual look and froze. Oh, God, he was wearing a tank top that said Denver Gents on it and a pair of purple jockey shorts decorated with yellow stars.

He must have noticed her regard, because he stopped and glanced down, as if just noticing what he had on. He made a gesture with his hand and grinned at her crookedly. "They send me dozens of these things," he told her, "and I thought I'd be alone."

"You can't just toss them away," she said, trying to return his smile. *Oh, Roy, I'm going to kill you,* she thought.

She'd seen Jeff's body, of course, she couldn't help it. She'd seen the thin white slanted scars on his knees, nice knees, she'd noted. Muscular thighs and curving calves covered with a fuzz of golden hair. Broad shoulders and corded arms and a practically hairless chest. A strong neck. Of course, plenty of men's swimsuits displayed a whole lot more. She bunched her pillow under her head and tried to close her eyes, but she kept watching despite herself as he turned toward the bed. He *was* beautifully put together, not tall and lean and elegant like Roy, but hard and chiseled and solid, an athlete. It suddenly occurred to her that she'd love to see him play hockey.

He had a firm round rear end—a skater's butt, she would later learn it was called. He leaned over and pulled back the sheets; the muscles rippled in his shoulder and one thigh contracted as he put his weight on it. Every nerve in her body quivered abruptly.

This wasn't going to work.

Lucy sat up, dragging the cover to her chin this time. "Ah," she began.

"Yeah?"

"Ah, I'm not sure." She swallowed. "Look, Jeff..."

For a long moment he stayed there, half in the bed, half out, and tipped his head at her. Finally it seemed to dawn on him. "Oh." He paused, then said, "Maybe I should, ah, head on over to your room."

"But that man..."

"He won't be back. At least, not tonight. You saw how he took off."

"Well, yes."

"And besides, I'm sure I could handle him, anyway."

"Are you positive? I feel really bad about this," she added, but he was already out of bed. She shut up wisely and watched while he tugged his pants on, up over his calves and scarred knees, over his golden-haired, muscular thighs, over his round rear end and zipped them up, pulling in his stomach in an automatic reflex the way men do.

"Sweet dreams," he said, picking up her room key from the table where she'd put it, shooting her an understanding, slightly rueful smile. "See you in the morning."

When he was gone Lucy closed her eyes and fell back against the pillow. A silly, childish relief washed over her, along with stinging guilt. She felt as if she'd sent an innocent man into dangerous exile. She prayed he wouldn't sit up all night waiting for the dark man to return. Poor Jeff.

She fell asleep, only to dream of a man knocking at the door of her bungalow, and when she let him in it was Roy, but his face melted into Jeff's features, then back to Roy's and then into the face of the dark-haired man who'd tried to get into her room. But the dark man was outside somehow and he kept tapping at the door, tapping, tapping...

Lucy jerked away. Sunlight streamed in through the blinds; it was morning and someone was knocking at her door. She got up, in a fog, and unlocked it.

"Morning," Jeff said cheerfully.

"Oh." She blinked her eyes and focused on him.

"I brought you some coffee and one of those sweet rolls they have down in the restaurant. It isn't too early for you, is it?" he asked.

"Oh, no, that's all right, uh, come on in." She backed toward the couch, suddenly realizing that all she had on was the black lace nightie, and pulled the sheet around her as if she did this sort of thing ten times a day. Jeff didn't seem to have noticed her, however. He was setting the coffee down and pulling the napkin off a roll on a plate instead.

"You sleep okay?" he asked.

"Actually I did. What about you? Did anyone try to get in the room?" she asked, relaxing now that the sheet was wrapped around her, toga-style.

"Slept like a baby. If someone tried, I never heard him. Sugar in your coffee? Cream?"

"Two sugars, please. Have you been up for long?"

He handed her the cup, sitting on the end of the pullout couch where she'd slept. "Yeah, I'm an early riser. I went for a walk on the beach. I've been thinking."

"About the money?"

Jeff nodded. "I've been going over all the angles, and I believe taking it to the authorities would be a big mistake. We're in a foreign country, a country already nervous about dope dealers and immigration and smuggling. I'm certain we'd get ourselves into a terrible mess."

"But what do we do with it?"

"That's what I haven't figured out yet," he said. "If we were in the States, I'd know, but here..."

"What would you do with it in the States?" she asked.

"Take it to the FBI, I guess, and make damn sure the newspapers heard about it so no one could keep it for themselves."

Lucy sipped the coffee, thinking, liking Jeff's Stateside solution. She sighed. "Boy, I wish we could just turn that bag over to somebody, somebody we trust, and wash our hands of it."

"You know anybody like that here? Anywhere in Mexico?"

"No." She stared across the room at Jeff's clothes hung over the back of the chair, at the towel still flung hastily. Her brother had kept his room like that, but she knew Roy's room was neat as a pin, with his suit hung on the standing valet and his shoes lined up in rows. What would Roy, sharp-witted, in-control Roy, do in this situation? "I do know people like that, but they're at home."

"Well, you're one up on me. I can't think of anybody who'd know what to do with a bagful of illegal money."

Lucy sat up. "Of course! He's just the person! Tom McLaughlin. He's the Hammond Foundation's lawyer, and my lawyer, too. He's been friends with my father forever. Tom'll know what to do!"

"But he's back in Denver?"

"I could call him, just ask his advice. Maybe he can help us out. If anyone can, *he* can."

Jeff spread his hands and tilted his head. "Hey, go for it."

The sheet had slipped when she sat up, and Jeff, as gallant as he'd been up to now, had definitely noticed. The instant Lucy saw the path of his gaze, she swung around in the bed and put her feet over the side, showing him her back. She felt clumsy and foolish, overreacting to an insignificant moment—any man who wasn't blind was going to steal a peek at a black nightie, for heaven's sake, and Jeff was a healthy, red-blooded man. She shouldn't make so much of it; it was no big deal. Heck, it was flattering. Still, when she stood up and left—escaped—she could feel her nerves prickling under her flesh like tiny, isolated electric shocks. "I'll dress and call Tom," she said over her shoulder, wondering if the bathroom had always been so far from the couch.

"Sure, good idea," Jeff replied quickly, and she heard him get to his feet. "Think I'll grab my bag and shower in your room. Okay?"

"Fine. See you later," she called, closing the bathroom door with a snick. *Phew*. Oh, how awkward, how stilted. If only Roy were here, she thought. It was bad enough finding the money and that man. Now this. Why *wasn't* Roy here?

Lucy turned, then suddenly caught her reflection in the mirror and drew in her breath sharply. Could that really be her? She hardly recognized the image that stared back, a stranger, not the casually dressed woman who normally slept in an old T-shirt. No, the woman in the mirror had sexily tousled hair, and her breasts showed in detail beneath black lace. Was that how she'd wanted to look for Roy? Was her plan seduction, that time-honored foil of womankind? Lucy stood there, horrified at how Jeff must have seen her that morning, and as she stared at the woman in the mirror, something teased her; some previously hidden knowledge about herself stared back at her from bewildered dark blue eyes that were her own. And suddenly she couldn't fathom why she'd bought the black nightgown.

She shook her head then, quickly pulled the black nightie off and stepped into the shower.

Afterward she felt much more herself, her hair washed and brushed back, her glasses on, her camp shirt tucked neatly into her white slacks. That person in the mirror had been an aberration, a momentary unreal vision.

She looked up Tom's law firm in her address book, placed her call and waited, nibbling on the roll Jeff brought her. Despite the unsettling moments between them that morning, he was really a nice guy. She wondered what he thought of her. But really, why did she care? It was Roy who counted. Roy whom she wanted, and Jeff was only his friend. Her friend, too, she supposed, if—when—she and Roy got married.

The phone rang. Lucy picked it up and heard Tom's secretary saying, "McLaughlin, Howard and Scott."

"Hello, Martha, this is Lucy Hammond. I'm calling from Cozumel. Can I talk to Tom?"

"Miss Hammond, how are you? Tom's just getting into his office. Let me buzz him."

Tom's hearty voice came on the line. "Lucy, where are you, Cozumel? Is everything okay?"

"Tom! Oh, it's good to hear your voice. Listen, I've got this wild story to tell you. You've got to promise you'll believe me. I'm not crazy, but I don't know what to do."

"Calm down, Lucy, and tell me. I know you're not crazy."

She told him about Roy, and Jeff arriving instead, and about the bag of money. When she finished there was utter silence on the other end of the line.

"Tom?" she asked, suddenly panicked, clutching the phone.

"I'm here, young lady. Well! You've got yourself in a pickle. Let me think. I may have to check out some legal opinions on this. You know, international intrigue and stolen money are not my specialties."

"Oh, mine, neither! What can I do!"

"It would have to happen in a foreign country. Goddamn." Tom sounded like a down-home Colorado rancher. He was a big man, balding and somewhat overweight, and his legal talents were legendary. "Lucy, let me think."

"Am I in trouble, Tom?" she asked.

"Not yet. As long as you don't leave the country, you're okay. You've got your little Bonanza down there?"

"Yes."

"Okay, this is what you do." His tone was so sure, so decisive, Lucy felt much better. "You sit tight. The money's secure for now?"

"In the hotel safe."

"Okay, leave it there. I'll fly down and take care of everything from your end. If I go to the authorities with it, I think things will be much less complicated."

"Oh, Tom, I hate to make you do that."

"The Hammonds are my best clients, Lucy. Don't worry about me. I'll catch a flight as soon as Martha can fix me up. I'll be there tonight. What hotel are you at?"

"The Cozumel Caribe."

"Got it. Now you be real careful, you and that boy."

"Jeff."

"You and Jeff be real careful."

"You think . . . ?"

"I think nothing, young lady. Just change your room, watch your step and hold tight."

She hung up, feeling relieved to have dumped the problem in Tom's capable hands, but also feeling a certain unease, a sense of peril that was disconcerting. Maybe they should just leave the bag in the safe and fly home and never think about it again.

The knock at her door made her jump. It was Jeff. "You call the old family retainer yet?"

"He's flying down here today," she said, letting him in. "He said to wait for him, not to do anything. He'll take care of it."

"Well, that's a load off my mind," Jeff said brightly.

"He won't be here until tonight, though."

"So you won't be leaving today then," he said. "Great. You'll be here tomorrow when Roy comes."

"It looks like it, doesn't it? But I'm afraid it's not going to be the uncomplicated vacation I had in mind. Maybe I should call Roy and tell him?"

"He's going to be hard to reach in those meetings. Better wait till tonight when he's back in Denver," Jeff suggested.

"Everything's gone wrong, hasn't it?" she asked.

"Not everything. The weather's beautiful, the water's warm, the company... Well, I did promise Roy to show you a good time." His voice was deep and soft, his green eyes fixed on her.

"Jeff..." Lucy hesitated. "Maybe you should just get out of here, you know, avoid trouble. Roy didn't send you here to get involved in this."

He looked disappointed for a moment, then covered it with a grin. "You're damn lucky it's me here *instead* of Roy," he said lightly. "I'm a scrapper, lady. Roy's the three-piece-suit type."

"Oh, really?" she replied, giving in to his charm. "You're the knight on the white charger?"

"That's it. So no more of this talk of me splitting on you."

"Okay. You're the boss. So, what do we do now?"

"We entertain ourselves," he said, tossing his bag back on the chair. For an alarming split second Lucy thought he meant... But no, Jeff would never...

"Snorkeling," he said, his mouth lifting at a corner in a smile, "I *meant* snorkeling."

CHAPTER FIVE

JEFF COULDN'T GET A HANDLE on Lucy Hammond. He'd been expecting a high-powered type with long, blood-red fingernails, or at least a tough drill sergeant sort, although he couldn't see Roy with one of those. He'd met rich women before, tons of them. All sports figures did. The groupies clustered around the top athletes like moths around a light, wanting to touch, to be close, to buy them drinks, to be able to say that they'd made love to a superstar.

But this Lucy had him really puzzled. What struck him the most was how normal, girl-next-door *nice* she was. She made no attempts to impress or overpower; she left a man room to maneuver. Which was pleasant, comfortable.

And she was ordinary looking, too. Well, that wasn't to say she was plain, only that she wasn't a spectacular bombshell. No long painted fingernails, no carefully dyed hair, no perfect makeup, no fancy clothes. She was pretty in a homespun way, though, with beautiful dark blue eyes, which she kept mostly hidden behind her glasses. It was as if, Jeff mused, Lucy Hammond dared a man to find her attractive.

Except for the black nightie. Well, he knew that little item had been meant for Roy, and she probably didn't own another one like it. She'd been real self-conscious in it, too, wrapping herself up in the sheet like a mummy. Jeff smiled, remembering.

Lucy Hammond, for all her traveling and do-gooding, for all her money, had some definite insecurities.

Jeff let himself out of his room, Lucy's old room, and, whistling, strode down to the shop to rent some snorkeling gear and a motor scooter to get around on.

He knew now why Roy had said Lucy was special. She was not the usual type Roy hung around with. Good, maybe Roy was getting serious; maybe his taste was improving.

And maybe Lucy was trying just a little too hard to impress Roy. Perhaps she was getting worried, passing thirty, looking for a husband before she was too old. Perhaps she was uncertain of herself because of disappointments in the past. Jeff certainly knew that routine. Money couldn't buy everything, he guessed.

He got the motor scooter, a bright red job with a big wire basket to carry their snorkeling gear. The day was warm and breezy, sunny, humid, wonderful. In Denver his Corvette, parked at the airport, was probably covered with a foot of snow and would have to be jump-started by the time he got back. Denver in January....

What a strange twenty-four hours he'd just had. Holy cow, Lucy Hammond and a bag of money and a tropical paradise. Was he dreaming, or was this really happening?

He knocked on the door of her room, still whistling. This could be fun, snorkeling in the warm blue water, lazing on the beach, waiting for her lawyer friend to show up and take the dough off their hands.

"Hi," she said, opening her door, "you got the stuff?"

"No problem. Fins, wet-suit tops, face masks. And a little red putt-putt to get there. The guy said the beach was *no muy lejos*, which I took to mean not very far."

She smiled at him. "Right. I guess we may as well enjoy ourselves till Tom gets here."

"Sure, why not?" It made sense. So why did Jeff have these sneaking darts of guilt? Was it because Roy was holed up in some stuffy conference room in Telluride, wheeling and dealing, while he, Jeff, was escorting a nice girl to the beach? A nice girl, *Roy's* nice girl, he reminded himself, and maybe Jeff found her just a bit too congenial.

"So that's our transportation?" Lucy said, pointing. "Will we both fit on it?"

"Sure, no sweat."

He piled the snorkeling gear in the basket, stuck his windbreaker and Lucy's bag on top of it and fastened everything down with the Bungie cord. Swinging his leg over the seat, he said, "Okay, now wait for me to start it, then you get on behind."

The motor scooter started right away, wheezing and popping and settling down to a tinny rattle. Lucy got on gingerly, and he could tell she didn't want to put her arms around his waist. "Hold on," he said, pulling her hands forward, "you don't want to fall off." He twisted the gas control on the handlebar, let out the clutch, and the scooter jerked forward. Lucy lurched against him for a second, so that he could feel her breasts press into his back and her arms tighten convulsively around him. "Sorry," he mumbled, glad she couldn't see his expression, getting the hang of the scooter as he turned out of the hotel driveway onto the road.

He'd gotten directions from the kid in the shop. Follow the coast road south through San Miguel, then go another two miles along the beach. There would be an old stone jetty and steps leading down into the water. "The best skeen diveeng," the shop attendant had said. "*Mucho* feeshes, *mucho* beautiful."

The sea on their right was sparkling, as if it were full of diamonds; the wind blew into his face, smelling of saltwater and jungle flowers. "What a day!" he called back to Lucy, but his words were snatched away by the wind. He was very aware of her arms around him and her body pressed against his. Maybe this scooter wasn't such a great idea. He should have stuck to a taxi. Would she tell Roy about this ride and would Roy get mad at him? Jeez, this escort stuff wasn't so easy, especially when the woman you were supposed to entertain found half a million in dirty money and then spent the night in your room. *Hell, would Roy get mad at that?*

He wondered exactly what Lucy Hammond thought of him. Oh, he could just imagine. No good, out of work, ex-jock, sponging off his rich pal, a sad sack. He bet Lucy never hung around with guys like him, probably didn't even *know* anyone like him, despite the fact that she was a real nice girl and didn't seem to look down on him at all. Gosh, when they got back to Denver, he'd make sure Roy took her to a Gents game. He'd send Roy a couple of his front-row passes and tell him to show Lucy a good time—she'd like that.

The beach was right where the kid had told him. It was deserted, a small, sandy inlet. A sailboat tacked across the horizon, its white sail reflecting the sunlight. The ferry to the mainland chugged across the water on its daily run, and not far up the coast a glistening white cruise ship was anchored. What a place.

"Great, huh?" he asked.

"Oh, yes." She got her bag off the pile of equipment and pulled out a couple of towels. "I thought you might need one," she said.

"Well, you're right. I forgot a towel. Say, how much snorkeling have you done? I did it once about twenty years ago, I think."

"Oh, quite a bit. It's easy. They say the diving here is about the best in the Caribbean. That's one of the reasons Roy wanted to come here."

"Roy can see it tomorrow. Today it's my turn. Now just tell me how to get into this stuff." Jeff took off his shirt and pants. Underneath he wore a garish pair of Hawaiian surfing trunks.

Lucy was unbuttoning her shirt, unzipping her slacks. She, too, had her bathing suit on underneath, a plain black tank suit. No itsy-bitsy bikinis for Lucy. But she had a good figure, he couldn't help but notice. Full firm breasts and a slender waist and hips. Nice legs. And her skin was as white and smooth as a porcelain doll. "Holy cow," he said without thinking, "are *you* going to fry!"

She looked down at herself and blushed. "I did bring some suntan lotion."

"Good thing." Maybe he shouldn't have mentioned it—now she knew he'd been staring at her body. And he had no right to look or to touch, or even to *think* of her as female. Lucy was his best friend's lady.

She spread the towels out carefully, folded her pants and shirt, then straightened. "Um, I can get the rest, but would you put some, uh, lotion on my back?"

He swallowed and took the tube from her. As he squeezed some into his palm, it smelled heavenly, of coconuts and bananas and all things warm and tropical. Her back was flawless, her skin white and the tiniest bit damp from perspiration. Fine blond down lay golden against her skin, and her waist narrowed, disappearing into the black elastic of her suit. He closed his eyes for a second, then began applying the cream to her carefully, leaving not a square centimeter uncovered. Up, down, pull the strap aside, over her shoulder blade, feeling the bone under her satiny skin, seeing the way the small bumps of her vertebrae pressed out against her skin and how the muscles ran in the hollows alongside her backbone.

"Thanks," she said, pulling away and turning to face him, and he wondered how long he stood there with the tube of lotion in his hand, looking like a dope.

She did the rest, legs, arms, feet, all by herself, then glanced at Jeff. "Do you want some?"

How would her hands feel on his back, smoothing that fragrant stuff on him? "No, uh, no, thanks, I'll be fine."

Lucy had a blue wet-suit top. She pulled it on and zipped it up. Jeff did the same with his black one. It felt funny, tight, sticky and constricting, but the shop boy had told him they kept you warm longer. Then they pulled on their fins, big, flapping things.

"Do you know about spitting in your mask and clearing your ears?" Lucy asked.

"No, but I bet you do."

"You spit in the mask and rub it around, then rinse it out with seawater. That's so it doesn't fog up. Then the snorkel is attached like this, on the side of the mask. Don't let the top of it get underwater." She showed him, leaning over to rinse her mask. "And see these hollows that fit over your nostrils? When you get deep enough to where the pressure hurts your ears, you hold your nose with your fingers and clear your ears. We won't go very deep, though."

"Sounds good to me."

They splashed down the stone steps and into the water clumsily, with big finny feet, but once in the cool-warm velvety sea, Jeff found he became a different creature, moving powerfully through the water with a kick of his fins, just as on the ice he moved with a push of his skate blade. With the end of the snorkel tube in his mouth he could breathe easily, and the face mask allowed him to clearly see a new, exotic world.

He turned his head, searching for Lucy. She was off to one side, gesturing for him to follow, her legs white and gleaming as the sunlight slid through mottled water and reflected off her skin. Her hair floated around her head in delicate whorls, a cloud of darkness like a halo.

And then he saw the fish. Thousands, millions of them swarmed in schools around him, just off the shore, so close he wondered why he hadn't seen them from the beach. They were brightly colored, flung like jewels hither and yon by the current, their round eyes sometimes staring right into his mask. Yellow ones, red ones, striped ones, ones with lacy fins, big ones, tiny ones. And fans of gloriously colored waving coral, long green feelers of seaweed, sea flowers and filmy plants, all swaying to a silent concerto.

He put out a hand to touch a rotund yellow fish with pursed lips and huge round eyes. It slid across his fingertip, cool and alive, magic. Wow.

A hand tapped his shoulder. Lucy. Her eyes were wide behind her mask. She gestured toward a shadow on the ocean floor, maybe twenty feet down. It was an old wreck, a boat, encrusted with coral and surrounded by schools of fish. She pointed down. *Let's go,* she was saying. Then she motioned to her nose. *Don't forget to clear your ears.*

He followed her down, holding his breath as he went under, watching her white legs scissoring in front of him, the muscles of her rear end working sleekly as she kicked. He felt tremendous pressure inside his head, in his ears, then remembered to hold his nose and blow, and miraculously they cleared.

The boat had been there for a long time. It was almost rotted away, decaying into the floor of the ocean. It made a handy place in which a fish could play hide and seek, though. It was cooler down here, a little dimmer, but still extraordinarily bright and beautiful, an alien environment.

His breath gave out and he kicked upward, bursting through the surface into hot yellow sunlight, blowing the seawater from his snorkel and treading water easily with his magic fins. A moment later, Lucy's smooth dark head broke the surface.

He pushed his mask up to his forehead. "Wow, is that something!" he said.

"Isn't it gorgeous?" She pulled off her mask, and her deep blue eyes sparkled. "I had no idea it would be so beautiful. And the fish!"

"The 'feeshes,' as they say around here," Jeff quipped, and they both laughed.

"And no one else is even here. I love it," she said. "You know what?"

"What?"

"If I hadn't found that money, I would have gone home today and missed all this."

"Yeah," Jeff said, "that's true."

"Let's go down again!"

Lucy was playful under the glittering surface, tugging at his fins, rolling over, diving under him, chasing fish. Once she took his hand and led him to a coral-encrusted anchor. Her fingers in his felt cool and silken; her eyes laughed from behind her mask, and he couldn't help being just a little bit glad that Roy had had those meetings and asked his best friend to go to Cozumel to meet his girl. . . .

By midmorning Jeff had had enough. His senses were overwhelmed by the colors and rippling, unreal scenery. He needed to get out and think about it, lie on the beach and relax. And besides, the torque from those big flippers was making his knees ache. He and Lucy both stood up near the stone step, chest deep in the water. Lucy pulled her mask off and took a breath.

"Time for a coffee break," Jeff said. "I'm a prune."

"Me, too."

But she hadn't been lying stretched out on her towel for fifteen minutes, when she announced that she was going back in. "I can't help it," she said, running her fingers through her salt-caked hair. "I've got to go back in. Do you mind?"

"Not at all, but stay close to shore. Aren't we supposed to be on the buddy system?" he asked.

"Oh, for goodness' sakes, you can practically see me out there, the water's so clear. I won't go far."

"Okay. I'm going to lie here and soak up some rays." But he didn't close his eyes until she had disappeared into the water again, watching her walk across the beach, her hips swaying, her calf muscles working as her bare feet trod the loose sand.

The sun was getting hotter as it rose in the sky. Sweat collected in droplets on his chest. Occasionally he opened his eyes to see sailboats or cabin cruisers or smaller motorboats gliding across the calm sea, out beyond the points of land that enclosed this little cove. Behind him, on the road, cars passed once in a while; otherwise there was silence, the cry of a bird, the hiss and lap of the gentle waves—and not a single person to disturb his solitude.

He dozed, warm and utterly relaxed. In his half waking, half sleeping imagination, Lucy came running out of the water, smiling, happy, rushed into his arms and kissed him full on the lips; he could practically smell the coconut suntan lotion she had on. Somewhere in his mind he knew he shouldn't be dreaming that particular dream, but it was so pleasant he didn't want to stop. A far-off drone, a speedboat, infringed upon his consciousness, and he grunted and rolled over, knowing he should put some of Lucy's lotion on, but too lazy to get up and find it.

He drifted off again, feeling the sun hot on his back, soaking up the pleasurable warmth of the sand beneath him. This time he dreamed he was on the ice in the middle of a hockey game. Lucy was there watching, cheering for him. He was invincible, receiving the puck, skating toward the goal; the crowd was howling. Nobody could catch him. He faked to the right; the goalie lunged; then Jeff shot the puck cleanly in on the left. The red light went on—a goal! And Lucy leaned across the boards and kissed him, while the crowd went berserk.

The dream was so clear in his mind he jerked awake, still in the process of reaching out for Lucy. "Wow," he mumbled to himself, blushing, "what an imagination."

It was then that he heard a thin, small sound, a voice, a woman's cry, fading in and out. Where? The breeze struck his hot face and carried the sound with it more strongly. Yes, it was a woman—and she was screaming! Jeff jumped to his feet and spun around. There was nobody down the beach or on the road behind him. He put a hand up to shade his eyes and squinted out across the water.

A white speedboat was rocking up and down in the cove as if someone had jumped out of it hastily. And there, in the water were two figures; it looked like they were struggling. Then he saw the sun glint off something bright blue, and he knew it was Lucy's wet suit. He heard her scream again, and he didn't even stop to wonder. His legs were pumping, carrying him across the sand and into the sea. He launched himself flat into a racing dive and began stroking like a madman. He tried to shout, to tell her he was coming, but seawater filled his mouth, choking him. He could see two heads bobbing around if he lifted his face from the water, but the motion slowed him down too much.

He was out of breath, gasping, and the figures still seemed so far away. He pulled as hard as he could, raised his head once more, saw splashing and arms thrashing about.

And then he heard the motor of the boat start, and Lucy was only a few yards away, alone, and two men were in the boat, speeding off, churning the sea into froth that filled his mouth so that he had to spit it out.

Lucy. She was sort of floating, moving her arms weakly, her face mask hanging off. *Oh, God, what would Roy say?* ran crazily through his mind as he reached her, pulled her head up and held her there while he trod water.

"Lucy! Wake up!" he shouted, shaking her, going under himself, coming up gasping, still treading water. *Got to get her to shore,* he thought in panic. *Artificial respiration. Brain death occurs in seven minutes. Cross chest carry.*

He turned her on her back, placed his hip up under her, his arm across her chest. *Scissors kick, strong, pull with the free arm.* Thank God she had on her wet-suit top; it made her very buoyant. He wished he had his and his magic fins.

Kick, breathe, pull. Her body was limp, not heavy, just limp. Who were those men? What in hell had they been doing to her? Oh, boy, she better not— He couldn't finish the thought.

The wedge of beach was getting closer. Jeff ignored his exhaustion, his aching muscles, his galloping heart. He could do it. He'd been trained all his life to push his body beyond normal limits. He had to get her to shore.

Finally his feet touched bottom. He stood, forging through the water, pulling her up onto the sand, dragging her, half collapsing on top of her.

"Oh, God, Lucy," he panted. "Come on, Luce, come on, kid!" He knelt by her head, pushed her jawbone forward as he'd been taught, pinched her nostrils shut and put his mouth over hers.

Breathe the air into her lungs, wait, breathe again. Seawater trickled out of her mouth. He took a huge lungful of air and breathed it into her; he could see her chest rise when he blew in. Good, the air was going into her lungs. Five times. He was getting dizzy. Ten times. *Come on, Lucy,* he coaxed silently. *Come on.*

Then she coughed. He sat back on his heels, a thrill shooting through him. She coughed again; her eyelids fluttered; she sputtered, choking, coughing, getting the water out of her lungs.

Jeff grinned from ear to ear. "That's it, Luce," he said. He smoothed wet strands of hair off her forehead.

Eventually she lay quiet, very still, her breathing spasmodic, her chest heaving, her eyes closed.

"You're okay, Luce," he said softly. "Can you hear me? You're okay now."

She lay there, only half-conscious, but he could see she was going to be all right, and his heart felt very full within him. Strange, new sensations bombarded Jeff: protectiveness, caring, profound relief. For a moment he stayed motionless above her, marveling at the whole thing, then without a single thought of the consequences, he lowered his head toward hers once more and found her lips with his, but this time it was all different, very, very different.

CHAPTER SIX

LUCY AWAKENED TO THE SENSATION of Jeff's mouth covering hers. Then, quickly, his lips were gone, and she could feel the bright sun splash across her face as he raised his head.

She felt waterlogged and confused and dizzy, as if she were in the middle of a bad dream, trying to wake up. Everything around her seemed surreal, hazy at the edges and out of kilter, and her chest hurt.

"Lucy" she heard Jeff say, and she was aware of his body still poised over hers, his hands on either side of her shoulders.

She licked her lips and tried to focus on his face. "What ... ?"

"You damn near drowned out there. Can you remember anything?"

It came back to her in snatches, a snorkel in her mouth, the sunlight filtering through the crystalline water, warm, lovely. And then hands at her back, wrenching her head around, ripping off her mask.

A sudden terror rocked her.

"Lucy?"

"Oh, my God," she whispered, turning her head away, feeling nausea rise in her throat.

"What happened out there? I saw a boat, a couple of men."

"He tried to *kill* me!" she breathed. "He tore my mask and my snorkel off, and he held me under! Oh, God!"

Jeff swore softly.

"I think I tried to kick him. Yes, I'm sure I did. I was swallowing water, and I got him with my knee. You know, in the..."

"I get the picture."

"But then I can't remember—" She stopped, her fear abruptly swept aside by embarrassment. She remembered, all right: Jeff looming over her the way he was now, but closer, and his mouth on hers. He certainly had a novel method of mouth-to-mouth resuscitation!

"You had water in your lungs, Lucy," he said as if in explanation, but his eyes didn't quite meet hers. "You think you can move?" he asked. "Maybe we ought to get an ambulance down here."

"Oh, no," she said quickly, propping herself up on her elbows shakily, "I'll be fine now. Really."

"I'm not so sure."

"Honest, Jeff, I'm okay."

Nevertheless, even with the hot yellow sun pounding down on her, goose bumps raised on her skin as he helped her to her feet, and she swayed slightly.

"Yeah," Jeff commented softly, "you're just fine."

"I'll be okay," she said weakly.

"You need to go to a hospital and get checked out."

"Why? I'm alive—I think. There's nothing they can do."

"Well, then, we'd better tell the police. Those guys shouldn't be running around loose," he muttered angrily.

"The police . . . They'll ask questions. Do you really want to start all that? Isn't it just what you wanted to avoid?" She started coughing. Her throat felt as if it were on fire.

"You okay?" he asked, coming close, patting her back.

Sudden queasiness heaved in her belly. "No," she mumbled, "I'm going to be sick." Waves of dreadful nausea rolled over her, and cold sweat popped out on her forehead.

"Uh-oh" she heard Jeff say.

She took a step, trembling, and headed for a stone wall, wanting to hide, to die, but Jeff was beside her, one arm around her, and she was too sick to care. Her stomach emptied itself, and the awful queasiness subsided, but then she realized that Jeff's hand was on her forehead, strong and warm and comforting—and utterly humiliating.

"Oh, no," she moaned.

"It's all right. Everyone who swallows saltwater throws up. I read that somewhere," Jeff said matter-of-factly.

"I'm so embarrassed," she whispered.

"Hey, it's okay." He was squatting in front of her, his hands on his knees. "You feel better?"

"Yes." She couldn't look at him; this was awful. *What would Roy have done?* her mind asked sneakily, treacherously. *Impeccable Roy.*

"Can you sit up here on the wall? I'll get you something to drink."

While Lucy sat on the old stone wall, trying to collect herself, Jeff walked to the small refreshment stand just down the shoreline. She hugged his windbreaker around her shoulders and followed him with her eyes.

Dear God, she thought, someone had actually tried to kill her. Or had he? It was more likely, she realized suddenly, that he'd been trying to subdue her long enough to get her on the speedboat. Of course! And there could be only one logical explanation.

"Jeff," she said anxiously when he returned with two bottled Cokes, "I'm not so sure he was trying to drown me out there."

"Yeah," Jeff answered, sitting beside her, "I've been thinking the same thing. They were going to get you on that boat and find out what you did with the bag of money."

Lucy cocked her head. "Are we looking at this thing right? I mean…maybe…" Carefully she sipped at her Coke.

"Come on, Luce," he said, "why else would someone attack you in the water?"

To that she had no answer. "So someone's desperate to get that money," she said pensively, feeling her stomach lurch, then grudgingly settle.

"Wouldn't you be?" Jeff laughed in irony. "Well, maybe *you* wouldn't be, but most of the rest of the world would be pretty anxious to recoup half a million."

She ignored his sarcasm. "So why, then, did he—or I guess it's *they*—leave it in that room in the first place?"

"Got me." Jeff shrugged. "Unless, of course, someone else left it there, and those guys in the boat are trying to get their hands on it. But what I can't figure is why they didn't just walk up to the hotel desk and ask for the bag."

"Because it's dirty money," Lucy concluded.

"Possibly." Jeff sighed. "But I guess we're never going to find that one out."

"Why not?"

"Because I'm beginning to think we ought to get off this island."

Lucy turned and looked at him in surprise. "You mean we should leave?"

Jeff nodded.

"But Tom's coming down. We can't just walk out on him."

Jeff's head was bowed, but she could see a faint smile on his lips. "You want to stay and give them another chance at you?"

"Well, no, but—"

"I can see me telling Roy. Oh, Lucy? Well, she found this money and someone drowned her."

There wasn't much she could say. Jeff had a point. But if they stayed together until Tom got there, stayed in a crowd . . .

And Tom could relieve them of that bag and go to the police. Surely they wouldn't suspect that a prominent lawyer would be mixed up in something illegal.

"I think," Lucy began as she set down her half-full bottle, "we should hang in here until Tom arrives. If we go back to the hotel and stay in a crowded area, we'll be all right."

Jeff looked at her through a squinted eye. "Roy never told me you were a stubborn mule," he said.

"Then Roy doesn't know me," Lucy commented dryly.

As they rode back together to the hotel, Lucy was struck by the paradox of their situation once again. Overhead, a brilliant sun shone, beating down on their shoulders, and a gentle sea-damp breeze stirred in the palm trees. The air smelled of suntan oil and salt and big, fragrant blossoms. Yet this was no paradise. Someone was out to get her. It was crazy, ludicrous, but undeniably real.

The town, a few blocks long on the waterfront, came into view. Ordinarily Lucy would have loved to stop and sit in the small sunlit plaza, watch the band play in the gazebo, look at the trinkets in the shops. That's what you did on vacation. But Tom was coming, and Jeff—not Roy—was here, and there were men out there trying to get their hands on her.

The wind plastered her salt-stiff hair to her face, and in spite of the vague chill she still felt, the sun beat down heavily on her thighs and knees, turning them pink.

I almost drowned, Lucy thought. *Almost.* Drowning, she'd always heard, was supposed to be pleasant after the initial panic, but her experience had been anything but peaceful. If it hadn't been for Jeff...

She could feel the warm, silky smoothness of his skin beneath her hands as she held on to him. The breadth of his back and shoulders hid the road in front of them.

Had he really kissed her? No, she'd imagined it. She'd been unconscious; she'd dreamed it. But she could not shake the memory of his warm, sweet lips.

Goose bumps pricked her all over again. Why did she find Jeff so attractive? There was nothing about him she could put her finger on exactly. In fact, his features were quite ordinary, maybe a bit unfinished. But if you put all his pieces together, the whole was quite pleasing, terribly masculine, rough around the edges, unself-consciously sexy.

She wondered about his ex-girlfriend, "Nance," he'd called her. Now why had she recalled that? But she was certain Jeff must have a dozen ladies pestering him all the time. How could they resist? Then, too, there was that youthfulness, that easy boyish charm that held a kind of vulnerability but also, unquestionably, a strength. Jeff fascinated her, even as Lucy realized he was too much like the other men in her past she'd been attracted to.

A thought crashed into her head abruptly: Roy was really not her type. But quickly, alarmed at the notion, she put it from her as nonsense.

"How are you doing back there?" Jeff called over his shoulder.

"I'm okay," she said against his back, and felt, rather than saw, his nod.

But was she? Her skin was still covered in goose bumps, and her heart was beating a little too rapidly. It was the incident in the water, of course. And the embarrassment of being sick in front of him. She'd be better in a few hours.

Jeff turned in the motorbike and snorkeling gear at the hotel's rental shop while Lucy waited. It occurred to her to offer to pay—Jeff did have money problems—but somehow he didn't seem the kind of man who'd let a woman pay the bills, or who even allowed a Dutch treat. She could have been all wrong about that, however, just wanting to think the best of Roy's friend. Jeff could easily be another Joel, or Art, or Monty.

"There," Jeff said, putting away his credit card, "that's taken care of. Now what?" He looked at her closely. "Are you positive you don't want to see a doctor? I'm sure the desk has a list of them.

"Hey, really, I'm okay. I'm not even chilled anymore." She turned away, uncomfortable at being reminded of Jeff holding her head while she was sick. How many men would do that? And he'd been awfully nice about it, as if he could take care of a woman when she needed help but not be overprotective. A strange contradiction. "Look," she added, "if I still feel sick tomorrow, I'll see a doctor, I promise. Okay?"

"Okay," he said, "just don't push it too much."

"I promise."

"Then how about the beach? Crowds, you know. And lunch. I'm starved."

"The beach is fine. As for lunch—" Lucy grimaced "—I think I'll pass on that for the moment. I'll just sit and wait for Tom."

"The beach then, and lunch for me."

Lucy dumped sand out of one of her tennis shoes while Jeff supported her arm. "I'll bet you can get something right on the beach," she said. "I just don't want to look at it."

They located two empty lounge chairs and dragged them through the soft sand, finding a shaded spot under a palm. "I really could use some sun," Jeff commented. "For years I saw only the inside of a hockey rink. You should have seen all the pasty white skin in those shower rooms."

"I can imagine," Lucy said, amused, the image of dozens of naked male bodies flashing unbidden through her mind.

Jeff was bunching a towel under his head, lying back. "Yeah, those were the days. I can't believe I'm only thirty-four and retired. My dad didn't retire till he was seventy."

"Are your parents still living?" Lucy signaled a waiter who was strolling the beach at a snail's pace, taking lunch and drink orders.

"Nope. I was a late-life kid, you might say. My folks both died within a year or so of each other."

"That's a shame. Both of mine are still going strong."

"Well, I've got an elder sister in Denver, and she's got kids and all. So I do have family."

"And there's Roy," Lucy added.

"You bet. I still keep in close touch with the team, too."

She looked at him thoughtfully for a moment. "Can your old teammates help you with this bribery business?"

That faint, crooked smile she was getting to know flickered across his lips. "I think I'm the one who's going to have to sort that out."

"It's been a while, though," she ventured.

"This is true." Jeff turned his head and shaded his eyes, catching her gaze. "But you know how it is when something's uncomfortable. You avoid it. Every day I get up and tell myself I'm going to start digging around, but somehow night comes, and maybe the best I've done is call some of the guys and shoot a game or two of pool with them."

"It's hard," Lucy agreed, thinking of the times she'd taken the easy path in her life, and somehow she thought of Roy just then, but the waiter came, and the idea just slipped right out of her head.

They lay in the patchy sun beneath the palm trees for a time, then Lucy followed Jeff to the water, but she really wasn't ready for a swim—she'd had her fill of water. She couldn't help looking around, scanning the beach, searching for—what—a dark man? Ridiculous, she told herself, but her eyes kept roving over the people.

"Coming in?" he asked, standing there with his hands on his hips.

She shook her head. "I think I'll pass. Maybe I'll build a castle or something."

Jeff turned and headed into the gently lapping waves. "I won't go far."

She did sit by the water and let the loose sand trickle slowly through her fingers, piling up in tear-shaped pyramids. But she was paying her sand art little attention. Instead she'd put her glasses on and was idly watching Jeff. He was swimming about twenty yards out, past the gentle breakers, and he was on his back. His wet hair was dark, glinting in the bright sun as he swam. One sinewy arm reached behind his head to pull through the water, and then the other arm was arcing through the clean air, again and again, fluid, easy, strong. Lucy couldn't take her eyes from his body, from his chest muscles working, the cords bunching at his shoulders as he flipped over into a breast stroke, his body sliding smoothly, lithely through the sea.

How long she sat on that beach staring she didn't know. And she hadn't realized, either, that Jeff had stopped swimming and was treading water now, facing shore, staring straight at her. It was as if time had stopped and there was only the moment. She knew her breathing had become shallow and that Jeff somehow knew it, too. It was in the pitch of his head, in the slow motion of his arms; everything in him seemed to be focused on her.

He was out of the water and drying off with a towel, and she was trying to collect herself.

"Great water," Jeff said, breathing hard as he sat beside her. "You ought to try it, Lucy. That is, if you're feeling better."

But she couldn't seem to find her voice. What had happened? What spell had this sunny isle cast on her? Had even the bag of money been part of some bizarre, otherworldly conspiracy to put her in this time and space?

"I think," Jeff was saying, "you'd better get out of the sun, Luce. Come on." He took her hands in his and pulled her to her feet, but she stumbled against him. The contact felt more like a soft, hot blow to her breasts than a mere brushing, just as his lips had felt.... Awkwardly Lucy mumbled something like sorry, but she wasn't sure. The next thing she knew, she was back under the palm tree on her chair, stretched out and breathing too rapidly.

"We're both getting way too much sun," Jeff said as he opened the tube of lotion. "You want some more of this on your back?"

"Oh, I'm okay."

"You're as red as a beet."

"Well . . . sure."

Lucy sat up in her chair, legs crisscrossed, while Jeff crouched on his haunches and put a blob of white stuff on the middle of her back. At the contact she shivered involuntarily. "Ooh, that's cold," she said, closing her eyes when his hand began to work the lotion in. He rubbed her back the way he'd done before, up to her shoulders, under the straps of her suit, down again, languidly, wordlessly. He made a circle and some dots with his finger, then a big curve at the base of the circle.

"What's that?" he asked.

"A happy face," Lucy replied dreamily, momentarily forgetting that it was Jeff doing it and not some childhood playmate. How easy he was to be with, carefree, adventurous, as if he'd held on to that curiosity that exists only in youth.

He wrote some words on her skin, chuckling at himself, and Lucy had to laugh, too. "That's the Gents," she said, suddenly feeling very young and untroubled.

"Right," Jeff replied. "Hey, my turn now. My back's burned to a crisp."

Reluctantly, sleepily, Lucy shifted in her chair and turned around to do his back. Her eyes widened. She poked at his skin with her index finger. "Oh, wow, Zany, you *really* have a sunburn going."

"No kidding."

"I'm serious. You should have let me put this on when we were snorkeling."

"Yes, ma'am." He saluted her facetiously.

She gave his back a good dose of protection, allowing her fingers to glide across his muscles, over his shoulders, down his long spine, tickling, until the waistband on his trunks stopped her.

"Feels great," he said lazily. "Don't quit now." He moved his head from side to side, as if easing tension. She watched, fascinated, as the cords worked in his neck, flexing, relaxing. She was aware of how much she liked touching Jeff, exploring his neck and back at leisure, and he didn't even know she was enjoying it—he never would.

"Say," Jeff asked, interrupting her reverie, "I'd like to ask your opinion about something."

She expected the question to be profound, about politics maybe, or religion or a problem with a woman, because his tone was sober and a little reluctant. "Sure, anything."

"I've been offered this job," he began hesitantly.

"Another coaching job? Well, that's—"

"No, not exactly a coaching job." He got to his feet and went over to stretch out on his own lounge chair. He was frowning.

"So, what is it?"

"It's another commercial, like the last one—but different."

"That's great, isn't it? Don't you get a lot of money for doing those, what with residuals and all?"

"Yeah."

"And you could do it while you're waiting for the coaching job to come through," she said brightly.

"Yeah."

"Well?"

"Ah, the commercial, well, it's not for underwear. It's for, uh, well, actually, it's for..."

"Jeff, you can tell me."

"It's for panty hose."

"Panty hose!" She giggled uncontrollably, getting an instant vision of Jeff in panty hose and a black negligee and...

"Hell," Jeff muttered, "that's what I thought."

The afternoon drifted along, the crowds on the beach lending Lucy a feeling of safety. Then, too, there was Jeff lying next to her, his breathing slow and cadenced as he napped. Lucy liked watching him, she discovered, almost as much as she'd like touching him.

Roy's buddy, she mused. No wonder Roy liked him, too. It crossed her mind that when they all got back to Denver, she'd enjoy seeing Jeff from time to time—with Roy, of course. Maybe she could go to a couple of ice hockey games, join the screaming, bloodthirsty horde. That would be a new experience. Exhilarating, if nothing else. The question was, would Roy have time for ice hockey games and maybe a beer and pizza afterward? Or would Roy be in a meeting?

Jeff seemed utterly content to doze. Lucy was beginning to feel much better and a little antsy as she gazed around the beach. There were people swimming, a few kids building sand castles that would have put hers to shame. Other people relaxed on chairs with books in hand and tall, tropical drinks stuck in the sand beside them. No out-of-place dark men.

A cold lemonade would taste great, she decided. She'd get Jeff one, too, wake him up. It would serve him right for napping all afternoon.

Lucy walked across the hot sand quickly, wishing she'd put on her shoes, then headed to the outdoor bar. She sat on the edge of a stool while she ordered, and felt the grainy sand scrape her skin beneath the elastic at the legs of her swimsuit. While the bartender poured the drinks, she glanced idly at a daily newspaper someone had left on the bar. It was a local paper, in Spanish, and she had fun translating the words in her head. She flipped a page, read, flipped another, scanning the column headings.

Local fishing tournament scheduled for next Saturday. Church supper Sunday night. So and so had a baby girl last Tuesday, and Juan Ortega, age eighty-one, died after a long—Lucy thought the next word was debilitating—illness.

There was a strange, out-of-place article near the back of the paper that caught Lucy's eye—strange because the paper was obviously tourist-oriented. *Don't want to upset the tourists with unsettling stories,* Lucy thought as she translated the Spanish in her head.

"Dos limonadas, Señora," said the bartender.

"'*Señorita,*'" Lucy corrected him pleasantly as she paid for the drinks, her nose still half buried in the paper. "*Gracias,*" she said, getting to her feet, the drinks and her wallet precariously balanced in one hand while she held the newspaper in the other.

Homicidio, *a murder,* Lucy thought, trying to finish the article while she crossed the beach. She'd bet murder was rare on this small, peaceful tourist island. Interesting.

"Hey, wake up, Zany," Lucy said, sticking their drinks in the sand. "I have something cool and wet for you. Rise and shine, sleepy."

"Um," Jeff groaned as he opened an eye.

Lucy pointed to his lemonade. "You want me to hold it for you, too?" she asked lightly.

"Not necessary. Say, that looks perfect. Thanks."

"My pleasure." Lucy curled up comfortably in her chair and went back to the article. "Pretty weird," she said to herself, still reading.

"What's weird?" Jeff sipped on his drink, then rolled onto his side, facing her, supporting his head with a hand.

"Oh, this article. It says there was a murder here the night before last. The victim was a caretaker for a doctor from Houston who owns a beach house here, a Dr. Malcolm Dover," Lucy said, rattling the paper. "It says the caretaker's body was found up near the north shore on an isolated beach."

"I'll bet they have about one murder a decade here," Jeff commented.

"Um... Well, it goes on to say that an empty briefcase was found near the man's body, and the police are sending it to a lab in Mexico City."

"Fingerprints," Jeff said, sipping on his drink. "Forensics, you know."

"Probably," Lucy put in pensively, something nagging at her mind, like a word or movie she was trying to remember. "A briefcase," she said, her brow wrinkled. She looked over at Jeff.

"Lucy," he began, sitting up suddenly. "Do you remember what you said last night when you found the money?"

She nodded slowly, her heart beginning to beat heavily. "I said a person would have to be dead..."

"Exactly."

"The empty briefcase," she said breathlessly. "You don't think... Is it possible...?"

"I don't know *what* to think, but something's not right here."

"A murder," she said, "the briefcase, the money I found."

Jeff got to his feet abruptly. "What's the caretaker's name, Lucy? Does it say?"

She scanned the paper, then tapped it with a fingernail. "He was an American, it says, named Lonny Taylor."

"You stay right here," Jeff ordered. "I'll be back in a flash."

Wondering where on earth he was going, Lucy sat trying to digest this new information, but there was something else stuck in the recesses of her mind other than the murder. She looked through the article again. Dr. Malcolm Dover, she thought—the name rang a bell. Dover. But why would a doctor with a vacation home in Mexico be familiar to her? Of course, there was mention of Houston, but she didn't know anyone in Houston.

Jeff couldn't have been gone five minutes before Lucy looked up to see him running back across the sand. "Come on," he said, panting, excited, "we gotta get out of this hotel!"

"What, what is it, Jeff?" she asked, alarmed.

"I went to the desk, Luce, to see who exactly had that room of yours before we checked in."

"Oh, my God," Lucy whispered. "Tell me it wasn't this Taylor. Oh, no!"

"Lonny R. Taylor," Jeff said in a strained voice. He snatched her hand. "We're getting as far from this place as possible. Come on."

The thought of going into her room to grab the rest of her things was utterly horrifying to Lucy as they hurried along the garden path. Someone had killed this caretaker, obviously for the money, and then had almost killed her.

"I'm not going in there," Lucy said firmly when they got to her bungalow.

"Give me your key, I'll get your stuff."

"Maybe you shouldn't."

"*Lucy*," he said sternly, "give me the key. It's all right. We'll get the hell out of here and check into a place as far away as possible."

"Tom..."

"I'll leave him a note at the desk. The key, Lucy."

She waited outside alone, feeling nauseous again, while Jeff went into the dim room to collect her things. What if someone was waiting in there? In the closet.... "Jeff," she called, poking her head in the open door.

"Be right out."

Lucy sighed with relief. *Hurry,* she thought, leaning against the stucco wall of the bungalow. *Come on, Jeff.*

While she stood there thinking about a dead body on the beach and her own near miss in the water earlier, she became cognizant of a man walking, a man in a suit maybe thirty or forty yards down the path. It was as if her worst nightmare was coming true, as if the man she'd been looking for all day had materialized in front of her.

Danger! her mind screamed. She recalled everything suddenly, felt her snorkel being pulled away, a hand on her neck, strangling, water in her mouth.

She tried to peer through the undergrowth, but the path twisted. She couldn't be sure. The man at her door last night had been wearing a suit. And where else on this vacation island had she seen anyone else in a suit?

Her heart thumping against her ribs like a mallet, she strained to catch sight of him again, but a moment later Jeff was back, her bag in hand, and he was pulling her along to his room.

When she told him about the man, all he said was "Hell, I wouldn't be surprised. Come on, Lucy, let's get checked out of here."

"The note for Tom," she reminded him.

"And the money, lady. We're not leaving that behind."

They got a cab almost immediately. Jeff tossed their bags into the trunk and joined Lucy in the backseat.

"Where to?" the driver asked. "*¿Aeropuerto?* Airport?"

Lucy thought quickly. Why stay on the island at all? Why not the airport? Heck, she had a plane, didn't she?

"Jeff," she said excitedly, "let's fly straight out of here—we can be in Merida by evening! That's the first place I'd have to stop on the way home, anyway. We'll call Tom from there, and he'll tell us what to do with the money."

"I suppose," Jeff began, "but what about Roy? I mean, he'll be flying in tomorrow and—"

"Oh, my gosh," Lucy breathed. "Roy. I'd forgotten. Well, I'll call him from Merida, too. Sure, why not?"

There was a lot to be done at the airport, Lucy knew. Documents to be signed and stamped, her flight plan to be approved and filed and the usual five dollar tips to each official with whom she had to deal. Jeff followed along dutifully, carrying their suitcases and his airline bag with the money. To Lucy, the bag stuck out like a sore thumb. But no one seemed to notice it.

They got through the formalities in a snap, and the *comandante* at the tower even remembered Lucy from the day before. The short, hook-nosed official, who looked exactly like an ancient Mayan, even said, "You come back to Cozumel soon, yes? Pretty place."

"Very pretty," Lucy agreed, and headed on out to the tarmac.

Her yellow Bonanza was parked, refueled and ready, at the far end of the runway complex, alongside three Lear jets and several other prop jobs. As she'd already taken care of the service bills at the tower, everything was in order. All she had to do was pay the boy who'd watched her plane overnight. And, naturally, he popped up, materializing from the bushes next to the runway, grinning and telling her he'd guarded her plane as if it were his own. "I never shut my eyes all night," he said.

"Bueno," she replied, handing him some pesos. She said to Jeff, "He says he never shut his eyes all night. I'll bet."

Lucy wasn't certain precisely what it was that first tipped her off. It might have been the unlatched door. Or maybe it was the corner of a blanket just showing from the closed luggage compartment. Whatever. But when she tugged open the door it was obvious someone had given her plane a thorough going-over. Everything was tossed helter-skelter on the seats and floor. Her maps, her box of tissues, her papers and receipts.

"Oh, God," she whispered, looking across the clutter to where Jeff stood at the open passenger door. "Oh, God."

"Damn."

"Jeff, they know about the plane. They know *everything*."

"Let's clean this up," he said, "and get out of here. The sooner the better." He looked at her sharply. "You okay? I mean, can you fly?"

"Of course I can fly," Lucy replied, irritated.

It took at least fifteen minutes to put all her documents back in their packets and to refold the maps, some of which were torn at the seams hopelessly, she was afraid. Nevertheless there wasn't time to brood.

Lucy went through her preflight check automatically. At least the plane had not been tampered with. She called the tower and asked for takeoff instructions, receiving immediate clearance, and she taxied out to the runway.

The air traffic controller called her when her engine was just about up to the speed at which she would let off the brake and roar down the runway. "Bonanza two-two-six-Lima-Hotel, be advised that a Mexicana flight is banking five miles out to the northwest on approach. Altitude, three thousand feet."

She pressed the button on her handset. "Bonanza two-two-six to tower. Thank you." She glanced at Jeff. "You ready?"

He swallowed. "Sure you know what you're doing, Luce?"

Her light plane used a third of the runway, then lifted off gently with the wind at its nose. Immediately she banked, avoiding the northwestern corridor and the approaching Mexicana flight. Below, the interior jungle fell away, and then they were out over the crystal-clear turquoise water, climbing, banking in a slow curve, the sun coming around to fall on Lucy's right shoulder as she headed west and north toward Merida.

"You sure we're headed in the right direction?" Jeff called, holding on to the instrument panel with both hands.

"I do have a compass," Lucy quipped, and gave him a sidelong glance.

"That was a great takeoff," he said, as if to reassure himself. "You don't do tricks in this thing, do you?"

"Like rolling over?"

"Something like that."

"No, not me. I'm like a little old lady in a '65 Buick."

"Good."

For a few miles they flew in silence, Lucy checking her compass every so often as the mainland and the popular resort of Cancun to the north dropped away behind them. What a hassle it was, she was thinking, all the airport rigamarole you had to go through in Mexico. In the States there were no regulations such as having to file flight plans. Lucy always did, however, just in case, of course. It was safer. A plane could go down somewhere, and the automatic locater might fail. With a flight plan someone could find you.

She thought about her yellow Bonanza being violated by those murderers. The creeps. And she wondered how they'd known she had a plane in the first place. Someone had done a lot of checking.

"You know," Jeff said over the constant drone of the engine. "I sure liked Cozumel, but I think I'll take my vacations somewhere else from now on."

"I know, it's crazy." Lucy could see the corner of Jeff's flight bag with the money stashed behind his seat.

"Maybe Roy should fly down," Jeff continued.

But Lucy wasn't really listening. Something was nagging at her—something to do with flight rules and regulations.

Suddenly she had it. "Oh, no," she whispered. "I should have thought! The minute I saw the inside of my plane, I should have thought!"

"What?" Jeff asked in a sober voice.

"The murderers," Lucy said. "If they got access to the runway and my plane, they can just as easily get access to my flight plan."

"So?"

"Jeff," she said, turning to catch his eye, "on a jet they can *beat* us to Merida. They could actually be there before us!"

Lucy never waited for him to digest the knowledge. Instead she pulled on the controls and banked sharply, only straightening the plane out when the late afternoon sun struck them both in the eyes blindingly.

CHAPTER SEVEN

THE DENSE STEAMY JUNGLE of the Yucatán Peninsula was below, dark green and undulating, without a road or a house or a clearing.

"So where are we going?" Jeff asked, trying to sound unconcerned.

"Chichén Itzá."

"I've heard of it. It's a Mayan ruin, isn't it?"

"Yes, and there's a landing strip there. I flew in once to visit the ruins. They'll never be able to follow us."

"Great idea."

"There's only one problem. It's a small grass landing strip that's been hacked out of the jungle. You know, for tourist flights. There's no tower, so I can't land there in the dark."

Jeff looked at his watch. "It's almost six. When does it get dark down here?"

"I guess around seven."

"And how far is this place?" he asked.

"About an hour away."

"Holy cow."

She looked at him and nodded. "It'll be close."

"Can you go any faster?"

"Not unless the headwinds change direction," she replied dryly.

Jeff said nothing. He was nervous, she knew, about flying with her in the plane. Lots of people were. But she was immensely glad he was along. Having him there boosted her morale, and what would she have done if he hadn't been there on the beach today? What if it had been Roy with her? She felt a cold wave of discomfort sweep over her at the thought. Would Roy have charged into the water and saved her, then held her head while she threw up? Of course he would have. Roy loved her.

The plane droned on, flying into the huge red orb of the semitropical sun. She checked her compass heading, her altimeter, her fuel consumption automatically.

"I didn't really thank you for saving my life," she said. "I owe you one."

"Anyone would have done the same." *Even Roy* were the unspoken words hanging in the air.

"Maybe," she said, "but I'm sure glad you were there."

"We're going to have to phone Roy, you know," Jeff said, bringing to life the specter that had been riding with them in one of the plane's empty seats all along. "Otherwise he's going to fly to Cozumel tomorrow."

"I know. We'll do it from the hotel. There's one right near the ruins." She sighed. "I'll have to phone Tom, too. He'll be having a fit. *And* I'll have to contact Cozumel control, because they think I'm landing at Merida."

"Will you get in trouble for changing your route?"

"Oh, I'll make up something, tell them I had engine trouble or compass problems and had to land."

She checked her instruments again, her mind elsewhere. She didn't really like to ask Jeff—it made her sound suspicious—but she had never liked loose ends or unanswered questions.

"Penny for your thoughts," he said just then.

"How about half a million?" she quipped. "Jeff, you know we *could* have left the money back there in the hotel safe."

"Oh, sure," he said, "except for a couple of problems. Sooner or later a desk clerk would have gotten curious and looked in the bag, and I'm afraid it would have been too tempting for some poor soul. Besides, Tom would have had a hell of a time getting that bag out of there—I had the receipt."

Yes, she thought, Jeff was absolutely right.

The sun was resting, half-obscured, on the jungle horizon, when Lucy saw the pale green strip cut out of the undergrowth. And nearby was the massive complex of gray stone pyramids that was the ancient city of Chichén Itzá. She checked the primitive wind sock as she circled the runway. The wind was coming from the northwest. She corrected her heading and descended, watching as the jungle sent long black fingers of shadow across the grass strip. She could actually see the sun setting lower into the trees. Soon the runway would be merely a black smudge against the jungle backdrop, and she'd be unable to land safely.

But she had time.

"We're going to land on *that*?" Jeff asked, pointing.

"Sure are. And real soon, too."

"Oh, boy" was all he said, but Lucy could see his hands, white knuckled, gripping the instrument panel.

There was no tower, no radio, no directions from an air traffic controller. Lucy was on her own. All she had to go by was a wind sock and her own instincts and skill. She lowered the landing gear, set her instruments, constantly checking the sock for wind speed and direction. She came in, lower and lower, until she was below the tops of the trees, in rapidly darkening shadow. Then her back wheels bumped down, bounced, her front wheel touched ground, and the plane went rocking and skipping down the grass strip as she braked.

"Jeez," Jeff said in an awed tone of voice. "You did it."

She taxied her plane to a safe place off to one side and turned off the key.

"Routine," she said, trying to sound sure of herself, trying not to scare Jeff, but it had been close.

"Routine, my foot. It's pitch-black out right now," he said.

She took a deep breath. "I don't know, until today I never was very good at living dangerously."

"Well, I hope you never have to get any better at it."

They had to walk about a quarter of a mile down the road toward the hotel before a truck driver gave them a ride. His vehicle was decorated with pictures and red fringe, painted with slogans, a veritable art gallery on wheels.

"*Gracias,*" Lucy said as he dropped them off in front of the hotel. "*Muchas gracias.*"

"*De nada,*" the truck driver said. "*Buenas noches.* Chichén Itzá very nice."

"Yes, very nice."

Going into the hotel, Lucy dug around in her bag until she found her wallet, and pulled out one of her credit cards. "Here," she said, handing it to Jeff, "will you check us in? I'm going to call Tom. He'll be frantic."

Jeff looked at the card she held out, then at her face. "Put that away," he said. "I'll take care of it. And wait until we get our rooms to call Tom. Or do you want everyone in the lobby to hear our, uh, problems?''

He was right. Also, he was a bit irritated. She had been correct in her assessment of him: Jeff was a man who didn't like women to pay his way. Touchy. Old-fashioned. Or, she wondered fleetingly, had Roy given him express instructions and a lot of cash?

By the time Lucy got to her room, she wanted a shower more than anything else—except a meal. She'd been too queasy to eat at lunchtime; saltwater on the stomach didn't help the appetite. Her hair was stiff with salt, she still had her bathing suit on under her clothes and sand still gritted under the elastic of her suit.

But she had to call Tom first. The Cozumel Caribe switchboard answered immediately, informing her that Señor Thomas McLaughlin had checked in and that they would ring his room.

She waited patiently, tapping her fingers as the phone rang. When Tom finally came on the crackling line, Lucy could hear the irritation in his voice. He had every right to be angry, she knew, having gotten all the way to Cozumel only to find her gone. He was worried, too, he admitted. And doubly so when Lucy told him exactly why they'd left the island so suddenly.

"And you think the murder of this caretaker, Taylor, is connected to the money?" he asked, settling down.

"I sure do," Lucy said, "because Lonny Taylor was checked into my room the night before I got there."

There was silence on the line for a moment, then he said, "You positive you're okay, young lady? You're safe there in Chicken—"

"It's Chichén Itzá, Tom, and I'm fine now. But you've *got* to get this money off our hands."

"I will, Lucy, I will."

She could almost hear those efficient wheels in his head turning. Patiently now, Lucy waited, crossing her legs, turning an ankle in circles.

"Dover," Tom said finally. "You said this caretaker worked for a Dr. Dover?"

"It does ring a bell," Lucy replied, "doesn't it?" Then suddenly she remembered. She snapped her fingers. "Tom! Do you remember that friend of my dad's, Andy Martin?"

"Vaguely. He's a banker, I think."

"That's right. God, I swear Andy was treated at a clinic in Houston, a Dr. Malcolm Dover's clinic."

"You certain about this?"

"Oh, wow," she said. "It's all coming back to me now. Dad had Andy over for dinner. Lord, it's been a year—*two* years, maybe—but I remember him telling us all about this cancer clinic in Houston. It *was* Dover, I'm positive. Andy told us the most gory stories. Mom turned white, I remember. There was something about these odd drinks the patients took, and the gossip around the clinic was that this doctor was using some kind of unapproved Mexican drug, you know, like laetrile."

"Mexican drug," Tom said meaningfully, and Lucy's heart skipped a beat. "I think," Tom went on, "I'd better make a few calls."

She put a hand to her head. "Tom, could the money I found have something to do with Dover?"

Tom gave a short laugh. "If someone was giving odds, I'd sure want a piece of the action."

Lucy let out a long breath. "I think," she said, "we've walked right into a hornet's nest. This is just great."

"Look," he said, "you hold tight there, and I'll do some fast checking. I may just contact the legal department of the American embassy in Mexico City. I'd really like to keep you and your friend out of it as much as possible. Where are you now? Give me the number, and I'll get back to you. Meanwhile, why don't you give Andy Martin a call and see what else he remembers about Dr. Dover's esteemed establishment?" He chuckled at his own brand of wit, then cleared his throat while Lucy rattled off her telephone number. "Now you're safe there till I get back to you?" he asked.

"For the time being."

"Okay. Give me tomorrow morning to make a call or two and I'll ring you."

"Fine. And, Tom, thanks."

"Oh, it'll cost you," he replied good-naturedly. "Say, where do I get a good steak in this town?"

"I thought you were on a diet."

Lucy hung up, relieved. She knew Tom would get them out of this mess. She wondered if Malcolm Dover really was connected in any way to the money, or had his poor, dead caretaker, Lonny Taylor, been doing a nasty deal on the side? She'd have to see what Jeff thought about it.

Lucy called the Cozumel airport, asked for the tower and explained that she'd had engine trouble, nothing serious, and had had to land in Chichén Itzá.

"Yes, Señorita Hammond, I will note that," said the man she spoke to, "but make sure you inform us of any further change of plans. What is your next intended stop?"

It occurred to Lucy that she could not make any plans until she heard from Tom. "Uh, I'm not sure yet. We may stay here for a few days—to see the ruins, you know."

Well, *that* was taken care of. She stripped off her clothes and stepped into the shower, the crazy events of the past twenty-four hours running through her head. A few minutes later the water turned cool. Everyone in the hotel must be taking a shower at the same time, she mused. Jeff, too. She pictured him in her mind's eye, standing under the water. Oh, his back! It was so sunburned—the hot water would sting. His sunburn would stop at his waist, though, and he would be white below, and those cute round buttocks... She recalled his mentioning the guys in the locker room and giggled to herself.

She scrubbed the salt out of her hair, still smiling, still thinking. He was right on the other side of this wall; was he whistling or singing in the shower? She couldn't help picturing his mouth, that same mouth that had moved over hers when she'd almost drowned. Had he really been kissing her, or was it just a waterlogged dream? She shook her head and chided herself to stop thinking about him.

It struck her when she was fishing around in her bag for a clean shirt. A horrible, cold hand grasped her heart as the notion hit home. Those men who wanted the money back, who'd searched her plane—they only had to check with the tower in Cozumel to find out where she'd landed!

Oh, God. All her trouble, all her cleverness in landing at Chichén Itzá had been for nothing! But wait a minute. If they'd already checked once and found out she was going to Merida, would they be likely to ask again? Or would they wonder why she hadn't arrived at Merida? How determined, how smart, how organized where they?

Who were they?

And she'd been such a good, dutiful pilot, calling in just as she was supposed to do. It was procedure, and she'd been trained to follow procedure; her safety, any pilot's safety, depended on it. But this time she might have made a drastic mistake.

Oh, damn! Abruptly she felt tired; her chest hurt from the saltwater she'd inhaled; her body ached. She was angry at Jeff for not wanting to turn the money over to the authorities, even though she knew he was probably right. That would only cause *more* trouble.

What were they going to do?

She pulled on a blue-and-white striped T-shirt and white slacks and combed her hair hastily. Letting herself out of her room, she walked the few yards down the hall and knocked at Jeff's door. He opened it in a minute, and she could see he was on the telephone. He motioned her in and closed the door behind her, still listening to someone on the other end of the line.

"Sure," he said, "I know it's crazy. Yeah, Chichén Itzá, the ruins. Hey, Lucy can really fly that plane.

He was silent for a minute, then continued. "No, Roy, it wouldn't do any good to head down here just yet. I don't know where on earth we're going to be. This lawyer Tom is going to manage everything. Yes, we'll be careful."

Jeff's eyes met hers over the telephone. She waited for him to tell Roy she was there, to say, "Here, I'll put Luce on, pal," but he didn't. His eyes held hers, a little sad, a little defiant, and the odd thing was, Lucy never said she wanted to speak to Roy, either.

"So, don't bother coming down here at all. It's a mess. We'll be back home in a few days, anyway. Some vacation." He listened again, his gaze still locked with hers, unblinking. She thought for a moment that she could drown in the depths of those sea-green eyes, but there was a hardness there suddenly, an aquamarine glint. "No, Lucy's in her room," he was saying. "Taking a nap. Yeah, it's been some day. Sure, sure, I'll tell her. Hey, fella, thanks. See you."

He hung up. The phone made an audible click as he set the receiver down. Silence filled the room to bursting.

"Uh, so, how's Roy?" Lucy finally asked.

"He's fine. Says the Telluride Hotel's going to go."

So there was to be no mention of his small lie. She felt like a conspirator; the deceit hung suspended between them, a living, breathing entity throbbing with portent. "What were you supposed to tell me?" she forced herself to ask.

"Roy said he misses you." Jeff's eyes slid away, their movement only too eloquent.

Somehow Lucy made it downstairs to dinner, her insides twisting with what she'd just done in Jeff's room. She kept the talk all business, relating her conversation with Tom to him, but lurking just at the corner of her thoughts was the deceit, a dark, shapeless knowledge.

"So this Dover is running a cancer cure scam," Jeff commented. "The Mexican connection..."

Lucy nodded. "It could be. People will do anything for a cure, I guess. I'd sure hate to be the judge of something like this."

"Was your dad's friend cured?"

"No, he went to the Mayo Clinic after he left Dover's, and I know he's still not well."

Jeff drank half of his glass of Corona beer. His Adam's apple worked, then he set the glass down and looked at her with a grim expression. "Lucy," he said, leaning across the table, "I don't like your being involved in this."

She gave a little laugh. "I don't like being involved in it, either, but I am."

"Someone, probably someone involved in this drug thing with Dover, has already tried to get at you."

"I know, and I forgot to tell you what I thought of after I checked in with the Cozumel tower," she said somberly.

"What's that?"

"Those men, they can find us here. All they have to do is check with the tower. I was so dumb, I should never have reported in, but I didn't think of that until it was too late."

Jeff frowned. "Maybe they won't be smart enough to ask the tower. We don't know."

"Let's hope so."

"Well, we'd better not sit around this place too long. We leave tomorrow," Jeff said decisively.

"Not until I hear from Tom," she reminded him.

He dropped the subject of leaving, of their possible peril, even of Dr. Dover and his expensive miracle cure. Instead Jeff began to tell her stories about his days in college, and how, in order to play hockey, he'd had to stay up half the night and study just to pass his courses.

"And by passing," he said, smiling ruefully, "I mean Ds."

"You're smarter than that," Lucy found herself saying.

"Maybe. But I was an awful student. I read twice as much now as I ever did then. In college it was Classic Comics."

"You're putting me on."

"No way."

Lucy sighed, relaxing a little. "Well," she said, surveying the table, "now that dinner's over..."

"Would you like to take a walk? I've never seen the ruins."

In truth Lucy was tired, very tired, but the notion of saying good-night to Jeff at her door in a few minutes was a letdown. "Sure," she replied, "I'd like that."

The hotel's van deposited them at the entrance gate to the ruins. It was dark out, humid and oppressively hot. A heat spell, the van driver had told Lucy. A fine mist curled along the ground, like dry ice in a theater production, and the ancient pyramids made an otherwordly spectacle, with their floodlit pinnacles rising out of the fog as if suspended on air.

Lucy found herself wanting to whisper. "Chichén Itzá is almost fifteen hundred years old," she told Jeff, and he whistled.

The ageless city had been cleared from the encroaching jungle, exposing huge pyramids and towers, walls and statues, all of heavy, gray limestone, all highly adorned with carvings. The castillo, the principal temple, covered an acre of ground and rose a hundred feet above the plain. Inside a thousand columns enclosed a huge central plaza of colonnaded halls, sunken courts, terraces and theaters. There was also an enormous ball court with stone bleachers for spectators, the jaguar temple, the astronomical observatory, the high priest's grave—and the altars where maidens were sacrificed to the fierce Mayan deities.

"No kidding," said Jeff, "they really did that! I thought that stuff was just in the movies."

"It was true." Lucy shivered as she always did when she thought of those young girls, the priests, the knives glinting in torchlight.

"Hey, come on there, Luce. That was a thousand years ago."

"I know—I'm silly."

He put an arm around her shoulders and gave her a tentative squeeze. "You're not silly—you're just sensitive."

She liked what he said, and, God help her, she liked the feel of his arm around her.

They wandered among the huge stones and stepped pyramids as if in a dream. Wisps of fog curled around their feet, and sounds were muffled. Only a few other tourists were there, and once in a while their voices, oddly hushed, disembodied, came out of the murky air to reach them.

The stones had been shaped into jaguars, plumed serpents, flowers, warriors with curved noses. "Hey," Jeff said, "that figure looks exactly like the kid I rented the motor scooter from." He was pointing to a Mayan warrior, frozen in stone forever.

"And the waiter we had at dinner," Lucy said.

"You think this fella is their great-great-grandpa?"

"Sure, why not?"

Anything was possible that night, Lucy thought. It was as if they walked on an alien planet deserted by giant, magical beings who'd left behind these formidable ruins.

They stood at the base of the castillo and craned their heads.

"Should we climb it?" Jeff asked.

"Yes, let's."

The steps were high, each a heavy block of limestone, and perilously steep. It took effort, especially in the heavy heat, and Lucy was sweating by the time they reached the top. Jeff climbed over the edge onto the platform and held his hand out to help her up. His touch tingled, as if electricity flowed through his fingers to hers. Lucy drew in her breath, lifting her eyes to see if Jeff, too, had felt it. He was watching her, his eyes shadowed in the darkness, a beam of light hitting his muscular forearm as he grasped her hand and drew her up beside him on the top of the pyramid.

They both stood in silence for a time, looking out over the floodlit expanse to the secretive jungle canopy beyond. "Wow," Lucy said, still breathing hard from the climb. She wiped her upper lip with a forearm.

"Yeah" was all Jeff said, but his hand was at her waist, as if he needed to grasp her, to share. His light touch burned, the heat radiating out until she felt weak, her knees going all rubbery. What was happening to her? She suddenly recalled the feel of his lips on hers when she'd come to on the beach. Warm, salty lips. Goose bumps rose on her flesh.

What about Roy? Was she so easily swayed by a handsome jock? Was she so shallow that, given a romantic setting, any man could excite her? Or was this attraction she felt for Jeff, this awful weakness, a mere passing whim, a matter of hormones?

She saw herself looking into the mirror in Jeff's room. The black lace, the disheveled hair. Was that her? And why did she feel it was so important to make things work with Roy? Why, oh, why, had Roy sent his friend to Cozumel to meet her?

Silently, with unspoken agreement, they started down the steps of the pyramid. Jeff helped her, his hand holding hers, their eyes meeting in wordless understanding.

Yet hanging over them, as heavy as the moisture-laden night sky over the ruins, was the knowledge that Roy stood beside them, behind their shoulders, between them.

Their steps were slow as they meandered farther into the ruins; the hot air pressed down on them like an invisible hand. Their shoulders occasionally brushing, they walked close together, hardly seeing the splendor around them anymore, not speaking, just feeling the excruciating, exquisite tension that flowed between them, that burst with sparks every time they touched inadvertently.

The unearthly atmosphere was intoxicating, and Lucy's thoughts stuck in her head, moving sluggishly. The universe was all sensation, and when Jeff put a hand at the small of her back to guide her, it became the focal point of her existence. She breathed deeply, fearing she would float away, afraid to speak in case she'd break the spell.

They had to leave the ruins eventually, and it was as if they were reentering a noisy and crass world, a world where magic spells had no power.

"It's late," Jeff said quietly, his hand dropping from her back, and Lucy almost staggered, as if she'd been cut loose from a lifeline, abandoned to flounder on her own.

"Yes," she whispered in reply, averting her eyes, feeling herself flush.

Back in the lonely haven of her room, she lay in bed, still feeling Jeff's hand, warm and solid, exciting, caressing her damp skin. Tomorrow, in the light of day, she told herself, his touch, his presence, wouldn't mean so much.

She couldn't let it.

CHAPTER EIGHT

JEFF OPENED ONE EYE and glanced toward the window. It was broad daylight, and a watery sun was showing through high, grainy clouds. He glanced at his watch: 8:35 a.m. He pushed the sheet away from his bare chest and felt the dampness on his skin. He'd been sweating, he guessed, in the close little room. If he had had the energy, he would have gotten up and switched on the air-conditioner. But he felt heavy and lethargic, unwilling to face the new day.

Why had he lied to Roy yesterday? Why hadn't he simply handed Lucy the phone?

"Here, Roy," Jeff could have said, "Lucy just stopped by. You can talk to her now. Yeah, she's a swell lady, all right. I'd sure like to be best man at your wedding, pal."

Why *hadn't* he given Luce the phone?

He lay beneath the damp sheet and felt guilt encase him like a suit of cement.

On the other hand, he mused, couldn't Lucy have spoken up herself? It wasn't as if she didn't know to whom Jeff had been talking.

Eventually he forced himself to swing his legs over the side of the bed. He rubbed a hand across the back of his neck, then stood, padding into the bathroom.

He wondered if Lucy was up. If it was as hot and humid in her room. If her soft skin was as covered in perspiration as his. He could almost imagine her skimpy black nightie, all damp and clinging to her breasts and hips—it would feel like warm silk. In fact, Jeff admitted to himself, he'd been lying in bed half-awake that morning, envisioning her in just that state of undress. And she was right on the other side of that wall, only a few feet away.

For crying out loud, Zany, get a grip.

The shower stall in his bathroom barely afforded enough room to turn around. He fiddled with the cracked plastic handle on the faucet until, protesting, brownish tepid water came spewing out of the shower head. The stall was metal, and mildew clung to the rusted-out cracks and seams. He avoided touching the sides as he rubbed the bar of soap across his chest and down his stomach.

Damn Roy, anyway. This whole mess was entirely his buddy's fault. And now here Jeff was, trying to protect Lucy from coming to harm in a totally alien environment, trying to keep his head clear, trying to keep his hands off her!

Damn you, Roy Letterman!

He dried off with a towel that looked as if it were made for a midget and wrapped it around his hips. Rubbing a circle in the steamy mirror, he reached for the razor in his shaving kit, then stopped. Why shave? Who was he trying to impress? Ordinarily he could make it two days without shaving, only looking a little ragged around the edges if he held off. The heck with perfection. If Don Johnson didn't have to shave every day, why should *he*?

It occurred to Jeff as he tugged on his trousers and zipped them that he could fly the hell out of this stinking hot place and be back in the States by midafternoon. Let Roy come down and take his place. Jeff *could* do that. And maybe, just maybe, he'd march himself into Lucy's room and tell her so.

"Look here, Ms Hammond, I've had it with this cloak-and-dagger business. You've got a boyfriend who should be here taking care of you. I've had it with worrying. Call Roy. Get him down here *today*." Sure, Jeff could plow right on into her room and let her have both barrels. But what if she was still in bed, still clad in that filmy little black thing?

He put on his last clean cotton polo shirt and rubbed his chin. Last night had been special, he thought, like walking through a time warp, a magical land with Lucy by his side. But today was a new day. And in the light things looked different somehow, and the guilty feelings about Roy, which he'd kept at bay, were closing in on him now.

With the bag of money safely tucked under his arm, he found himself tapping on Lucy's door, still uncertain what to say to her. He knew one thing, however. She was Roy's lady—not his—and somehow he was going to have to let her know he'd drawn the line.

Lucy's hair was still damp when she let him in, but she was fully dressed in a khaki skirt and blouse, a little red scarf tied around her neck. She was on the phone, however, having carried it with her to the door. She put her hand over the mouthpiece for a second. "I've got Andy Martin on the line," she whispered, then went back to her conversation.

Jeff closed the door behind him and went to sit on the side of the bed. The black thing was there, too, only a few inches from his fingertips.

"I'm glad to hear you're doing better," Lucy was saying into the receiver. "I guess traditional treatment is the way to go." She listened for a minute, then spoke. "That's very interesting, Andy, and I appreciate your telling me this. It explains a lot." Silence for another minute. "Oh, it's a long story, Andy. I'll fill you in when I'm back in Denver.... Yes, Mom and Dad are quite well.... Okay, I'll give them your best. Bye, Andy, take care."

She hung up and turned to Jeff. "Wait till you hear this! Just like we thought," she said excitedly. "Our Dr. Dover has been the object of a couple of lawsuits lately. Andy said that some former patients tried to prove he was using an unauthorized drug on them and giving them a cock-and-bull story about vitamin and mineral treatments."

"Did the patients get anywhere with the suits?" Jeff asked.

Lucy shook her head. "Andy didn't think so. He said that by the time they sued, the medication was out of their systems and there was no evidence."

"You'd think this doctor would stop the treatments," Jeff said, "before someone nailed him."

"Before you came in," she said, "I asked Andy just that. In his opinion, Malcolm Dover is an egomaniac, a man who thinks the rest of the world is crazy not to see the benefit of his treatments."

"So our doctor is probably still buying the stuff illegally, maybe through his now-dead caretaker, and smuggling it across the border," Jeff said.

"It would explain the half million," Lucy put in.

"And it sure seems like this caretaker was double-dealing. Maybe he was on that beach in Cozumel to make an exchange. You know, the drug for the money, only he never intended to give the Mexicans the money that night."

"The empty briefcase," Lucy said pensively.

"It would explain plenty."

"But... Say he *was* making an exchange, Jeff. Then how did he expect to give his contacts an empty briefcase and get away with it?"

Jeff thought for a minute, while Lucy paced, her hands on her hips. "Okay," he said finally. "We know Dover has been giving these treatments for several years at least. Maybe there have been quite a few exchanges on that beach, and maybe the Mexicans have been getting careless. You know, trusting the caretaker. I mean, if it had been going on without a hitch for years..."

"That's logical," Lucy said, stopping to face Jeff. "But why was the money in that hotel room? And why did the caretaker get a hotel room in the first place, when he lived in Dover's house on Cozumel?"

Jeff shrugged.

"There has to be an explanation," Lucy said.

"Yeah, well—" Jeff shook his head "—I'd say it doesn't matter. What does matter is that I'm betting the guys that half drowned you and trashed your plane are the same ones who did in the caretaker."

"And chances are they know by now," Lucy said grimly, "just where we are."

"We better assume they do."

"And they know we have the money."

Jeff only nodded.

They ate breakfast that morning in a subdued mood, both of them soberly eyeing the bag of money that sat on the tabletop. Jeff was beginning to wish, more and more, that Roy could get down there and be with Lucy. This was a heck of a big responsibility, and one that Jeff would just as soon relinquish. Over and over he thought about Lucy's welfare. If those men caught up to them, could he protect her? Then again, could Roy do any better?

He glanced across the table at her. She was playing with a piece of toast, turning it around in her fingers, studying it. Her brow was creased in thought, and she seemed a million miles away from him at that moment.

What was going through her head? Was she worried about her safety, or was she thinking about Roy, wishing he were here to watch over her?

While she fiddled pensively with her food, he found himself unable to stop watching her. Over the rim of his coffee cup, he saw the graceful curve of her sun-browned neck above the red scarf, her small, pointed chin and the distinctive, full mouth, made fuller by her narrow chin. Her bone structure was strong yet graceful, feminine, and she had the loveliest blue eyes behind her glasses. Her short brown hair was cut in an attractive style and framed her face nicely. A very pretty lady....

"I wonder if Tom's talked to the embassy in Mexico City yet," Lucy said, putting down her unfinished toast. She looked at her wristwatch. "Surely he's been able to reach the right people by now."

"Should we try his room on Cozumel?" Jeff suggested. "I'd feel a whole lot better if we could ditch this money."

Lucy smiled dolefully. "So would I, Jeff. This vacation's turned out to be a total disaster."

"Sure has," he agreed readily. *Except for meeting you, Luce,* he thought.

He stood by the window in Lucy's room and stared out at the tops of the pyramids that showed over the jungle canopy, while she made the call to Cozumel. In the distance he could hear the sound of a plane's engine, a puddle-jumper that brought tourists in and out of Chichén Itzá. Those men in their conspicuous dark suits could be on that plane, or any of the flights, for that matter. How long would it take to find Lucy at the single hotel here? Not long. And what if they had guns? How was Jeff going to protect Lucy from hard, cold weapons?

In the background he could hear her speaking in Spanish on the phone, then in English. He liked her voice; it was never shrill or too loud. It was sometimes full of humor, sometimes melancholy, sometimes upset. He was beginning to know all of Lucy's moods, to recognize the lifting of an eyebrow, the gesture of a hand, the curve of her lips, the way she moved and laughed and shrugged. *Dangerous,* he told himself.

Roy should have known better than to send him. But how could Roy have guessed in a million years that he and Lucy would hit it off? Roy was his best friend, for God's sake, and you just didn't do that to your best friend! You turned off your hormones and your feelings; you put yourself into neutral. You didn't feel the way Jeff did about Lucy or want to touch her so much or worry about her or just plain *like* her so much.

The worst part of it was that he couldn't leave her. He was trapped into staying until this ridiculous situation was resolved. Maybe he should have left the damn bag of money outside her hotel room that night before last; it would probably have been gone yesterday morning and they would have been in the clear.

But, of course, then he never would have pulled her out of the sea; he never would have kissed her or walked through the ageless, fog-shrouded ruins of Chichén Itzá holding her hand, feeling closer to her than he'd ever felt to anyone in his life. It had been scary and wonderful at the same time; the two of them had been lost in another world together, as if they could have walked on into the mist, into the past, and just vanished.

"Tom," he heard Lucy saying, "yes, we're fine." She caught Jeff's eye. "No, we haven't seen anyone." She paused, listening. "Okay, I see, uh-huh. Yes. So it's all set? Oh, good.... But I *have* to file a flight plan, Tom, I just can't land there, *especially* there, without one. They'd have my license in a minute." Again she paused, nodding, biting her lower lip. "Okay, we'll be careful," she said. "And you be careful, too. I've got a feeling these are no amateurs we're fooling with.... Okay, see you there."

"So?" Jeff asked when she was off the phone.

"We're flying to Mexico City," Lucy said. "Tom's made contact with someone at the embassy who's going to get to work on this. We can be rid of the money, Jeff. We'll be safe."

"Mexico City?" He appeared doubtful.

"I know," she said, "it's a lot more than either of us bargained for, but we don't have a choice right now."

"I guess not," Jeff replied. "What was that about a flight plan?"

"Oh." She stopped stuffing her things into her bag for a moment and looked at him gravely. "It can't be helped," she said. "We have to file our plan with Mexico City."

"Lucy, I really wish—"

"We *have* to. It's a major airport. Believe me, I know. They wouldn't even let us land..."

"You realize," Jeff said, "that they'll probably put it on computer there and anyone, *anyone*, Lucy, with a lick of sense could check. We've lucked out so far, but God knows how long it'll hold."

She let out a long breath. "I know."

Getting to the landing strip at Chichén Itzá was a whole lot easier during daylight hours. The hotel even had a van, such as it was, to shuttle overnight guests back to the hourly tourist flights that flew in from several different resorts.

While they loaded their gear on the plane, Jeff thought about Roy. They really should have called him before leaving, to let him know their plans. For all either of them really knew, Roy might have taken a plane to Mexico already and decided to rendezvous with them here in Chichén Itzá.

Lucy went through her preflight check, while Jeff sat in the passenger seat, glancing out at the myriad tourists who were milling around and wondering if the men after the money might be among the throng. He was feeling melancholy. He wished he had the nerve to ask Lucy more about her relationship with Roy Letterman. For instance, had the two of them discussed marriage? Roy had never said, and the subject had not come up with Lucy, either. Jeff had assumed that was the direction in which the relationship was heading, but he could have been totally off base.

It saddened him to think of Roy and Lucy together. And the sadness made him feel guilty. He was a complete fool for allowing himself to like Lucy so much. Couldn't he get a lady of his own, for goodness' sake? Did he have to covet his best buddy's girl?

Lucy put her clipboard with the preflight check on it behind her seat. "Boy, you sure look anxious," she said as she turned the little plane and began to taxi down the grassy runway. "The takeoff will be easy. Don't worry."

He gazed at her for a moment, shrugged and said nothing.

It was a smooth ascent until they hit the line of gray clouds; then the plane lurched and bumped for a few minutes, and Lucy had to climb sharply before they broke out into the sun at sixty-five hundred feet. Jeff admitted to himself that the view was spectacular from up there. There were breaks in the clouds below as they headed west, and the sunlight filtered down through the openings in brilliant yellow columns, illuminating the sea of the Yucatán jungle below.

"Pretty, huh?" Lucy turned her head and smiled at him.

"Beautiful," he agreed. "Too bad we can't really enjoy it."

"Well, all of it hasn't been bad," she said. "The diving was terrific—for a while anyway. And I loved the ruins."

Jeff nodded, watching her face.

"Mexico's a great place," she added, "if you know where to go. Now, on the west coast around Puerto Vallarta and Acapulco, well, it's real touristy. Expensive. But central Mexico and places like Cozumel are cheaper, and not everyone is after the good old dollar."

"They're poorer," Jeff said.

"For sure. I was really glad to get that children's orphanage together last week. You can't imagine how badly it's needed. But the red tape." She made a face.

"You mean it's hard to give money away down here?"

"It really can be. To do things right, that is."

"Will you go back to—what was the place called?"

"Yaxcaba."

"Will you go back from time to time?"

Lucy laughed. "You bet. And not only me. Once the funding is established, authorities from Mexico City will keep a close tab on spending, corruption, you know. Hopefully," she said, "the place will be successful and some of the wealthy Mexicans will take an interest. Frequently the Hammond Foundation operates these kind of homes as joint ventures."

"How many homes are there?"

"Let's see . . . seven in the States and now three below the border—one in Panama, two here in Mexico."

"I'll bet they keep you busy," he said.

She rolled her eyes. "I *could* get the foundation to hire someone to do my job, but to tell you the truth, I like being busy. I love flying around and seeing the kids at the homes we've started. It's great to see those children all well fed and clean and neat and taken care of. I've seen them on the street, where they're starved and scared, and it's such a change." She glanced over at him. "I know what people think, that the foundation is just a tax dodge, but we really do a lot of good."

Jeff recognized sincerity when he heard it. She really meant all those trite things that a lot of people might mock as being naive. It was obvious she cared a lot. "You like kids," he said.

"I *love* kids. All kinds, all ages."

He stirred in his seat, half-afraid to ask the next question. "You going to have kids someday, Lucy?"

"Oh," she said airily, "I hope to. Don't you?"

"Sure. Does, ah, Roy want children?" he asked.

"Roy? Well, we haven't really gotten that far yet."

Good, he thought, then felt that knife of guilt dig deeper into his chest.

It was about an eight-hundred-mile flight across the fertile Yucatán and over the eastern Sierra Madre to Mexico City. To be on the safe side, Lucy refueled in Veracruz, where they grabbed sandwiches and coffee to take along in the plane.

When they took off into the afternoon sun the land began to alter drastically. No longer was it as green and flat, coastal; instead the plane climbed above deepening valleys and over twisted hills as they wound their way through the ancient, rolling mountains of the arid Sierra Madre. Jeff found himself duly impressed by Lucy's flying skills. She was careful, checking her compass and instruments frequently, giving wide berth to the taller mountains, following procedures to a tee. He relaxed, confident at last that she really did know her stuff.

"You ever sky dive?" he asked once.

"Me?" Lucy groaned. "Why would I step out of a perfectly safe airplane into midair? I'm not *that* crazy."

"Me, neither," he said.

"Yeah, but you're crazy enough to go out on the ice and get your head bashed in by professionals."

"It's fun, Luce, honest. And you give as much as you take," he said, smiling. "Sometimes a whole lot more."

"Macho? Is that what you are?" she asked lightly.

"I kind of like to think I am," he replied, then felt the heat on the back of his neck when she laughed.

The spreading metropolis of Mexico City sat on a high, alarmingly arid plateau surrounded by mountains. Once, eight hundred years ago, the plateau had supported a vast lake system that had been the center of Aztec civilization.

"No kidding," Jeff said as Lucy contacted the tower for approach instructions. "What happened to the lake?" he asked.

"Well, the Europeans—the Spanish, that is—came here and used up all the water. They built over the marshes. The land settled—they built some more. Pretty soon there *was* no lake left."

"The ecologists would go nuts today," he said.

"I'm sure the old Aztec priests would have, too. They'd have gladly sacrificed every European in sight if they could have."

Landing in Mexico City was no simple feat. There were jets from all over the world circling at various altitudes, on hold, and small private planes at lower heights vying for position on an outlying runway that ran north and south.

"Wow," Jeff said, "I hope air traffic control knows what it's doing."

"They're pretty good here," Lucy answered, checking her altitude, banking as per instructions. "Now you know why I had to file a flight plan. Can you imagine this airport trying to control the air space without prior knowledge?"

Lucy circled for fifteen minutes until the tower instructed her to make her final approach. The skies were a little too crowded for Jeff's liking, and he was darn glad to feel the tires make contact with the oily black tarmac. "Glad you know what you're doing," he commented, letting out a breath.

"You ought to learn to fly," Lucy said as she began to taxi. "I could help you..." Her voice trailed off. "Well, I could tell you how to get started."

"Maybe" was all Jeff replied.

They were to meet Tom in the heart of the city at the Hotel Camino Real, where the lawyer had made reservations for three rooms. Jeff assumed that Lucy's friend had already arrived by jet and would be there waiting. While Lucy arranged to have her plane serviced, he glanced around and wondered if this was to be their last few hours together. They'd turn the money over to McLaughlin, stay the night, of course, then go their separate ways. Roy might even fly down to Mexico City and accompany Lucy back to the States, Jeff thought. That would be natural, wouldn't it? Maybe the two of them would even stay in Mexico for a few days together. *How nice for them.*

It was taking Lucy a long time to show her documents to the authorities and arrange for service on the plane. Too long for Jeff's comfort. Whereas in Chichén Itzá there hadn't been a man in a suit around, here in this airport, almost every man wore a suit or sport jacket. It was conceivable that their pursuers could have arrived ahead of them. Any one of these men could be after the bag of money tucked under Jeff's arm.

He glanced at Lucy, who was having a document stamped by an airport official, and wondered if she was aware of the danger, if she was looking at the many faces questioningly.

They caught a cab in front of the main terminal. "It's quite a drive in," Lucy said, settling back, "and not exactly scenic."

Jeff was already getting the picture. Because of the high altitude, the air was far cooler than in Cozumel or Chichén Itzá, but it was smog filled and dirty, a worse brown cloud by far than Denver's considerable one.

Virtually every square inch of land was occupied, mostly by families living in shacks. Sewers ran in ditches down the middle of the dusty, makeshift streets of the shantytowns, and children played along the littered roads, clad in torn rags, their big brown eyes looking hopelessly toward the passing cars as if for salvation.

The city's outskirts were wide avenues lined with chaos, Jeff decided. There were broken walls, goats, adobe huts, and corrugated iron fences defaced with graffiti he couldn't read; drunks on the pavement, outdoor barbecues. A constant racket filled the air, deafening, overpowering, malevolent: car horns and engines overrevved by anxious drivers, the din of people packed too close together and old machinery working too hard.

"God," Jeff breathed.

Lucy only nodded.

The highways seemed to run in no particular direction, twisting and turning. And he'd never seen so many vehicles in his life. Cars and buses and trucks of every description clogged the main arteries of the immense city, as well as every side street, every alley, every thoroughfare. The exhaust from the hundreds and thousands of vehicles formed a black sooty cloud over the streets.

"Awful," Lucy said.

"Scary," Jeff replied.

But then there were heartening sights. As they neared the core of Mexico City the highways widened, becoming boulevards, and there were actually trees growing on the center islands. The boulevards ran into innumerable traffic circles that held statues, lush greenery and park benches. The populace was better dressed, too, than it had been in the overcrowded outskirts of the metropolis. Better dressed and colorfully dressed. Obviously the Mexicans loved color: bright red and orange, royal blue and deep green contrasted sharply against their brown skin and dark hair. Shops crowded together, and tall skyscrapers pierced the cloudy sky. Jeff recalled the terrible earthquake of a few years back and could picture the destruction.

He sensed that they were very near the heart of the city when the buildings appeared older and there was more fancy ironwork in windows and on doors. He'd been to Europe on tour once with the hockey team and thought that the flavor of central Mexico City was decidedly European. Madrid, perhaps....

Every so often Jeff found himself turning in his seat, staring out the back window. As far as the eye could see there were nothing but long lines of cars and trucks jammed bumper to bumper, their headlights now coming on. Was one of those cars following them? Had those men on Cozumel checked with air traffic control and gotten Lucy's flight plan? It wouldn't have been difficult, Jeff knew.

He turned back around in his seat and found Lucy looking at him. Her expression was uncharacteristically solemn.

They passed by an immense park, a complex of modern museums, a zoo and many acres of open green space. Nannies pushed babies in strollers; tourists snapped pictures in the growing dark.

"If I recall," Lucy said, "the hotel's right on that circle ahead." She pointed.

The Hotel Camino Real sat on the north side of the traffic circle, an elegant, turn-of-the-century gray stone building that climbed ten stories into the smog. On the side street that met the roundabout was a pedestrian mall, European in style, with myriad shops, boutiques and outdoor cafés lit cheerfully by lights, tall trees, colorful striped canopies and umbrellas advertising affordable wines.

"It sure is a city of different faces," Jeff commented as he took Lucy's hand and helped her out of the cab.

"They say there are only two kinds of people here," she replied, "the very rich and the very poor."

Tom had checked in, all right, and had left a message at the front desk. He'd gone to the American Embassy to have dinner with someone who could help them. "Enjoy the sights," his note read. "I'll see you in the morning—Tom."

"Well, that's something, at least," Lucy said as she stuck the note in her purse.

"I only hope," Jeff said, "that this thing gets straightened out soon. Maybe the embassy can really help."

"They'd *better* help," Lucy said under her breath.

They followed the bellhop onto the elevator and stepped out into a dimly lit hallway on the eighth floor. Tom would think of something, Jeff knew, no matter what happened with the embassy. Shortly Jeff would be out of it entirely. He knew they had to get hold of Roy, too, and let him know about their change of plans. Roy would fly down for sure. Maybe even tonight.

He followed the bellhop and Lucy down the hall and felt regret swamp him. It had been a wild two days, nerve-racking, but exciting, too. Now he would take a flight back to Denver and have to face the real world once more, get those videotapes and try to find some way to clear his name. His prospects for the future seemed pretty dull compared to sharing life with Lucy Hammond. Fleetingly, grudgingly, he wondered why *he* hadn't met her first. The luck of the draw, he supposed, and his draw had been damn lousy of late.

The bellhop opened their side-by-side doors, deposited their bags and waited for Jeff to tip him. Lucy, as well, lingered in the hall, and it ran through Jeff's head that she was hesitant to leave his company. Or was that wishful thinking on his part?

Jeff stood at his door and stared at her silently. A thousand things he'd like to say to her flew through his mind but stuck in his throat when he tried to voice them. Finally he came out with "I suppose we'd better call Roy and let him know what's going on." Why was it so hard to say?

"Yes," Lucy agreed, shifting her weight to the other foot, gripping her purse in front of her. "I guess we'd better do that."

Jeff took a step toward her, then stopped, rubbing a hand across the back of his neck. "Lucy," he began, his voice low and intense, "do you *want* me to make that call?"

It seemed to Jeff as if all the air had suddenly been sucked out of the hallway. He felt the heavy rise and fall of his chest as he waited and waited for her reply.

She stared down at the floor, and all he could see was the top of her head, her fine, dark, glossy hair and her white knuckles gripping her purse. What was she thinking? Did she want to spare Roy the bother? Was she worried about him being annoyed? Or was she looking forward with a rapid heartbeat, a surging stomach and excitement to Roy's arrival?

Jeff didn't dare guess; he was afraid of the answer. He shouldn't have asked the question in the first place.

Finally she looked up, and her expression was troubled. He wanted to soothe those anxious lines away and hold her close, kiss the top of her head and breathe in her special scent, but she was trying to say something to him, struggling with her words.

"I don't know," she said. "I just don't know anymore, Jeff." Her eyes begged him to make the decision for her, and he could do that. He could spare her that much. "I'll take care of it, Lucy," he said softly. "Don't worry about it."

"Thanks," she murmured.

"Lucy..." Why was he prolonging this? What did he really want from her?

"Jeff, I'm really tired. I'd like to get cleaned up," she was saying, looking down again.

"Yeah, sure."

She was backing away from him, distancing herself physically and emotionally. He'd pushed too hard. "Luce, look, let's get something to eat. It'll make you feel better."

"Maybe later." Her gaze slid away, and she reached for her key.

"Okay."

Her door was open and she was inside; still he stood there in the hall like a jerk, unable to end the scene.

"I'll call you," he said.

But she was closing her door and didn't hear him, and his words echoed foolishly in the empty corridor.

Jeff leaned against the wall and let out a ragged breath. What kind of a heel was he? He'd put her in a terrible spot, selfishly, cruelly. Why, why had he gone off the deep end like that?

There was an answer, he knew, but he couldn't let himself contemplate it. Suddenly he spun away from the wall, strode into his room and slammed the door.

CHAPTER NINE

LUCY AWAKENED TO THE RACKET of rush-hour traffic: the honking horns, the police sirens, the shouts of irate drivers. *Only in Mexico City,* she thought.

Almost instantaneously she found herself thinking about Jeff, wondering if he was up yet, wondering if he'd slept as poorly as she had. She tried to tell herself that it was the money and all the hassle it had caused, but she knew it was much, much more that had made her toss and turn half the night.

She dressed in a clean, coral-colored shirt with rolled-up sleeves and the same khaki skirt she'd worn the previous day. They had even grabbed a bite to eat together last night at the hotel, and still Lucy avoided any mention of Roy. The shrinks called it "denial" or "blocking." Good terms, she mused.

Leaving her room, Lucy glanced at Jeff's door. Was he still asleep, or was he downstairs eating breakfast? And where was Tom?

She found them both in the dining room, having coffee and freshly baked rolls laced with honey. "I see you two have met," she said, letting Jeff pull out her chair.

"It wasn't hard to spot him in the dining room," Tom McLaughlin said. "I must have seen Zany Zanicek on the ice in Denver a thousand times."

Lucy signaled the waiter for coffee. "And then we've *all* seen Jeff in those TV ads," she put in with a teasing smile.

"Let's just skip that subject," Jeff said dryly.

Lucy poured two sugar packets into her strong Colombian coffee and took a sip. "So, Tom," she began, "any thoughts on how we can get rid of this money? I'd sure like to be able to breathe again."

"I was just filling Jeff in," he answered. Tom shifted in his seat, a strapping man, tall and weighing over two hundred pounds, with a pleasant square face above a fleshy chin and small, wide set eyes that lent him a shrewd look. He was hounded constantly by his diminutive wife to watch his cholesterol and stop smoking his filthy black Havana cigars.

"You two have really opened a can of worms," he was saying. "I checked out what you told me, Lucy, about Andy Martin's experience at Dover's clinic. Well, I found out plenty. A few years back, Malcolm Dover tried to open a clinic here in Mexico City." Tom leaned forward on the table, tapping its surface with a blunt finger. "He needed a Mexican national to sponsor him, because a foreigner can't operate here without the proper licenses. And guess who he had lined up?"

"Who?" Lucy asked dutifully.

Tom leaned back, grinning smugly. "A man who just happens to work for a large pharmaceutical company right here in the city, Fuentes Químico. And guess what this Fuentes company makes?" He answered his own question. "Planifolia."

"I've heard of that, haven't I?" Lucy asked.

"Yes, it's a drug, perfectly legal in Mexico, but not approved yet in the States, that's been hailed as the new miracle cure for cancer," Tom concluded triumphantly.

"Oh," Lucy said.

"And where did you dig all this up?" Jeff asked.

"The embassy already had a file on Dover. He'd been there a lot, trying to get help setting up his clinic. It never flew, though, because the Mexican government refused to license this fellow Morales, who was going to sponsor Dover. Something about a previous criminal record."

"So when the good doctor couldn't start a clinic here, he began smuggling planifolia into Houston," Lucy said. "Through this Morales."

"Apparently. *Allegedly,*" Tom replied.

"Can't someone check out his clinic in Houston?" Jeff suggested. "If they found the planifolia there…"

"There's no probable cause for a search warrant," Tom said. "But that money you've been toting around might help convince someone. Of course, we can't connect it to Dover. Not yet."

"All right," Lucy said, "what do we do with the money then?"

Tom looked from Lucy to Jeff and back. "It may take a little longer than I thought."

"Uh-oh," Lucy said, sighing.

"The embassy is trying to decide whether to call in the Drug Enforcement Agency or not. We're talking here about a controlled substance. But there's interagency rivalry, because the embassy lawyer I'm dealing with would like the credit for nailing Dover. You know, the usual. And the DEA has a way of stepping on toes down here, both the Mexicans' and our own."

"Great," she said, exasperated. "So here we sit with half a million and thugs on our tails, and the authorities are squabbling over who gets credit for the bust!"

Tom nodded apologetically.

"Meanwhile," Jeff put in, "there are patients in Dover's clinic who're suffering because they belive in the miracle cure."

"It didn't help Andy Martin," Lucy said angrily.

"It's an unapproved drug in the U.S. of A., folks. There's supposed to be an announcement on its effectiveness soon, but it'll probably amount to nothing, like laetrile," Tom reflected.

"Those men after me, the ones in Cozumel who wanted their money back," Lucy said thoughtfully, "must have something to do with that man Morales, the one who's selling Dover the planifolia. Maybe he was even one of them."

"You could easily hypothesize that." Tom nodded. "And maybe Morales was selling it through Dover's caretaker, Taylor, the one who planned to skip town with the money."

"The caretaker," Lucy added, "who is now deceased."

"Damn," Jeff muttered, "if you're right, we've walked right into Morales's home territory."

"Oh, boy," Lucy whispered.

"Look," Jeff said, catching Tom's eye meaningfully. "I think the primary concern is to get Lucy out of here as quickly as possible. She almost got killed back on Cozumel. Maybe I should go talk to these embassy people."

"Jeff," Lucy said, "I'm sure Tom will clear everything up today. In the meantime, we'll put the money in the hotel safe. Those men can't know exactly where we are in the city. Not yet."

"I'm doing everything possible," Tom said. "You can best help her, Jeff, by staying with her for a few more hours. Take her to see the sights. Stay in the crowds."

"Which isn't hard to do in this city," Lucy said, forcing herself to be cheerful.

"And I may as well tell you," Tom said, lowering his voice, "if I get any more of a runaround from that lawyer at the Embassy today, I may just contact the DA in Houston and dump the whole thing in *his* lap. If we were on the other side of the border, I would already have turned the money over. As it is . . ."

"Can you take the money across the border just like that?" Jeff asked.

"Hardly," Tom replied. "There are legal channels, but it *can* be done."

"Maybe that's the route we should take," Lucy said. "Get out of Mexico City."

"Well, let's see what happens today," Tom said, rising. "The easiest way to get you free of this is to leave the money in the hands of the authorities right here."

"When will we know?" Lucy asked.

"Tell you what," Tom said, "you two go and see the sights, and I'll meet you back here at four. Say the cocktail lounge, the one that's decorated like an Aztec temple."

"Fine," Lucy said as she watched Tom hitch up his belt and head out of the dining room.

"He's a character," Jeff commented, reaching for a roll.

"He is that, and I'm sure he's doing everything he can."

"Well," Jeff said between mouthfuls, "we'll get the money locked up here, and then maybe you could show me around."

For a moment Lucy thought he'd been about to say, "We'll call Roy," but somehow she knew he wouldn't.

While Jeff stood at the front desk and got his receipt for the bag, Lucy waited by the little florist shop in the lobby and fingered the cut flowers.

Why *hadn't* she called Roy? There had been ample opportunity, and yet it was as if some unseen force held her from doing it. She admitted to herself that she liked Jeff, that in his company she felt alive, really alive, for the first time in years. Of course, the feelings she'd developed for Jeff came from the closeness, the crazy adventure they were involved in. And undeniably he was a very attractive man. Heck, she thought, millions of women saw him in that sexy ad and drooled. Why should she be immune? A passing fancy, Lucy told herself firmly, that's all he was....

"Beautiful, aren't they?" Jeff said at her ear.

"What?"

"The flowers, Luce, they're beautiful. And in January. I can't get over it."

She did like being with Jeff. She liked the way he pushed open the hotel door for her and steered her through. She liked the way he took her arm tentatively and led her down the street through the hordes of pedestrians.

"So, where to, Luce? You're the guide." Yes, she even liked the timbre of his voice, the boyishness, the youthful curiosity that sparked in his eyes.

"The museum? Do you like museums?" Lucy asked, wanting to show him everything, wanting to share the city with him, wanting this day to go on and on—this last day with Jeffrey Zanicek. "There are lots of Aztec exhibits. Everyone enjoys them."

"Lead the way."

They walked, as the museum complex was only a few blocks from their hotel. Their route followed alongside one of the largest parks in all Mexico, a lovely, serene open space of trees and gardens and wrought-iron benches. Policemen patrolled, couples picnicked on blankets, university students kicked a soccer ball high into the air.

"Let's cut through the park," Lucy suggested. "We'll get away from the traffic."

Jeff even stopped at an outdoor drinking fountain, but Lucy shook her head. "Ever heard of Montezuma's revenge?"

"Oops," he said, grinning, passing up the drink of water.

The museums sat at the far end of the park, a sprawling gray stone complex that housed the history of this ancient land, as well as its modern arts. It was crowded that morning, with tourists lined up at the entrances already. Schoolchildren in their crisp navy uniforms filed in and out of the buildings with their teachers, and artists stood behind their easels at various points on the sweeping marble terrace.

"Here," Jeff said when they reached the entrance to the museum of antiquities, "I'll pay." And Lucy felt that twinge, that question: How much had Roy given him?

Roy. Tall and handsome and refined. He had such an elegant way about him, smooth and debonair, pol-

Harlequin's

Best Ever "Get Acquainted" Offer

Look what we'd give to hear from you

6 FREE GIFTS 6

Return This Sticker
and Get 6 Gifts—FREE
Compliments of Harlequin

▲ **GET ALL YOU ARE** ▲
ENTITLED TO—AFFIX STICKER
TO RETURN CARD—MAIL TODAY

This is our most fabulous offer ever...
AND THERE'S STILL ⟫⟫➤ **MORE INSIDE.**
Let's get acquainted.
Let's become
friends—

Look what we've got for you:

... A FREE digital clock/calendar
... plus a sampler set of 4 terrific Harlequin Superromance® novels, specially selected by our editors.

... PLUS a surprise mystery gift that will delight you.

All this just for trying our Reader Service!

If you wish to continue in the Harlequin Reader Service®, you'll get 4 new Harlequin Superromance® novels every month—before they're available in stores. That's SNEAK PREVIEWS with 7% off the cover price on any books you keep (just $2.74* each)—and FREE home delivery besides!

Plus There's More!

With your monthly book shipments, you'll also get our newsletter, packed with news of your favorite authors and upcoming books—FREE! And as a valued reader, we'll be sending you additional free gifts from time to time—as a token of our appreciation.

THERE IS NO CATCH. You're not required to buy a single book, ever. You may cancel Reader Service privileges anytime, if you want. All you have to do is write "cancel" on your statement or simply return your shipment of books to us at our cost. The free gifts are yours anyway. It's a super sweet deal if ever there was one. Try us and see!

*Terms and prices subject to change without notice.

Get 4 FREE full-length Harlequin Superromance® novels.

Plus
this lovely lucite clock/calendar

Plus
a surprise free gift

▼ PLUS LOTS MORE! MAIL THIS CARD TODAY ▼

Harlequin's Best-Ever "Get Acquainted" Offer

PLACE STICKER FOR 6 FREE GIFTS HERE

Yes, I'll try the Harlequin Reader Service® under the terms outlined on the opposite page. Send me 4 free Harlequin Superromance® novels, a free digital clock/calendar and a free mystery gift.

134 CIH KA7E

NAME _____

ADDRESS _____ APT. _____

CITY _____

STATE _____ ZIP CODE _____

Offer limited to one per household and not valid to current Harlequin Superromance Subscribers. All orders subject to approval. Terms and prices subject to change without notice.

PRINTED IN U.S.A.

Don't forget...

. . . Return this card today and receive 4 free books, free digital clock/calendar and free mystery gift.

. . . You will receive books before they're available in stores and at a discount off the cover prices.

. . . No obligation to buy. You can cancel at any time by writing "cancel" on your statement or returning a shipment to us at our cost.

If offer card is missing, write to: Harlequin Reader Service,
901 Fuhrmann Blvd., P.O. Box 1867, Buffalo, N.Y. 14269-1867

ished. And he was a good man, honest and caring. There were few faults to Roy Letterman, so few they hardly mattered. The important thing was that he cared deeply for her, that marriage was in the air, that he couldn't care less about her money and position. *That* counted for a lot, considering the number of times she'd been burned in the past.

Okay, she thought, he *was* too busy. But so were a lot of executives. It was the age they lived in, the pressure of a career and family, the balance a person had to find. Roy would find his. Of course he would.

"Coming?" Jeff was asking, and she had to tear her mind away from Roy and the icy fingers of Denver in January. She was here with Jeff, for a few more hours at least, in sunny, warm Mexico. And despite it all, she wanted those short hours to last.

Inside the museum it was cool and dark as they stood at the head of a wide marble staircase that opened up below to a huge central lobby, guarded on the far wall by one of the largest sun gods unearthed to date. "Which way?" Jeff asked, looking around, craning his neck for a better view of the vast glass ceiling.

"Let's do the whole place," Lucy suggested. She noticed that Jeff, however, kept glancing around frequently, behind them a lot, too. Did he really think they were being followed? She tried to put the notion from her, to cling to the sense of youthful enthusiasm she felt when they were together. If Morales's dark men in suits were tailing them, Lucy did not want to think about it, not today.

As she'd guessed, Jeff was fascinated by the relics of the Aztec Empire. There was, admittedly, something compelling about the Aztec preoccupation with death.

Aztec artists painted a brutal picture of the frequent human sacrifices to the sun god.

"And all in the name of their religion," Lucy remarked as they stood together in front of a particularly graphic bas-relief. She felt a shiver up her spine.

Jeff studied the artwork carefully, his corded neck thrust forward as he read the little typed card at the base of the display. "I know a few guys on the hockey team who'd do this stuff if they could get away with it," he said, and she saw a twitch at the corner of his mouth before he put an arm around her shoulder and led her on.

They covered almost the whole building before returning to the warm, sunlit day. "I'm starved," Jeff said as he put on his sunglasses.

"After *that*?" Lucy nodded toward the museum.

"Hey, I'm just an animal at heart," he teased.

Lucy ignored his attempt at humor. "If you're really hungry, we could go to the market. It's outdoors, and we could shop, too. They sell everything.

"Sounds fine."

They took a cab, as the huge cobbled plaza that twice weekly became a busy marketplace was some distance away. Again Jeff paid the driver in pesos, and she found herself trying to see how much he had left in that wad of bills. Why should she care? Lucy asked herself. Jeff was, after all, only a paid escort. Sure, he had money problems, and that ugly scandal hanging around his neck like an albatross. Fleetingly she wondered if he was really going to try to clear his name, or if he would simple roll with the punches. He professed to want that coaching job at Denver University, though, and she couldn't imagine them hiring him with a cloud over his head.

Oh, well, Lucy told herself, it was none of her concern.

While Jeff stared out the cab window, Lucy glanced down at her folded hands, then across to his legs—strong legs, well shaped beneath the trousers. She'd seen those legs in his swimming trunks, the smooth skin over the long muscles, the crisp, curling blond hairs. She caught herself and turned her head away abruptly, only to find the cab driver watching her in the rearview mirror, a smile glued to his lips. Lucy colored hotly, rolling her window all the way down.

Roy's got great legs, too, she reminded herself firmly.

"This is really something," Jeff said as he steered them along the cobbled street.

"I told you," Lucy said, feeling relaxed and happy, "they sell everything."

She felt childishly proud to show Jeff all the stalls and booths and pegboard displays, the flowers and bright handwoven cloth, the caged birds that sang cheerfully and the colorful *piñatas*, the ripe vegetables and fruits and silver jewelry. There were whole blocks of used, broken furniture and an alley full of old auto parts, right down to secondhand spark plugs. There was a half a block of exotic animals for sale, too: strange, slinky cats and noisy parrots; several overly friendly little monkeys; lizards and iguanas; even spiders and crawly things, which Lucy steered clear of.

"Want a tarantula?" Jeff asked, trying to pull her toward a cage, grinning. "I'll buy you one."

The foods were as exotic as the rest of the goods. A large part of the marketplace was taken up by food stalls and outdoor seating areas. Hundreds of Mexicans sat around eating and drinking and smoking, and talking—it seemed that chatting away passionately for hours was a national pastime.

"Everything looks great," Jeff said. "What're you hungry for?"

They looked over the charcoal-grilled meats, the goat heads turning on spits above open fire pits, the crackling pork and the hog ears, the steaming rice and chicken and bean concoctions, the hand-tossed tortillas and Mexican pizzas, the marinated cactus plants.

"I don't know," Lucy said, overwhelmed, "maybe a real taco. Or some chilies. They say," she began, then paused.

Jeff stopped and looked at her with his head tilted to one side. "What *do* they say?"

Lucy shrugged, seemingly unconcerned. "They say that if a man eats hot chilies, it makes him strong and virile."

"Oh, really?" He hid a smile. "You know," he said offhandedly, "some chilies might just hit the spot at that."

Jeff was a practiced tease, she decided as she ate her taco and watched him brazen his way through beans and tortillas covered with hot chili sauce. He had that little smile on his lips and his eyes danced, playing with her, sending her messages, making her want to tease him in return.

"No wonder they asked you to do that underwear ad," she said. "You think you're the sexiest thing since Tom Selleck."

"Sexier," Jeff said, his face straight.

"But," Lucy put in, ignoring him, "I don't notice any of the women around here falling at your feet."

"Guess they didn't see me in my underwear here, then."

He *was* fun. There was none of the quiet intensity in Jeff that Roy possessed. There was no fear of looking foolish or uninformed or immature—Jeff was too spontaneous. He accepted what came along; he enjoyed himself; he played hard at life.

It ran through Lucy's head that he really was much more her type than Roy. But then she caught herself. Jeff might be fun for a fling, a fast-paced couple of months. But in the crunch, where would he be? If it hadn't been for his friendship with Roy, would he even have stayed around with the bad guys chasing them?

Lucy sipped on a bottled Pepsi and checked her watch. "We have to meet Tom at four," she said. "And I'll need to change." She tugged at the collar of her coral blouse; it pulled away from her warm, moist skin, then stuck to it again. She looked up to catch Jeff watching her silently.

"Well, we have an hour or so. Don't you want to buy something, Luce?" Jeff finished off his *pulque*, a drink make from the sap of a cactus plant, so powerful it was drunk only by the locals, and Lucy saw the red in his eyes.

"You're going to need a nap," she commented, laughing. "That stuff can kill you, Zany."

"A tough old jock like me?"

He took her hand when they stood, and Lucy let him. His skin was warm and soft against hers, firm yet gentle. She felt heat spreading into her cheeks, a delicious heat, as if she'd been lying in a spring sun. It must have been the salsa she'd put on her taco....

They strolled hand in hand through the racks upon racks of clothing, and she saw a beautiful man's shirt, white with hand-embroidered stitching around the buttonholes and cuffs. *Roy could wear it to a barbe-*

cue, she thought. *It would look great on him.* But, no, she'd be too ashamed to buy a gift for him while her hand was in Jeff's.

She noticed, too, that Jeff had relaxed, even before the white lightning he'd imbibed. She supposed it was impossible to notice a tail in this mob scene. Lucy was glad. No one had a right to spoil her afternoon.

"Let's look at the jewelry," she said, tugging him across the crowded street. "I got Mom some earrings in Merida, but there wasn't nearly the selection there."

She looked through table after table of lovely jewelry. There were silver trinkets, and brass, gold and copper. There was lots of turquoise, handmade by the Mayan Indians in small villages in the same way they'd been doing it for centuries. She glanced at the next booth.

"Come on," she said, taking Jeff in tow. "I think I see something I have to have."

He stood by patiently while she fingered a silver concho belt. Fastening it around her waist, she asked, "What do you think?" She turned around for him and held out her arms. "Is it me?"

"It's you," he said quietly, watching her intently.

"It's awfully overpriced," she said, avoiding his scrutiny, feeling uncomfortable suddenly. "Maybe I'll wait."

"If you like it," Jeff said, leaning back and folding his arms across his chest. "get it."

"Oh, I don't know." She had no right to be putting Jeff through this. Roy, sure. But not his friend. It was somehow too intimate, too personal. "I think I'll—" she began, but he'd stepped forward already and was unclasping it from her waist, and whatever she was about to say stuck like cotton in her throat when she felt his touch against her skirt, her hips, as the belt slid away. Oh, God, she thought, what was happening to her?

"How much?" Jeff was saying to the saleslady, and he was digging money out of his wallet, not even caring that the woman was taking him to the cleaners.

"Jeff," Lucy protested, "you can't...I won't let you..." But his look took her breath away. It said: *Let me do this for you while we have time.* Then he was handing her the paper bag and taking her hand again. This time, however, there was no tenderness in his grasp; there was only urgency.

They caught a cab to the hotel, and Lucy sat next to him in the back, her face averted as she gripped the bag with white fingers. She felt as if all the blood had drained from her cheeks, yet paradoxically she was hot. Her heart was squeezed in a tight fist; she couldn't seem to catch her breath.

Why had she let it go so far? She should have refused the belt. It was more than a gift. It was a sign, a symbol. And they both knew what it was, as clearly as if it had come in a tiny jewelry box, nestled in pure white cotton.

How had she let this happen? What in God's name had become of her good sense?

Jeff sat there stiffly, wordlessly. If she turned her head, she'd be able to see his profile, the lumpy nose, the thrust out chin, the strong neck. But she wouldn't turn her head; she wouldn't look.

The traffic was heavy as the start of rush hour gripped the frenzied city. The cabby kept getting stuck in long lines, honking his horn, waving his fist out the window, yelling Spanish obscenities. Yet the silence in

the back seat was so gravid that Lucy thought she
might scream.

I'll give the belt back to him, she thought frantically. That'll solve everything. But would the implica-
tions of his gesture go away then? Would the fact that
she'd accepted his gift be erased?

Oh, God.

She felt frightened suddenly, as if her mind would
not obey. It was drifting away from her, out of control. She tried desperately to think about Roy, to re-
gain her balance, yet Jeff's male scent seemed to fill the
close space, to envelope her like a fragrant, musky
perfume, irresistible, seductive. *It's Roy I want,* she
thought wildly. *He's right for me.* But Jeff's face su-
perimposed itself over her thought, his handsome,
blunt face, his wide mouth, the little crooked smile....

The cab pulled up in front of the hotel, and as if
suspended in a dream, Lucy stepped out unsteadily.

"You tired?" Jeff asked in concern.

"Oh, no," she managed to say. "Well, maybe." She
had to get away from him immediately; she had to re-
gain her equilibrium. She'd give the belt back to him,
show him how it had to be between them. She'd made
a terrible mistake, but it could be remedied.

CHAPTER TEN

JEFF RAISED HIS HAND to knock on Lucy's door at five minutes to four, but, oh, boy, he sure didn't want to face her. The belt had been a mistake. He knew it, and so did she. If he'd bought it with Roy's money, the gesture wouldn't have been so fraught with meaning. But he'd spent his own. As a matter of fact, he'd been spending his own money all along, ever since he'd met Lucy. And he hadn't intended to do that. He had meant to blow every dime of Roy's cash right up until the moment he'd first looked into Lucy Hammond's eyes.

He rapped on her door finally, then shoved his hands in his pockets. When it swung open, he saw that she had changed clothes; she was wearing a blue denim dress he hadn't seen before, and around her waist was the silver belt. A perverse elation washed over him. "Ready?" he asked.

"All set," Lucy replied as she stepped out into the dim hallway, but he noticed that she hadn't looked him in the eye yet. That was okay, though, because she had worn the belt.

"I gave Roy a call," he said, breaking the silence as she pushed the elevator button.

"Oh?"

"I thought I better keep in touch."

"What did you tell him?"

"Not to bother coming. At least not yet. It's too up in the air right now."

"Thanks." Her voice was barely audible.

"Was that what you wanted me to do, Lucy?"

"Oh, that's fine," she said, but he wondered if she really meant it.

The elevator swished up and the doors opened, swallowed them and closed. Jeff pushed the lobby button.

"Well, this'll be over soon," he remarked, trying to sound cheerful.

"Yes, I'm sure Tom has it all set," Lucy replied. "I, ah, bet you'll be glad to have this over with. Then you can go home." Her eyes finally met his, and he saw a kind of sorrow there.

"Lucy, hey," he began, but he couldn't find the right words. What was he going to say to her, anyway?

He stood there feeling as if he were about to burst. How long, for God's sake, could they keep this up without one of them popping?

"Look," he said, "this isn't going to work any-more." He could see her swift intake of breath, as if she'd been running and suddenly stopped. "Lucy, we have to talk. We've shared too much."

"Jeff, don't," she whispered.

"I *have* to. Hell, it's been coming. You know it and I know it. I think you like me, and I *know* I like you— too much." He turned around in the gently falling car, trying to think of how best to say it. Lucy stood absolutely still, her gaze downcast, her hands clasped tightly on her canvas bag. "Damn! Lucy, just tell me. Give me an idea. Is there anything . . . is there something in the future for us?"

"Oh, Jeff," she said, twisting her fingers in the strap of her handbag. "Don't ask me, not now."

"When then? When all this is over and you're back with Roy?"

"No, no, I didn't mean that."

"Do you love Roy?" There. He'd said the words. He couldn't believe it, but he had. Now he had to be able to cope with the answer.

"I . . ." she began, but her voice faltered.

Jeff reached out and gently touched her cheek with his finger. "You're wishing I hadn't asked," he said.

"You have a right to know." She took a quavering breath as the elevator whispered on, the silence filling the small cubicle to bursting.

He could see moisture glistening in her eyes and felt like a total heel for putting her through this.

Lucy gave a short laugh finally. "I don't know how to answer you," she said softly. "I don't seem to know anything anymore. Can you understand that, Jeff?"

"I guess so," he said slowly, and he supposed he had his answer. If Lucy did still love Roy—if she had ever really loved him—that love was splitting at the seams. A part of him rejoiced; another part was swamped with guilt and frustration. The doors opened onto the lobby then. "Come on," he said, taking her arm, "Tom's waiting. Come on, we'll talk about this later."

She only nodded and let herself be led—not the Lucy he knew at all.

But Tom McLaughlin was not in the Aztec bar yet. They sat at a table for three, the third seat conspicuously empty, and looked around at the plaster renditions of Aztec gods, the stepped pyramids and the copies of ancient masks on the walls. A mural of the sacred mountain of Popocatepetl covered one wall.

"Nice," Jeff murmured politely.

"I like the real thing better," she said quietly.

"Where's Tom, anyway?" he asked. "It's a quarter to five."

"He's always late. Don't worry, he'll be here." She didn't seem to really care, though.

Jeff sipped at his drink and drummed his fingers on the table. The bar was filled with cigarette smoke. Businessmen in silver-shot suits drank martinis; beautifully attired women spoke with animation over glasses of champagne. These were the rich folk of the city. What an incredible contrast to the poor sections, Jeff was thinking.

"I'm sure you'll be able to fly back to Denver tomorrow," Lucy was saying.

"Yeah, well, as long as I know you're safe."

"Oh, Tom will see to that."

"Sure, good old Tom. And where is he?"

She looked at her watch and frowned. "I don't know. I just spoke to him on the phone a few minutes before we came down here."

"Maybe you should call him again."

"All right."

"There's a house phone right outside the door of the bar," Jeff said. "Want me to do it?"

"No, I'll call him. It'll just take a second. He's probably on the phone. You know, with the embassy or something."

But Lucy returned with a puzzled expression on her face. "There's no answer."

"Good, he's on his way down."

"I guess so."

But fifteen minutes later Tom still hadn't shown up.

"This is ridiculous," she said, glancing at her watch for the hundredth time.

"I agree."

"Why don't we just go on up and see if he left us a note or something," she suggested.

"Pretty strange," Jeff remarked as they headed to the elevators, "but I'll bet it's something silly."

"Oh, I'm sure it is," she said too brightly.

They walked down the eighth-floor hallway, their footsteps hushed on the thick carpet. "Was this his room—807?" Jeff asked, stopping in front of the door.

"Yes."

He knocked. No answer. "Where the devil is he?"

"I don't know. I wonder..."

Jeff tried the doorknob. Before his mind could register surprise, the door swung inward; it hadn't even been latched. "It's open," he mumbled to himself in puzzlement.

"Jeff..." Lucy said, her voice an odd mixture of warning, of premonition.

He pushed open the door and went in. The room was neat, a suitcase on a luggage rack, the curtains open at the French doors, billowing gently in the breeze. The din of traffic wafted in from the street below, and with it the faint stink of diesel fuel.

He was on his way to the open doors, thinking that Tom might be out on the balcony—in a faint, having a heart attack?—when he kicked something with his shoe. A cigar, half-smoked, still warm and smelling awful. Tom could have set the place on fire!

Jeff's eyes moved from the floor to the curtains stirring in the wind, and at that instant he knew. Automatically, coolly, despite the heavy thudding in his chest, he strode to the balcony and the iron grillwork that served as a barrier. He took a deep breath and looked down. "Oh, God," he muttered. His knuckles turned white on the rail.

"What is it?" he heard Lucy ask faintly behind him. "Jeff? What is it?"

He went to her, to where she stood in Tom's room looking scared, her eyes wide, her body tensed as if for flight—or to receive an impact. He took her in his arms and held her head to his chest.

"What happened? Where's Tom?" she cried, her voice muffled against him. "Oh, God, it's Tom, isn't it?"

"Don't look, Lucy. Don't look" was all he could say.

"Is he . . . ?"

"Yes."

"Oh, no. Oh, no. Oh, no," she sobbed into his chest, and he could feel her shaking.

Scenarios raced through Jeff's mind. Men, dark men in suits, came into Tom's room. They'd just missed him and Lucy. They wanted the money back. Tom wouldn't tell them anything. Of course not. There were threats, but Tom McLaughlin was a tough old guy, and he couldn't believe anyone would hurt *him*. There was a struggle. Tom was a big man and would have put up quite a fuss; and then fell or was thrown off the balcony.

Eight floors.

"What do we do?" Lucy was pleading. "Oh, my God, Jeff, what do we do?"

The sound of a siren could be heard, faint at first, but growing louder with each heartbeat. The police, an ambulance, perhaps, explanations, no Tom to smooth things over. The money in the safe. And Jeff hadn't the slightest idea who Tom had spoken to at the Embassy. There had been problems, Tom had explained that morning. Delays and problems...

"We get the hell out of here fast," Jeff said harshly.

"But Tom—"

"Tom will be well taken care of," he said bitterly, "through all the proper channels."

"But—"

"*Lucy.*" He held her at arm's length and gave her a shake. "They won't stop with Tom. They followed us. They know where we are! There's only one thing we can do now—run as fast as we can back home, to the States. Dump the money with that D.A. in Houston Tom was talking about."

"Jeff, I can't just *leave* him."

"You have to. Those men could be down there waiting for you, for us."

She went white with shock and swayed against him.

"Can you fly?"

"Yes...I...I think so."

"Let's go. We won't take our bags. We won't check out. We just leave, quick. You have your plane documents?"

She gestured to her handbag.

"And the money," Jeff said in a hard voice. "I'm not leaving the money for those killers to get hold of. Not after this!"

A different world awaited them as they raced out the front door of the Camino Real Hotel to hail a taxi.

It was rush hour. But worse, the wide boulevard in front of the hotel was bedlam—a mass of police cars and people, with screaming and flashing red lights and old women fainting and street urchins crawling on the roofs of stalled cars to get a closer glimpse.

"Tom," Lucy breathed, but Jeff only nodded grimly, leading her away to a less congested corner, where they stood waving futilely for a taxi—for hours, it seemed.

The huge sun, settling lower in the west, was colored bright red by the city's ever-present layer of smog, and it seemed to be squeezed between the tall glass buildings of downtown Mexico City, buildings that were dyed with its light. Lucy shivered. "It looks like blood," she whispered.

A taxi finally stopped, a Volkswagen Beetle. Its interior was battered and dirty, but there was a large statue of the Virgin of Guadalupe on the dashboard. The driver was dressed like a banker, in a white shirt and dark tie.

"*Aeropuerto*," Lucy said.

The driver nodded; he was a young man, smooth skinned, with a curved nose, an ancient Aztec driving a modern German car. Skillfully he pulled his small vehicle out into the traffic and said something in Spanish to Lucy.

"He says it will take a long time because of the rush hour and he doesn't want us to be angry if we miss our flight," Lucy explained dully.

"Okay, it'll take anyone else just as long," Jeff replied, settling back against the seat, taking a deep breath, clutching the airline bag of money. He was sweating, clammy all over, and he was sure his hands were shaking. The image of Tom's body on the pavement... "Are *you* all right?" he asked carefully, turning to Lucy.

"I don't know," she whispered. "I'm shaking all over. I can't believe it. Tom, poor Tom. Oh, what's going to happen now?"

"I know one thing that's going to happen. I'm getting you out of Mexico so fast your head's going to spin."

"Are you sure? Maybe we should go to the Embassy, find out who Tom spoke to."

Jeff gave a snort of derision. "And start all over again, meanwhile providing live targets for the bad guys? No, Lucy, not on your life."

"I'm scared, Jeff," she said, her eyes wide, her face pallid.

He felt a wave of protectiveness surge up in him, so strong, so pure, that it was like a flame. Taking her hand in both of his, he felt how cold it was and how her fingers trembled. "Lucy, don't worry. We'll get out of here okay. They probably don't even know we left the hotel."

"They know about my plane," she said.

"But they can't follow us in the air, not unless they have a private plane ready right now, and I have a problem believing they're *that* smart." He chafed her hand in his, feeling the delicate bones under her skin.

"Tom . . ." she began.

"I know."

"I'll never forgive myself. It's all my fault."

"Stop that," Jeff said firmly. "Tom was a grown man. He knew what he was getting into. He knew about the guy murdered on Cozumel, didn't he? He told *you* to be careful."

She took a long, quavering breath. "Yes, yes, I have to believe that."

The minuscule car moved in fits and starts in the crawling traffic. All six lanes of the great boulevard Insurgentes were practically halted. Jeff held on to Lucy's hand and stared out the window. *Mexico City must be where old cars come to die,* he thought irrelevantly. There were dented cars, rusty cars, crudely painted ones in garish colors.

And entertainment for the masses, too, as they withstood the awful but routine traffic jam. Newsboys flourished evening papers with the abandon of fan dancers, screeching their wares. Women sold flowers. There was even a kid hawking lottery tickets, which were trailing from a roll like toilet paper.

The noise crashed at Jeff's ears; the air stank of exhaust fumes. A handsome man in jeans walked through the traffic, stopped and tilted back a bottle of gas, igniting his breath so that he breathed fire. The crowd howled their approval, leaning out of their cars to toss him coins.

Mexico City.

It was six o'clock before they were finally on the outskirts of the city, and the traffic had thinned out some. The red sun was touching the tops of the surrounding mountains, turning the world pink. It should have been exotic.

The cabbie was speaking to Lucy, but Jeff was still thinking about Tom, lying on the sidewalk back there. "Oh, God," he heard Lucy say.

He roused himself. "What is it?"

"The driver says—" she took a deep breath "—he says he thinks we're being followed . . . a black limo."

Jeff immediately twisted around in his seat and stared out the back window. He saw a universe of cars, crawling along, honking and lurching forward and braking. "Where's the black limo?"

The cabbie spoke again.

"It's behind the blue Chevvy, the one in the far left lane," Lucy translated. "Do you see it?"

A light changed to green up ahead, and the traffic surged forward. "Yes, there it is, a Cadillac," Jeff said.

"Oh, my God, do you think they're really following us?" Lucy asked.

"I can't see who's in it, not yet. Tell our pal here to keep an eye on it. There's a big tip in it for him."

Lucy clutched at Jeff's hand, but leaned forward and told the driver calmly enough.

The cabbie drove on, slowly, stop and start, doing maybe fifteen or twenty miles an hour. They could see the big jets taking off and landing at the airport far ahead; the planes made dirty vapor trails across an already dirty sky.

Jeff craned his neck, trying to see. *Could* their pursuers, Tom's murderers, be so clever? He supposed they could have had someone watching him and Lucy in the Aztec bar while the killers "talked" to Tom.

While Jeff watched, the Cadillac swerved, changing lanes too fast, cutting a car off dangerously, and horns blasted. It was only two cars behind them now, and one lane over. "Tell the driver to step on it," Jeff warned.

Lucy spoke quickly to their cabbie, and he started darting in between other cars, a symphony of horn-honking trailing them. The Beetle careened through openings so narrow Jeff held his breath. Once the driver even drove up on the sidewalk to get around some cars. No one seemed to mind, though, except the Caddy that followed them, maneuvering adroitly through the traffic.

"Oh, no," Lucy said. "They're catching up."

Their driver shot through an intersection on a newly turned red light, causing brakes to lock, tires to squeal, horns to blare. The limo had to wait at the light, but charged forward as the signal turned, and made up the distance rapidly.

Jeff thought fast: he and Lucy could get out and run, but they'd be easy targets on foot, lost in the immensity of Mexico City, and how would they get to her plane? No, they had to stay with the taxi and hope to outdistance the Cadillac. He clenched his jaw.

A huge intersection loomed; the light was turning red. Their driver stopped short, but kept gunning the engine, ready to take off.

"Oh, Jeff! They're coming!"

He turned. Sure enough, the black limo with its ominous dark windows was only two cars behind them now. Quickly Jeff glanced at the light, which was still red, and pounded his fist on the back of the seat. "Move over," he said to Lucy, "let me out."

"What . . . what are you going to do?" she cried.

"I'm going to buy you time," he said. "Now move! You get to your plane as fast as possible and take off—"

"You are not!" she said suddenly, her face growing taut with determination. "Unlock that bag," she demanded, blocking his way.

"Lucy . . . What?"

"Hurry!"

"Okay," he said, unzipping it, watching as a line of traffic in the left turning lane began to move. "Here." He pushed the bag over to her and watched in mounting astonishment as she dipped her hands in, coming up with bundles of fifties and hundreds. Then, before he could grasp what was happening, Lucy was climbing out of the car, tearing open the bundles and scattering the bills, throwing them all over the intersection. They lifted in the breeze and fluttered like strange, rectangular butterflies, settling onto the pavement, on the tops of cars, on the heads of motorcycle drivers. With her hand held above her head and her arm stiff, she looked like the Statue of Liberty, Jeff thought inanely, gaping in mute amazement as the bills twisted and turned on the breeze, darting and falling, leaping into outstretched hands.

Wordlessly Lucy ducked back inside the Beetle, and their cabbie laughed like a maniac as he floored the gas pedal and roared away. Behind them the intersection was hopelessly snarled in stopped traffic as everyone screamed and dove for the money, picking up fifties, grabbing at hundreds, yelling in Spanish.

And in the middle of the gigantic, hysterical traffic jam sat the Cadillac, blocked on all sides, utterly unable to budge.

"There," Lucy said with tight satisfaction.

Jeff looked at her, at her now serene profile, at her neatly folded hands, and he could only shake his head wonderingly.

CHAPTER ELEVEN

LUCY THRUST HER DOCUMENTS under the nose of the guard who stood at the gate. She could see her yellow Bonanza pulled up to the gas pumps clear across the service area. She looked over her shoulder nervously, despite the fact that she knew the Cadillac couldn't possibly be there yet.

"So, what's our route?" Jeff asked at her side.

"Well—" she put the papers back in her bag and hurried on "—we'll just be able to make it to Matamoros, right on the border. It's at the limit of my fuel range. Then we have to give U.S. Customs in Brownsville, Texas, an hour's notice. Ridiculous, it's a five-minute flight, but rules are rules. Then we go to Houston."

"Customs, huh?" Jeff rubbed the stubble on his chin thoughtfully.

Lucy stopped short. "My God, the money! I forgot."

"Let me think," he began. "Tell you what, you head on over to get your papers stamped, and I'll take care of the bag."

"But what are you going to do with it?"

"That's for me to figure out" was all he would tell her. "Now go. I want you out of here, and quick."

Lucy hurried away, her heart pounding. She still felt the adrenaline rush of the chase, of those men. Oh,

God, poor Tom. Who would tell his wife and children? The authorities? Her brain threatened to start its whirling descent into despair, but she stopped it by sheer willpower. She couldn't afford to lose control, not here, not now. Later, perhaps, she'd have the leisure to mourn for Tom properly, but not now.

Thank heaven for Jeff. He'd gotten them away from the hotel when Lucy would probably have stayed there, paralyzed with horror, and been grabbed by those men.

She went through the red tape, impatient, worried about whether her plane had been serviced, worried about the dark men, who might arrive any minute. She left large tips in each outstretched hand, larger than usual, to forestall any snags in the bureaucracy. She even flirted with the *comandante*, a fat little man with a dapper beard, when it became obvious she'd never get her papers stamped unless she did.

"Gracias," she kept saying, *"muchas gracias,"* smiling and thanking them and holding out her packet of papers, in nerve-racking, ceremonious ritual.

At last she was done. She ran across the oil-spotted concrete toward her plane, but then stopped abruptly. *Oh, no.* There was her little yellow plane, all right, but it was still pulled up to the row of gas pumps, the mechanic in greasy overalls poking his head into the engine. Anger simmered within her. She'd paid extra to make sure everything would be done yesterday. *Darn.*

Lucy walked up to Jeff and frowned. "How long?" she asked him, and noticed that he glanced past her to the gate.

"I don't know," Jeff replied. "He keeps telling me just a little more *gasolina.*"

She approached the mechanic carefully; it would not do to aggravate him. "How many liters to go?" she asked in Spanish.

"A few, *señorita*, a few."

"We are in very great haste," she said politely, handing the man a bundle of pesos.

"Ah, *muchas gracias*, but the *gasolina* only pumps so fast," he said, spreading his hands to demonstrate his helplessness. But he took the money.

Lucy paced, watching the numbers click on the gas meter.

"Take it easy, Luce," Jeff said once.

She flashed him a wry smile. "I wish I could."

"Yeah, I know it's hard."

"Say!" She stopped and faced him. "Where'd you put the money?"

"I'll never tell, not even if the customs agents torture me," he replied mock seriously.

She remained facing him, studying his expression, then she sighed. "I guess it's better if I don't know."

She noticed Jeff stiffen then, and focus on something beyond her shoulder. Whirling, she pushed her glasses up on her nose and strained to see what he was looking at.

"The black limo," he said through clenched teeth. "Damn it."

She gasped. Yes, there it was on the road outside the chain-link fence, heading toward them. She raced over to the mechanic, shouting to him that the tank was full enough.

"No, *señorita*, it is not full yet," he said mildly.

"It's enough!" Lucy yelled. "We're leaving! Pull out the hose!"

"We made it, though," Jeff said, abruptly grinning from ear to ear. "I'll be damned, we made it!"

They looked at each other, pumped up with triumph, grinning like kids who had gotten away with something. "We made it!" Lucy chortled. "Free and clear!"

"U.S.A. here we come!" Jeff yelled.

"They can't catch us now!"

Jeff leaned over and planted a big kiss on her cheek. "There, that's for getting us out of there."

But Lucy didn't answer. She was flushing, feeling the place his lips had touched, recalling without a connecting thought that uncomfortable taxi ride back from the outdoor market that afternoon. The silver disks of the concho belt dug into her waist.

Jeff was quiet, too, as if reading her thoughts. The night enclosed them, huge, black, infinite, as they flew north. Only the winking lights on the wing tips of the plane kept them company, and the rush of wind at the cockpit.

"About the fuel," Jeff finally ventured. "Is there enough to get us to Matamoros?"

She checked the gauge. "I think so, unless we hit headwinds or turbulence. Take a look at the flight map. I think we can stop in Tampico if we have to, but there'll be more red tape."

"Yes," Jeff replied. "Tampico's halfway."

"I hope we don't have to stop there. We're going to need all the energy we've got for customs in Brownsville."

It was past midnight by the time they landed in Matamoros, refueled a tank in which only fumes were left and notified U.S. Customs in Brownsville, Texas, right across the border. They sat in the fluorescent light of the Matamoros airport, drinking coffee, waiting until the Brownsville tower gave the clearance to fly over—and to go through customs.

"What a day," Lucy said. "I can't believe it ever happened. None of it."

"I know." Jeff finished his coffee, set the cup down and leaned toward Lucy. "You were great, Luce, really great. Cool as a cucumber."

She looked down, embarrassed by his praise. "I was scared to death the whole time, terrified. You were the one who kept me together."

He reached for her hand and took it, playing with her fingers, not quite meeting her eyes. "Well—" he gave a little laugh "—I guess we just make a good team, kid."

"A good team," she whispered, feeling his strong fingers hold hers, wanting to say something more but not sure what—or how to say it.

"Señorita Hammond," said a voice next to her, "you are cleared for customs in Brownsville."

She looked up at the official, drawing her hand swiftly from Jeff's. "Oh. Oh, thank you."

Customs was as trying an experience as anything Lucy had ever been through. She was exhausted, but so keyed up that she kept yawning out of nervousness. There were questions and forms to fill out, her papers to show. But these men were Americans, edgy, suspicious Americans, used to owners of private planes trying to smuggle across the border anything from illegal pre-Columbian art to immigrants to bales of marijuana.

"I'm working for the Hammond Foundation," Lucy explained. "We're building an orphanage at Yaxcaba. I was just there setting things up."

"It says here, ma'am, that your flight originated in Mexico City," one of the customs men pointed out.

"Yes, well, we stopped off for some...uh, some sight-seeing."

"And shopping," Jeff added.

"Oh, yes, I want to declare my belt," Lucy said hastily.

"And what is the value of that, ma'am?"

Jeff handed him the receipt, and the agent studied it with great intensity.

Meanwhile, another agent was looking through Lucy's purse. Did they wonder why she and Jeff had no suitcases with them? My God, everything made them appear so guilty. They'd search the plane for sure. She glanced at Jeff; he was as relaxed as a cat in front of a fire. Where *had* he put the money? Her hands were shaking, but she pasted a smile on her face and tried to keep from yawning.

"Where were you born, ma'am?" the agent was asking.

Out of the corner of her eye Lucy could see the other man, his head practically buried in her purse. Would they search the plane?

"Denver, Colorado," she replied automatically.

"U.S. citizen?" he asked Jeff.

"Sure am," Jeff replied, and Lucy noticed that the agent was eyeing Jeff very carefully. *Oh, God,* she thought, *they think he's a smuggler!* It was his clothes, the worn look, and his hair—why hadn't she made him get a haircut? And did Jeff have to stand there looking so darn cocky? Was he crazy?

"Oh, my," Lucy said suddenly. "My it's late. Why, I had no idea. Maybe my watch is wrong. What time do you have?" she asked the agent who was still scrutinizing Jeff. "Do you have the correct time?" she repeated, practically nudging him. Her heart was in her throat. Any minute now, any instant, they were going to tear her plane apart!

"I got it!" The agent broke out into a wide grin, a foolish grin. "Zany Zanicek! That's you, isn't it? Number thirteen!" He beamed, then turned to his fellow officer. "Hey, Van, get a load of this, Zany Zanicek!"

On it went. The handshakes, the embarrassed chatter, even an autograph for Van's nephew. Lucy stood aside and felt like laughing or crying, she didn't know which. It didn't matter. And even when they were safely back in the air, heading toward Houston, Jeff only said affably, "It pays to have friends in the right places, doesn't it, Luce?"

The Houston airport was enormous, practically a city in its own right, and Lucy was in such a fog by then she just let Jeff lead her around, arrange for the plane to be serviced, grab a taxi and tell the driver to take them to the nearest hotel.

He bundled her into her room and shut the door behind them. "You going to be all right?" he asked.

"Yes," she answered, sinking down into the bed. She was so tired.... "I just need some sleep."

"Okay, I'm right next door." His face swam above hers, moving in and out of focus. It loomed closer, and she lost focus again, but then she felt his lips on her forehead. "Good night, Luce," he said.

There was something she wanted to ask him, but she was so tired she couldn't remember. Something important. "Good night," she murmured, sinking into oblivion.

Lucy awakened late and had to think a second before she remembered exactly where she was: Houston, Texas. She sat up in bed, looking down at the wrinkled blue denim dress and the lovely silver belt, and realized she'd slept in her clothes.

Yesterday Jeff had bought the belt for her in Mexico City. Had it only been *yesterday*? So much had happened. It all came flooding back to her. Tom... No, she wouldn't think of him, not yet.

She rubbed a hand over her face. There was so much to do. First they had to get rid of the money. She'd have to make some phone calls. Then there was Roy, waiting in Denver, not knowing what was happening. Jeff had called him yesterday, but Roy must be worried. Yes, she'd have to call him. She owed him that, at least. She wondered, feeling guilty, at her reluctance to talk to him. It wasn't as if she'd done anything wrong. And Roy himself had sent Jeff to meet her. No one had counted on the money, those men—or Tom.

The whole thing was insane. She could hardly believe it had happened, but it was over now. They were safely back in the United States, far from the men in dark suits, and someone else could unravel the mystery of the crumpled paper bag.

Jeff. She recalled the feel of his lips on her forehead. Oh, yes, she liked him a lot. She liked his looks, his sense of humor, his courage and quick thinking. She felt safe and secure with him. Appreciated. He was a great guy.

He was also unemployed, with no future to speak of, a little too easygoing and, well, let's face it, poor.

Still, she liked him a lot—too much. But today was the end of it. She'd call the D.A. here in Houston, tell her story and hand over the five hundred thousand—

minus a few bills she'd thrown away on the street corner. Had she *really* done that?

The phone rang, and she jumped. But that was silly, a hangover from the past few days. It was over.

"You up?" Jeff asked on the line.

"No, I'm actually asleep."

"Right. Listen, I took the liberty of setting up an appointment with the D.A. here."

"That quickly?"

"You bet. I told his secretary it had to do with a murder and whole lot of cash, and that her boss was about to be a front page hero."

"The things you come up with, Zany," she said. "*That's* what I forgot to ask you last night! Where on earth did you hide the money?"

"Think this line is bugged? I hate to give away trade secrets."

"Come on!"

"I jammed it in around the battery, behind that little door in the fuselage."

"Really?"

"Sure, it was a tight fit, but I managed. They could have found it, I admit, but why should they have looked? Good old Zany Zanicek is as honest as the day is long, right?"

"Oh, Jeff," she said.

"Hey, it worked. Now, there's something else." He paused, and she could hear him clearing his throat. "One of us has to call Roy."

"I know."

"I'll do it if you want," he offered, "but I think, that is, you haven't talked to him. I mean, he must be wondering..."

His words trailed off, but Lucy finished them in her own mind: *he must be wondering why you don't want to talk to him.* "I'll call him," she said. "I'll do it now."

"Okay." His voice was brisk, businesslike, utterly unlike the humorous, caring one she was used to. It hurt to hear him sound that way. "Well, I'll talk to you soon."

"Yes, thanks, Jeff," she said.

She *had* to call Roy. What would she say? Oh, something. Something like: *thanks for sending your pal to save my life and buy me a silver belt and...and make me care for him too much.*

It was an hour earlier in Denver, so she dialed Roy's home number. Familiar digits; she'd dialed them dozens of times. She could picture the phone and where it sat on a polished black-lacquer sideboard. She could see Roy's apartment. Classy, expensive: the latest styles, all in black and white and chrome and glass. Elegant. And she wondered about Jeff's house in Lakewood. What did it look like? She'd probably never see it.

Roy's phone rang, once, twice. Then he picked it up, and she heard his voice, bright, clear, carefully modulated. So familiar—and yet so strange.

"Roy, it's me, Lucy."

"Honey! Where *are* you?"

"We're in Houston. We're safe. Yesterday was crazy, awful."

"This story Zany was telling me, is it true? About money and some guys after you? I mean, Lucy, sometimes Zany's imagination goes wild."

"It's true, Roy. Yesterday those men killed Tom McLaughlin."

Stunned silence met her ear, then a hoarse whisper. "Lucy?"

"It's true, Roy. They threw him off the hotel balcony in Mexico City. It was horrible. We ran—we almost got caught by them, too. Jeff was great. I don't know what I would have done without him. He saved my life."

"Lucy, honey, this is terrible. Are you all right?" Roy asked.

"Yes, I'm fine. We're going to the D.A. with the money. Today. And then it'll be all over."

"Houston." His voice was decisive, the way it must sound when he made business decisions. "I'll be done here today, Lucy. It's a short flight. Hang on, I'll be there as soon as I can. All right?"

She closed her eyes. She'd known this was coming.

"Lucy?"

"Yes, yes, I'm here. I just wonder if you should come, Roy. I know how busy you are. And I'm sure we'll be home tomorrow."

"Wild horses couldn't keep me from you right now. After what you've been through? Give me some credit, Lucy."

Her eyes were still closed. "Well, if you really want to..."

"I'll take care of everything. Don't you worry about a thing. What hotel are you at?"

"Oh, the airport..." She fingered the matches in an ashtray. "Um, the Airport Hilton."

"I'll be there late this afternoon. I've got a couple of things to clean up on my desk, nothing serious. You take care of yourself." He paused. "I love you, honey."

Lucy's heart sank to her feet like a stone. "Oh," she managed to murmur, "me, too, Roy."

"And, Lucy, give Zany a real big thanks from me."

THE DISTRICT ATTORNEY, Harry Fields, was as receptive as Jeff had promised. While Lucy sat in his downtown office she watched the political machinery working, grinding. Fields leaned back in his chair, his hands clasped behind his head. Frequently he nodded as Jeff spoke and then Lucy spoke, and all the while his secretary took notes, even though a tape machine was running.

"Dover," Fields said when they'd told him everything, "Malcolm Dover." He grunted, then turned to his secretary. "Carla, that'll be all for now. Why don't you type up some statements for these folks." Dutifully Carla left.

"I don't like to point fingers," Fields said, "but Dover has made himself quite a reputation around here. Lawsuits, the usual, but no one has nailed him yet."

"Will our statements help?" Lucy asked.

"I expect they will." Fields, a man in his fifties with thick black eyebrows and a long, narrow nose, gave her a reassuring smile. "With some cooperation from the Mexican government, we might be able to stop the smuggling of this drug, planifolia."

"And the money?" Jeff asked.

"We'll keep it as evidence."

"I take it we get a receipt," Jeff said lightly.

"Standard procedure," Fields replied humorlessly.

"What about Tom?" Lucy asked. "Someone has to call his wife. I . . . can't. I don't know her well enough. I just can't."

"Miss Hammond," Fields said, "I'm quite certain the American embassy in Mexico City has already handled everything."

Lucy could only nod.

"Yup," Fields continued, his Texas accent pronounced, "I'd sure like to stop the flow of planifolia into the States. It's a hoax. A big, moneymaking hoax." He shifted in his seat. "Well, I suppose you two are free to go. But I have to warn you, there may be more depositions, a trial hopefully, but that could take a long while. You'll be available?"

Both Lucy and Jeff said they would.

Fields steepled his fingers and stared at Jeff from under his heavy black brows. "You expect the Gents will make the Stanley Cup playoffs this year?" he asked as if he were about to place a bet.

Jeff half smiled. "They're going to win, I think, but it'll be hell on them without me there on left wing."

Houston was huge, and their hotel was miles from the D.A.'s office. The taxi driver who took them past the accoutrements of the American road show—the fast-food joints and shopping centers and motels and Ford dealerships—was not small and hook nosed with gold teeth. He drove sedately, too, bored. But, then, Lucy was not looking for a black limo out of the back window, so she didn't care.

"So," Jeff said eventually, "that's it, Luce."

"Well, Mr. Fields said we should stick around until tomorrow, in case he needs to ask us anything more."

Jeff didn't answer right away. He stared out the side window, his face turned from her. All she could see were the strong cords of his neck and the collar of his shirt. It was gray and drizzly in Houston, with a pewter-colored sky that pressed on the city relentlessly.

Lucy looked down at her hands and felt a lump in her throat. No words came to mind, no polite phrases that would erase the reality.

"Roy's coming. Soon, I guess." Jeff glanced at his watch.

"He'll want to see you. He told me to, ah, thank you, but I'm sure he'll want to tell you himself."

He whirled to face her. "So he can *pay* me for a job well done?"

She recoiled. "No, no, I didn't mean that."

"Sorry." He scrubbed a hand through his hair and attempted a crooked smile, but it fell short. "Roy's my best friend." He shook his head sadly. "I just don't know..."

"Neither do I," Lucy whispered as the wet, gray trappings of Houston slipped by the window.

Jeff paid the taxi driver at the door of the hotel. He was quiet, withdrawn, unlike himself. Was it because the adventure was over or was it something more?

Quit kidding yourself, Lucy thought. *It's because he likes you and you like him and you both feel as guilty as the devil about it.*

"I think we better talk," she said quietly as Jeff dug in his pocket for his key.

He stopped and glanced at her warily.

"Please," she said, "we haven't had time to talk. It's been so, so confusing."

He sat stiffly in the chair in her room, uncomfortably. *Oh, God, where has the closeness between us gone, the ease, the laughter, the liking?* Lucy wondered.

She sat on the bed and searched desperately for the right words. "Jeff, this is so hard. We've spent a few days together, crazy days. I'll never forget what you did."

He averted his face as if she'd slapped him.

"I care for you a lot. I think you're a wonderful person. I'm very fond of you . . ."

"Yeah, like a pet dog."

"No."

He got up from the chair and began to pace angrily. "Look, Lucy, I know I haven't got any money, and I know Roy's a great guy. I'm really stuck. Damn it, this is a hell of a position to be in."

"I know. It's not much fun for me, either."

"Because you like me a little too much, isn't that it?" Jeff demanded. "Come on, Luce, admit it. Then I'll tell you that I'm crazy about you, but we can't do this to Roy. Star-crossed lovers, is that it?"

"Oh, Jeff," she said miserably.

"Do you love Roy?" he asked.

She put her face in her hands. "I don't know. I still don't know. But how could I do this to him? He's on his way here. He said he loves me."

Jeff was silent for a moment. "I don't know what to do," he said at last. "Lucy, I love you. That's the only reality there is for me. But if you tell me you don't love me, that you love Roy, I'll never say another word to you, I swear."

Her heart froze, caught on a point so sharp there was no escape from pain however hard she struggled, no escape from pain even if she pulled herself free. Their eyes locked and held, the question hanging between them like an unexploded bomb. "Jeff, I . . . I don't know." She gasped, unable to catch her breath. What was the truth? Who did she love? "I do love Roy, I do, but . . ."

He held a hand up. "That's it then. I don't really feel like hanging around getting slammed into the boards in a game I can't win."

"Jeff, please, don't hate me."

"Hate you?" He took a step toward her and thrust his face close. "I *wish* I could hate you!"

She gazed up at him and despised herself for hurting him like this.

"Lucy, don't look at me like that." Then his fingers were on her shoulders, and he was pulling her up to face him, pulling her close, his hands strong and urgent on her back. He groaned when her body touched his, and he clutched her more tightly to him. "Luce, do you know how much I—"

"Don't, Jeff," she cried. He had to stop. She was drowning in a sea of need for him, unable to breathe, hot and cold all over. Her body burned where it touched his, ached.

But he lowered his head and kissed her, softly, tenderly, with infinite care, and she gave up trying to fight the tides of passion that inundated her in waves. She moaned and held on to him and met his lips, opening to him, smelling, feeling, tasting this man who moved her as no one ever had.

His lips pressed on hers with more urgency, and her breath quickened. "No," she whispered against his mouth, but he only said, "yes," and held her head between his hands, tangling his fingers in her hair, kissing her relentlessly.

Yet a grain of sanity remained in Lucy's mind. She couldn't do this. It was wrong. It was wrong for both of them.

"No," she cried again, trying to push him away, but he was strong and he held her close, and she almost forgot that it was wrong. "We can't," she protested, pushing at his chest with both hands.

He stiffened then and drew back from her. Pain darkened his eyes. A flush spread up from his neck. "I'm sorry," he said.

"We can't," she whispered. "Don't you understand?"

He only stared at her, his hair mused, his shirttail out, his jacket hanging askew.

"Don't torture us both," she said, trying to catch her breath, feeling her pulse in her ears. "There's Roy...to consider."

"Yeah, Roy."

"I *want* him to come," she said. "I have to find out."

But Jeff only turned and let himself out of the room. When the door was shut behind him, Lucy sank down on the bed, her face in her hands. She knew what she felt; she didn't need to see Roy. She'd lied. She'd lied because she was afraid of her feelings, afraid of Jeff and the kind of man he was, afraid of being hurt again. Roy was an excuse, a cowardly excuse.

CHAPTER TWELVE

JEFF SAT ON THE EDGE of his bed and idly fingered an ashtray on the nightstand, tilting it to one side then the other, turning it on end and trying to make it spin. She *wanted* Roy to come to Houston. What more did Jeff need to know? He sighed. His chest swelled; he sighed again.

She'd responded to his kiss, though. There was no mistaking that. He could still feel where her breasts had been pressed to him, her soft breasts, the firm peaks....

"Ah, hell," he said, spitting out the words as if they tasted sour. Why should he feel guilty? He was a man; she was a woman. It was simple chemistry. Big deal. This notion he'd gotten into his head that Lucy was the *only* woman was bull. Why, by the time Lucy and Roy tied the knot, he'd be at the wedding with a lady equally as great as Lucy. Plenty of fish in the old proverbial sea.

Suddenly Jeff noticed the ashtray in his hand and flung it across the room, where it struck the wall, shattering. Who was he kidding? There were no Lucys in his future. She was a one-of-a-kind woman. The trouble was, no matter how hard he tried to forget it, she was Roy's woman.

Jeff looked at his watch as he knelt to pick up the pieces of the ashtray. It was almost five o'clock. Roy would probably be arriving around six, on a business commuter flight from Denver. In the meantime, Lucy was alone in her room. Jeff didn't really think the bad guys had followed them to Houston, but there were no guarantees. It was foolhardy to leave her alone; yet he didn't have the guts to face her, not after he'd grabbed her as if he were some kind of Neanderthal.

He paced the room, rubbing the back of his neck, thinking. He stopped and stared at the phone. Maybe the way to handle this was to meet her on neutral ground. The cocktail lounge?

He dialed her room. "Lucy? Yeah, it's me," he said, wishing his voice were steadier. "I don't think you should be alone.... Well, I know they probably didn't follow, still.... Look, how about we meet in the lounge or something? Roy'll be here soon and... I know, but it's just a safety precaution. Okay, I'll see you down there in ten minutes. And, Luce...what happened just now, well, I'm sorry. It wasn't fair to either of us. Let's forget it." He listened for a moment, then hung up slowly, unable to believe he'd heard her right.

But she'd said those words. "I'm not sorry," she'd said in a whisper, in a lovely, beautiful whisper.

Jeff punched the elevator button and stood waiting, his hands thrust deep in his pockets. He'd felt guilt before. He'd felt it when he'd disobeyed his folks as a kid; he'd felt it with Nance, when he wasn't there for her, and she'd packed her stuff and left. Sure, he'd felt it a hundred times during hockey games when a shot had been off or he could have checked an opponent harder. But he'd never known this all-encompassing pain in his chest, as if a knife were stuck in his breastbone. Roy was as special a friend as a man could have. They'd been close since childhood, and nobody had a right to come between them, especially a woman. But, then,

Jeff thought as he stepped onto the elevator, this was no ordinary woman.

Lucy looked great when he spotted her at a table in the dim lounge. She'd changed into a navy shirtdress with lots of pockets and pleats. She must have bought it in a shop in the hotel, because their bags were still back in Mexico City. And here he was, still in his rumpled shirt and pants, a slob. Her hair was swept back, too, clean and shiny and natural looking. Small gold earrings winked from her shell-pink earlobes, and her glasses were gone for now. Fresh, wholesome Lucy Hammond. Rich, she lavished her time and money on the less fortunate, and she was so bright and alive. What would he do, Jeff wondered, if Roy asked him to be his best man? He supposed he'd have to say yes, but it would tear him to pieces.

"Hi," she said, then looked down at her folded hands, those same hands that had grasped the back of his shirt.

"Hi." He sat, knees splayed, and glanced around the room. "Guess Roy isn't here yet."

"Not yet."

"Um. Want a drink?"

"Oh," Lucy said, "I think I'll pass."

But I need one, Jeff thought, *bad.* "An iced tea? A soda?"

"Tea, please."

Jeff flagged the waitress. "One iced tea," he said, "and a double Scotch, neat." He caught Lucy's eye accidently and looked away. Maybe by the time Roy arrived he'd be so blitzed he wouldn't even notice their intimate reunion. *Good way to handle it, Zany.*

The Scotch, which he prudently sipped, did take the edge off his uneasiness. But the sick feeling in the pit of his stomach remained.

"Look, Jeff," Lucy began once, then slipped back into silence.

In silence, he thought, there was supposed to be healing. He wasn't so sure of that. "Well," he said, letting out a breath, "at least the money is out of our hands now. I'm glad for your sake, Lucy."

"For both of us," she replied, and gave him a weak smile.

"Sure, for both of us." *Now we don't have to stick together like glue.* "I'm really sorry about Tom, too. I can't get it off my mind."

"It was awful."

Why wouldn't she *look* at him? Why did she have to be subdued, so obviously unhappy? Did she think her troubles were any worse than his?

Anger bubbled up inside him. She had Roy. He had nobody.

"Listen," he said, and paused, his head tipped to one side. "Lucy..." But there wasn't anything left in him but frustration. "Never mind." He polished off his drink and set his glass down too hard.

Roy arrived at 6:15. Jeff, whose back was to the door, didn't have to see his buddy to know he was there. All he had to see was Lucy's face when she looked up kind of startled, her rose-red lips parted, her eyes wide and expectant. Jeez, what Jeff wouldn't do to get a look like that from her.

"I should have known where to find you two," Roy said in a friendly tone as he put a hand on Jeff's shoulder. "Sorry if I kept you both waiting." Jeff could feel Roy's hand tighten then, as if to say thanks,

and he was aware, also, of the fact that Lucy was hesitant, trying to smile, and that she held her glass in both
hands. He thought he could hear the ice cubes tin-
kling.

"Lucy," Roy was saying as he stepped around the
table and took her hands in his. "What an ordeal
you've been through." He leaned over and kissed her—
long and soft—and all Jeff could see through an
agonizing red haze was the lovely, delicate curve of her
white throat.

Don't, Roy. Don't do this to me, man! he wanted to
yell.

The kiss must have lasted a minute, Jeff was sure, a
brutally long minute. He'd never known such fierce
jealousy or raging anger, and there wasn't a goddamn
thing he could do about it. Finally—what was his pal
going to do, kiss her all night?—he called the waitress
over and ordered them all drinks. "Roy," he said
brusquely, "what're you having? Hey, Roy."

At last Roy's head came up. "Oh, how about a wine,
red. The house wine will do." He smiled at the waitress, that good-guy, winning smile that had always
knocked them dead in the boardrooms, then turned his
full, riveting attention back to Lucy.

Jeff spent the next hour studying his friend through
that crimson haze, seeing Roy in an entirely new light.
This was no ordinary Joe. Roy had charisma, tons of
it, charm and competence and terrific male good looks.
Jeff tried to find some niche in Roy's armor, some
dent, even a nick. But damned if he could. The man
was perfect. If there *was* a flaw—and some thought of
it as an asset—it was Roy's powerful drive, his stress-
ful life-style. Although at that moment Jeff would be

darned if he could see just how that fast-paced life was truly hurting his friend.

"I'll tell you," Roy was saying, his fingers possessively entwined in Lucy's, "I don't know how you two held up under all that pressure. It blows me away to think of those men chasing you clear across Mexico."

Lucy glanced at Jeff and back at Roy. "Jeff was terrific. He held me together, Roy. You have one brave friend here."

Why did her eyes have to be so blue, her voice so soft, her lips so full and inviting? "You're all right, too, Luce," he said, his tongue loosened by the Scotch.

"I told you, didn't I?" Roy replied, grinning in pride. "And she's rich as hell," he teased, "so maybe I'll just marry this lady and retire."

"Roy," Lucy protested, her cheeks flaming in the wavering candlelight.

"All right," he relented, "I'll keep my job."

They talked about the hot pursuit through Mexico, and about the D.A. in Houston and maybe having to appear as witnesses should Dover's case ever come to trial. "I hope we're out of this now," Lucy said quietly.

Jeff was sure she was hurting, or maybe he only wanted to believe that. But her eyes looked troubled, and she'd lost that radiant glow. God, how he wanted to pull her away from Roy and cradle her to him, to hold her until she laughed and grew playful and her lips parted to meet his and her hands... He closed his eyes and took a deep breath. An image flashed before his mind. Two young lovers under a hot yellow sun, innocent, carefree, the blue Caribbean caressing their sunburned flesh as they played in the water, brilliantly colored schools of fish swarming around their masks,

Lucy tugging on his arm, smiling, pointing to a coral reef below, her hand in his hand now, soft and cool and silky, her skintight suit stretched across those firm breasts, the peaks hard, tantalizing, promising. He could even recall her natural scent, the sweetness of her hair drying in the sun, the apricot-blossom fragrance of her skin and the harmony of all the components that yielded a perfume so balanced, so magical that it stole his reason.

Suddenly Jeff couldn't take another second of it. He surged to his feet, banging his thigh against the table and making their drinks slop onto the polished wood. "Sorry," he mumbled. "Look, I'm pretty beat. I think I'll head on up to my room."

"At seven o'clock?" Roy asked.

"What about dinner?" Lucy asked.

"I'm, ah, not hungry." He turned to leave. If he didn't get a breath of fresh air, he was going to explode.

"Jeff." It was Lucy's voice, caring, bell-like in his ears, and did he note a hint of panic? "Please, you have to eat something. Have dinner with us."

"Absolutely," Roy put in.

Jeff shoved his hands in his pockets and turned back to face them. "Look, you two want to be alone," he began.

"Nonsense," Roy said. "We want you here. Come on, Zany, don't be a party pooper. We want to celebrate your safe return, don't we, Lucy?"

"Of course."

"You're a hero, buddy," Roy added embarrassingly. "Come on."

In the end it was Lucy's eyes that made him say okay. He saw in them the same uncertainty, the same torment—a mirror of his own. He couldn't leave her alone with Roy, but neither could he stand to see his pal touch her cheek with his manicured finger one more time.

They ate in the Oil Rig dining room, a swank restaurant done in garish reds and blacks with a big steel rig in the center of the room that housed a salad bar. The prices were nothing to sneeze at, either. Jeff put his napkin in his lap and decided that Roy could damn well pay for this meal.

"Mmm," Roy was saying, holding the menu over in front of Lucy and pointing, "chateaubriand for two. Are you interested?"

I could have a pork chop, Jeff thought sourly.

"Oh, I don't think I could eat that much," Lucy replied, and Jeff could see her shift in her cushioned seat uncomfortably. "Do you mind?"

"Of course not," Roy said, and he picked up her delicate hand and held it to his lips. "The seafood should be decent this near the coast. Would you like a shrimp dish, crab, something Creole?"

"Maybe shrimp," Lucy said.

Roy ordered a bottle of champagne, a Tattinger, and insisted on opening it when it reached the precise temperature in the ice bucket. Anyone else who usurped the wine steward, thought Jeff, could have come off looking like a number one jerk, but not Roy Letterman. Oh, no, never Roy. He was too smooth, too polished, too almighty *nice.*

"Do you mind?" Roy asked the steward. "It's a very special occasion." He gave the man one of those white smiles.

"Certainly, *monsieur*, enjoy."

Oh, yes, Roy always did things correctly. Hadn't he sent Jeff, his best buddy, his *loyal* friend, to Cozumel to entertain his lady?

There was caviar and melted Brie with fresh raspberries and the sweet bubbly champagne that made Jeff's head buzz. And there was Roy, his deft hand feeding Lucy little crackers with dabs of salmon pâté on them and touching her arm intimately. There were quiet whispers in her ear, and a wink or two for Jeff, who, God forbid, should feel left out. And there were jokes, the latest Denver "in" jokes, to which Roy naturally was privy. Lucy smiled at all the right times, and her eyes grew a little pink from the fizz of champagne, and a smidgen melancholy, too. Dinner arrived with a flourish, a flaming this, a sautéed that, a grilled, lightly seasoned whatever. Roy talked, never too much, and entertained them, while Jeff sat there morosely trying to think of some witty remark, some hitherto before-unheard-of witticism. Nothing came into his brain, though, not one single word.

"Jeff," Roy said, "you're awfully quiet tonight. I feel selfish for monopolizing the conversation. I guess I'm just so glad to see you two out of that country, safe and sound..."

"Sure," Jeff muttered. *I could have had her, old buddy. I could have Lucy now if I wanted. Look at her. Look at how miserable she is!*

What was he thinking? Was he crazy?

Lucy was as withdrawn as Jeff. Obviously Roy chalked it up to the letdown from their wild escape; *Lucy's just tired.* But Jeff knew better. Oh, yes, on that score Jeff was one up on his pal.

When Lucy excused herself and went to the ladies' room, Jeff looked—stared, actually—at Roy's face.

There was no denying that the man had those debonair Gregory Peck features, and eyes that were both warm and intelligent at the same time. And Jeff couldn't fault him for personality: Roy was friendly, outgoing, trustworthy. So why did he hate Roy Letterman's guts?

"I don't mean to put a damper on your evening," Roy was saying, "but I tore this article out of the Denver paper yesterday. I thought you'd better look at it, Zany." He handed it across the littered table. "Does, ah, Lucy know about the trouble with the Gents?" he asked.

"Yeah, I told her about it." Jeff shrugged and held the strip of paper toward the candlelight. Denver Gents on Winning Roll, it read. Fuel Added to Fire Over Last Season's Losses: Was a Certain Nationally Known Player Not Doing His Best? "Hell," Jeff swore, "they just won't let it lie, will they?"

Lucy came back then and sat down. "Who won't let what lie?" she inquired, putting her napkin on her lap.

"It's nothing," Roy stated, catching Jeff's eye.

"Just my life," Jeff replied gloomily.

"What?" Lucy asked.

"It's that business with the Gents again," Jeff admitted, and he thought, *might as well air it. I couldn't feel any worse.* "The newspaper is on my case again." He handed her the article.

"Look, Jeff," Roy said carefully, "you've got to quit sitting around and do something to clear your name. I know you have your suspicions. Follow them up. I'm sorry if I'm being tough on you, but damn it, buddy, I can't stand to sit by and watch your life go down the drain."

Jeff felt a fist of anger tighten in his chest. "I've got some ideas," he said defensively. "I'm not just sitting around, *pal*."

"Jeff," Lucy said cautiously, "Roy's only trying to help."

"I know." He rubbed his neck. "But even if I review those tapes a hundred times and spot something, I can't prove it."

"Maybe you could force the guy's hand," Roy suggested. "You know, go to him with your suspicions, make him look at the tapes—"

"Threaten to take what you have to the hockey commissioner," Lucy interjected.

"Sure, sure," Jeff said dully. "Don't you think I've thought of that?" He sighed, feeling like an idiot—they just didn't get it. Abruptly he looked them each in the eye one after the other. "It's not easy watching the papers smear your name all over the place, you know. It hurts. I was hoping everything would die down on its own. I *was* hoping that Denver University would give me that job."

"Things don't disappear so easily," Lucy said softly.

"Don't I know it," Jeff replied. "So I'll get back to Denver and do what I can."

Roy reached across the table and touched his arm. "If you want, Zany, I'll front you the cost of a private investigator."

Jeff swore again. "Sorry," he said quickly, "but I can't let you do that. Besides," he added, forcing a smile, humiliated, "I know more about the game than any private investigator ever could. I've got to go this alone."

Alone, he thought, boy did *that* description fit his situation.

Thank God Roy had the good sense to change the topic finally. He turned his attention back to Lucy and began asking her about the new orphanage in Yaxcaba.

Lucy's voice drifted in and out of Jeff's consciousness as he finished off his champagne. The last thing he'd needed tonight was to be reminded of the scandal, not to mention the fact that his bank account was just about drained. He'd always been an upbeat person, enjoying life, enthusiastic, optimistic. It had never occurred to Jeff that he could feel so low.

There was another aspect to his evening that was equally as depressing but infinitely more painful. Had Roy gotten a room at the hotel, or did he plan on staying in Lucy's? Images of the two of them together in that bed of hers kept swirling around in his head. Of course, Roy would stay with her, he thought. Why else would he be in Houston if not to comfort her, hold her, do things to her lovely body that would make her forget?

Damn.

The pork chops Jeff had devoured began to sit heavily in his stomach. And the champagne, on top of the Scotch, was making his head throb as if there were drumbeats in his temples. As bad as he felt, Jeff wondered why he was hanging around. Did he really want to see Lucy and his best friend get up and head to her room? Did he really want to watch Roy put a hand at the small of her back and lean close to her ear as they entered the elevator?

Roy was occupied with the waiter, ordering dessert, and Jeff caught Lucy's gaze and grasped it for a long, painful moment. The room seemed to swim in a fog at the edges of his perception, as if he were underwater.

But Lucy was clear, as clear as a bell. He could see the uneven rise and fall of her chest, the way her hands seemed to shake, the strained set of her shoulders and the unspoken words on her lips. What would she say if Roy weren't there? Would anything change between her and Jeff, or would there still only be vast regret and that suffocating guilt?

Unable to look into those velvety blue eyes another instant, Jeff got to his feet abruptly.

"You don't want dessert?" Roy was asking him.

"No," Jeff managed to say, "I'll pass on it." He reached into his pocket, pulled out his wallet and tossed a credit card on the table.

"Hey," Roy said, "dinner's on me."

But Jeff wasn't in the mood to argue. He motioned the waiter over to their table. "Run the bill up for me," he instructed, "and put your tip on it, will you?"

"Certainly. Thank you, sir," said the man. But Roy was still protesting, and Lucy had her head ducked in between her shoulders.

"Will you quit it, Roy?" Jeff finally demanded in a hard voice, and his friend subsided. The waiter returned with Jeff's card in his hand, but there was no receipt to sign.

"I'm sure there's some mistake," the man said lamely, apologetically. "But the charge was refused."

Jeff would never quite remember how he got out of that dining room. He could recall saying something about it being a mistake, that maybe he'd done some wrong figuring in Mexico. Lucy, oh, God, had pulled out her own credit card in a rush. Roy, who stopped her with a firm hand, had accused Jeff of foolishly using his own money the past few days, and, damn it, Roy would never have asked Jeff to go to Cozumel if he'd thought Jeff was going to pull a stunt like that.

Yet somehow Jeff had escaped, his pride left back on the table like a pile of cold leftovers no one wanted, and made his way, shoulders sagging, feet dragging, to the lounge. "A double Scotch," he told the bartender as he hitched himself up onto a padded stool and tossed a few of Roy's bills on the bar. "Make it a triple," he said glumly. Somewhere in the background he could hear a pianist. He thought the tune was "Climb Every Mountain." Swell.

Half-obscured by the dim shadows of the bar, Jeff sipped on his too large drink and stared at himself in the mirror. He'd really made a mess of things. He'd behaved like a love-smitten sophomore, and Roy, if he gave it any thought at all, was sure to figure things out. Damn. On the other hand, if they really were friends, shouldn't Roy be told the truth? Could Jeff go on, month after month, and pretend that Roy's lady hadn't ripped his guts out?

He was vaguely aware of the bar crowd, of the low din in the cushy lounge, of a couple of women who'd taken the stools next to his. He stared at his drawn face in the mirror, though, and thought only of his dim prospects for the future. Every so often he'd imagine Lucy's face in that mirror and his chest would squeeze painfully.

"Hey" came a voice from somewhere out of the haze around him. "Excuse me..." It was a timid voice, he registered, shy, female. Lethargically he swiveled his head and saw that the lady sitting next to him was speaking. "I'm sorry to disturb you," she was saying, "but aren't you ... well—" she blushed "—aren't you that guy... you know..." He saw her friend on the other side of her give the woman a poke in the ribs. "Aren't you…Jeff Zanicek?" she finally got out, and tittered, showing an overbite.

"It's him," the other woman, a bleached blonde, said. "I see those ads all the time."

Jeff managed to shrug. "Didn't know they were still showing them." He went back to his drink.

"Oh, yes!" the lady next to him assured him loudly. "They show them all the time in Houston. Honest."

"That's nice," Jeff replied, sipping.

"Hey, Sharon," the other one said, "we're bothering him." She leaned across her friend. "Sorry we disturbed you."

"Oh," Jeff said distantly, "that's okay."

"Come on," one woman said to the other. "Let's get a table over there. Mr. Zanicek doesn't look like he's in the mood." The women gathered up their purses and cocktails and slid off the stools. "Sorry if we made pests of ourselves," said the timid lady who'd first spoken. "Bye."

Idly Jeff watched them go. Both wore miniskirts, shiny things, their hips wiggling as they made their way across the room in their spiked heels. When they were seated in front of the piano, Jeff went back to his drink. A minute passed. He turned and glanced at the women; as depressed as he was, they were looking better and better. He wouldn't mind some company.

"Hey, bartender," Jeff found himself saying. "think you could muster up a bottle of champagne and three glasses?"

When it arrived, Jeff tore off a wad of bills from Roy's roll and tossed them on the bar.

"Say, buddy, what about your change?"

Jeff was already heading toward the ladies, balancing the champagne bottle and glasses in one hand. "Keep it," he called over his shoulder. "This night's on my best friend, anyway." He threaded his way through the crowd, took a deep breath and plastered a smile on his lips.

CHAPTER THIRTEEN

LUCY HAD NEVER BEEN SO HAPPY in her life to see someone's back. Roy had finally left her hotel room, and only when the door had been closed and locked behind him did she feel as if she could breathe again.

It had not been conscious on his part, but Roy had been trying to smother her. He had kept *touching* her, holding her hand, stroking her arm, patting her shoulder. Had he done that before when he'd been with her? She didn't know—she couldn't remember. Or perhaps she'd *liked* it when he'd touched her then.

The scene at dinner had been awful. Jeff had put a good face on it; he'd tried, at least, but it had been hard. Dreadfully hard. And then the final calamity of the evening: his credit card. She should have known all along that Jeff was paying the bills. She'd compared him to the men in her past and never seen—or *let* herself see—the truth, the decency and honesty in Jeff. Oh, how it had hurt to see him suffer that humiliation this evening.

There was something else, too, that made her want to curl up into a ball and hide. Wherever Jeff was right now, he thought that Roy was in here with her. He had to be thinking that. *Damn.*

She wished he knew that she was alone. That she'd sent Roy to his own room with the excuse that she was exhausted, upset about Tom, which was true enough, and upset about the money and the chase.

But it was all false. She *was* upset, but for a completely selfish reason: she liked Jeff too much and Roy not enough, and she felt the worst kind of awful, tearing guilt.

Lucy got up from the king-size bed, the bed on which Roy had sat, stroking her forehead and telling her how proud he was of her, what a wonderful person she was. She was wearing the new nightgown she'd bought that afternoon, a weightless shadow of fabric that clung to her breasts and hips. But it didn't make her feel sexy; it made her feel dirty. It was too much like that black thing she'd gotten to attract Roy, to reel him in, and from the way his eyes had lit up when he'd seen her in this one, her ploy had worked. But now, like a spoiled child, she didn't want him; she wanted another toy, a new toy.

Jeff. Jeff ''Zany'' Zanicek. He had everything in the world going against him; he was absolutely wrong for her. But she liked him so much. No, she loved him. She loved the way he moved. She loved his strong square hands and the blunt features of his face and his round rear end. She loved his sense of honor, his ridiculous, knight-on-a-white-horse romanticism. She loved the way he talked and laughed, the way he read her mind and let her handle the things she was good at—like flying and speaking Spanish—but took over when he needed to, competently, quietly. He'd been brave and cool and uncomplaining. He'd saved her life more than once. Heck, their crazy three days together had been almost *fun*.

Except for Tom, of course.

Lucy paced the carpeted floor. She was too tired to sleep, too on edge to relax or to forget a moment of the excrutiatingly awkward dinner through which Roy, poor unsuspecting Roy, had dragged them. She wanted to leave her room and find Jeff, explain to him, apologize to him. But she didn't have the nerve. And she didn't know where he was. And what if Roy checked on her or found out?

What would she say?

Jeff was imperfect, flawed, but she adored his every fault. Roy was perfect, but she didn't love his perfection. What was wrong with her?

She went into the bathroom and turned the light on. Staring into the mirror, Lucy studied her face, just as she had in Cozumel. Had it been only three days ago? No, it couldn't be; an eternity had passed, and a different person stared back at her. Yet it was the same face, the same blue eyes, smudged with shadows, the little scar on her cheek where she'd fallen as a kid, the same plain nose and pointed chin, the same few freckles and dark, wavy hair.

But in her brain there were new connections, nerve cells bridging gaps, sending impulses, where before there had been none. Knowledge, a changed sensitivity. Connections that created new logic.

She felt shaken. Everything she knew, had known, was shifting. All the turmoil she'd felt, all the guilt and uncertainty, was coalescing into a vague sense of fear. She wanted desperately to love Roy, to have everything back to where it was—secure, in control, safe.

And Jeff Zanicek was dangerous. He *touched* her core, made her feel. She was scared. She could see what he offered, but was she willing to change the entire structure of her life to accept him?

She frowned at her reflection. It was simple, but so difficult. People didn't change their patterns so easily—and if she was willing to try, if she *did* change, would Jeff want her? Could he handle the responsibility? Could *she*?

She had to decide, to be fair to Roy, to Jeff, to herself. She turned the light off and went back to the big, empty bed. The room was cool, neutral. The heating unit whispered monotonously; it gave no answers to her problem.

Roy. Jeff. She put her face in her hands and felt panic and despair claw at her. What was she to do?

ROY KNOCKED ON HER DOOR at nine sharp. When she let him in he gave her a smug grin and held out a breakfast tray: coffee with two sugars, no cream, croissants and jam and a single white orchid.

"Oh, Roy, you shouldn't have," she said uncertainly.

"Only the best for my girl. You could use a little pampering," Roy said.

Luckily she'd been up already and showered and dressed. No more intimate black wisps, not until she'd decided what to do.

"The flower is beautiful, Roy," she said, picking it up. "And did I ever thank you for the flowers in Cozumel—and the champagne?"

He waved a hand as if the gift were nothing. And it wasn't anything to Roy, only money. An orchid. A white orchid, with pale mauve freckles on a yellow center—fragile, cool, odorless.

Jeff, she thought, would have picked a handful of wildflowers.

Jeff.

"Eat, honey," Roy urged, seating himself on the side of the bed. "I already called the D.A., Fields. He doesn't need you anymore. I made sure of that. So we can fly home today if you're up to it."

"Oh." Why did she feel just the tiniest spurt of irritation?

"We can stay over till tomorrow if you'd rather. I do have a meeting in the morning, but I can always call Linda and tell her to cancel it," Roy said.

"No, I'm fine. There's no reason to stay." Why *didn't* she love Roy? He was so handsome, tall, with razor-cut hair, an aquiline nose, manicured nails, two hundred dollar Gucci loafers, a cashmere sweater of shell pink and a pink-and-gray-and-white striped shirt. He was gorgeous. And intelligent and successful and thoughtful.

"I had breakfast with Zany this morning," Roy remarked. "He was a little under the weather. Too much champagne, I guess."

"Oh?" Casually Lucy broke off the end of a croissant. Her fingers shook.

"Isn't he a great guy?" Roy asked. "I mean, could a fellow ever have a better friend?"

Guilt smote her a bludgeon blow. "No," she tried to say, then cleared her throat and repeated it. "No."

"You liked him, didn't you?"

"Uh-huh." She tried to chew the piece of croissant, but her mouth was dry. She reached for the coffee.

"I *knew* you would. You know how long we've known each other?"

"Uh, yes, he told me."

"A great guy."

"Does he, ah, I mean, is he flying back to Denver with us?" she asked.

"Oh, no, Zany left already. I saw him off in a cab an hour ago. He's catching the early flight." Roy reached out a long, slim-fingered hand, took a piece of croissant and chewed it.

Her heart thudded down to the pit of her stomach. Misery filled her, a choking, cloying miasma. He was gone. Without saying goodbye. Gone. He'd left her behind, her life torn irrevocably, a tattered fabric, flapping in a cold, impersonal wind. Then she despised herself, because she'd never even told him how she felt. He'd tried to level with her, tried to be frank and truthful, but she'd only avoided her own responsibility in this awkward triangle and put him off.

And now it was too late. He was gone and that was that.

IT WAS SNOWING LIGHTLY in Denver that afternoon, but the ceiling was at eight thousand feet, so Lucy had no trouble landing at the small airport south of the city where she kept her plane.

"You sure you're going to be all right?" Roy asked as she gave him a ride to his office.

"I'm fine," she said. "Don't fuss over me. It's over now, isn't it? Fields has the money and our statements." Her tone must have given away her feelings, because Roy looked hurt.

"Sorry," he said, "I'm only concerned about you, that's all. You had a bad experience."

She stopped at a red light. Her windshield wipers swept back and forth methodically. The streets were wet. "No, *I'm* sorry, Roy. It's just that sometimes, well, you have a way of overpowering people, of taking control."

"So I've been told," he said wryly. "I'll try to watch it, Lucy. I know you need room. You're independent and I love that about you. Just ignore me when I get bossy."

"Okay," she said lightly. "Are you sure you want me to drop you at the office? It's pretty late."

"Linda will still be there. I just wanted to check on a few things."

She pulled up to the sidewalk in front of his office building and let him off.

"Bye, Lucy, thanks. Can we get together this weekend, honey?"

She forced a smile. "Sure, call me."

"I will," he said, reaching across the seat and giving her hand a squeeze.

Lucy parked her Volvo in the underground parking garage, took the elevator up and let herself into her apartment. She turned the thermostat up to banish the damp cold; it seemed as if her blood had thinned out in the tropics and she just couldn't get warm. The place was neat as a pin, as she'd left it, the plants watered by her cleaning lady and her mail piled neatly on her dining room table.

The big picture window overlooked Cherry Creek and the boulevard that followed its banks. It was dusk, and the commuters had turned on their headlights, which reflected off the shiny, wet road surface in long streaks.

It was a familiar scene, and she stood by the window and watched it for a few minutes, until, abruptly and without warning, her eyes filled with tears and she started to cry.

What was wrong with her?

She laughed at herself, the sound harsh and strangled in the silent apartment. "Stop it," she said out loud, through her tears. "Stop feeling sorry for yourself."

But the feeling that everything was altered persisted. Her world was askew. Or maybe the world was the same, but Lucy was different.

She went to bed that night without eating or unpacking or phoning her parents. She felt as if she could sleep forever, but it was a tiredness of the spirit, not of the body. And in her dreams she relived those three days in Mexico, over and over again. This time she wasn't afraid because Jeff was there, grinning and cracking jokes, and she knew, with the unquestioning surety of one who dreams, that he loved her and everything would turn out to have a happy ending.

JEFF WAS NOT CRACKING JOKES. He'd gotten back to Denver that morning with one whopping big headache from his evening with the ladies in Houston. They'd had to pour him into bed, or so he recalled in a moment of self-reproach.

There was nothing to do, he decided, but get out of the house, out of the city and away from his problems for a time—he had to forget.

He got up the next morning and threw his ski gear into the car. He'd drive up to Copper Mountain, use Roy's hidden key to his posh condo there and spend a couple of days in the cold mountain air. Cobwebs, that's what he had in his head, a sticky morass of cobwebs. A few days on his own would clear them.

He started up his car, letting it warm gently, then banged his forehead on the steering wheel. "Oh, sure,

Zany, let's go on a ski vacation. And what're you going to use for money?''

He got out of the purring Corvette and pulled out his house keys from his parka pocket. Maybe his Visa card was full, but the good old Discovery card they'd sent him in the mail, when he'd been a man with a job, was sitting on his dresser, unused. And to think he'd been ready to throw it out last summer. ''This'll teach them to give away credit,'' he mumbled.

At a good solid eighty-five miles an hour, the Vette took the foothill highway that rose from the plains of Denver. Jeff could have pushed it to ninety-five, but the Colorado Highway Patrol had new unmarked vehicles, and all he needed was to lose his license. Of course, if he couldn't drive, he could sit like an eggplant in his house, kinda like Howard Hughes. He could grow his hair to his waist, let his fingernails and toenails get so long he could pick a penny up from four feet away. The only difference was, Jeff thought, Hughes had had a whole lot more money in his checking account. A hundred million or so more.

How long the red lights had been flashing in his rearview mirror Jeff didn't have an inkling. ''Oh, no.'' Automatically his eyes switched to the dashboard. Ninety-two miles an hour. *So long, license.* Sighing, he pulled over.

''Ah, officer,'' Jeff began.

''Step out of the car and remove your license and registration from your wallet, sir.''

The officer looked like one of those cops who was always chasing Burt Reynolds in the movies somewhere in the South: high dark boots, blue uniform, lots of brass, aviator glasses, a big hat with a wide brim, a grim expression.

"Look," Jeff said, pulling his wallet from his back pocket. "I had no idea I was speeding."

"Is that right."

Zero sense of humor.

"Well, I maybe thought I was going a *little* fast."

"The license, please, sir."

Jeff waited while the officer ran his driver's license and car plates through the routine computer check. With his luck, the Vette would probably come up stolen.

"I'm going to write you a ticket, Mr. Zanicek," the officer said upon his return.

"Couldn't you make it a warning?"

The man shook his head. "I might do that, but seeing how you're sort of a celebrity, Mr. Zanicek, my boss might take it wrong."

"When it rains," Jeff muttered, "it pours."

"What's that?"

"Oh, nothing. Say, this won't mean losing my license, will it?"

"Not unless you have other point violations."

"Oh, just a couple...."

It was afternoon by the time Jeff made it to the Eisenhower Tunnel which bored through the Continental Divide, splitting the U.S. into two disproportionate pieces. Supposedly if a raindrop fell on the top of the divide, half would eventually run to the Pacific Ocean, the rest to the Atlantic. Jeff snorted, turning up the car radio. He'd like to see *that*.

Copper Mountain ski resort, near Vail, Colorado, was only another thirty miles or so. It occurred to Jeff that he might arrive and find the locks changed on Roy's place or an important business connection staying there. Or Roy and Lucy. It would be just his luck.

But the place was empty, and the key was under the snow on the back window ledge. Jeff knew Roy wouldn't mind him using the place. Why should he? He had Lucy. What else did he need?

Hoisting his skis over his shoulder, his boots dangling from his other hand, Jeff trudged up the snow-packed walk and deposited his stuff inside. He turned up the heat, switched on the *real* gas-burning logs, checked the fridge—beer only—and sat down in the empty, vaulted living room.

Now what?

Dinner, cruise a few of the local watering holes, maybe talk to a few people about skiing, the weather, the new ski lifts rising from the east side of the mountain. Sure. But no mention of Mexico or bags of money or lawyers being tossed out of hotel windows. And none of this self-pity business.

Jeff ate alone that night at a local steak house, then strolled the cold streets of the spanking new resort, looking for—what? He didn't really know. He found himself drinking strictly soda water and lime in a stained-glass-and-fern place with a few other tourists, all men. That suited him fine. They were all belly-up to the polished bar, discussing the runs on the mountain, the powder in the trees, the group of vacationing airline stewardesses staying at a lodge down the way.

"I wonder where they're partying tonight?" said one man in perfect après-ski wear.

"Who cares?" Another replied, downing a double Scotch.

"I agree," a third man put in. "I've had my fill of women for one winter."

Jeff was getting uncomfortable.

"Yeah," the third said, "my wife packed it in right after Thanksgiving. Took the three kids and went home to Mother."

"So," Jeff said, loudly, cheerfully, "what's the snow depth on top? I haven't been up from Denver yet this winter."

"Yeah," the third said, "I'm better off now than I was. Who needs them?"

"It can get lonely," the first man remarked. "I ought to know. I haven't even had a date in over a year. My wife left and—"

"Well," Jeff said, growing edgy, "the forecast sounds good for this coming weekend. Snow expected."

"We could check on those stews, guys," said the second man. "I mean, what else do we have to do?"

"We could try to live without women," Jeff said. He finished his soda, set the glass down and marched away.

"Wasn't that...you know..." he heard someone say as he opened the front door.

"Sure was," another voice answered, "and did you read in the paper about that scandal...?"

THE NEXT MORNING was cold and clear. Jeff put his ski gear on and walked out to the ski lifts. Enthusiasm wasn't his middle name that morning, but if you drove all the way up to the mountains, you damn well had to ski. He charged his lift ticket and attached it to his parka just like all the other tourists were doing. He rode to the top of the mountain on the chair lift with a senior citizen from Denver; naturally the man turned out to be a Gents fan.

"*You're* Zany Zanicek? You look older in person," he cackled.

Jeff chose a run, taking it easy, getting the feel of skiing again. He turned great on his left side, but his right knee reminded him of its condition in no uncertain terms: *Stress me, buster, and I'll hurt all night!* It'd loosen up, though, after a couple more runs.

Lunch was a sandwich in the cafeteria restaurant on top of the mountain, and a nice rest on the sunny deck, his legs stretched out in front of him, his head back. The sunlight was warm on his face, and for a moment he was reminded of Cozumel and the beach and Lucy. But this cold winter sun wasn't the same one that pounded down hard on that subtropical isle. It couldn't possibly be.

He wondered what Lucy was doing now. Working probably. He tried to picture her in an office, poring over papers, pushing her glasses up her nose automatically, but he couldn't. He'd never seen her office. He never would, either.

He tried a steeper trail after lunch, but his knee screamed at the effort, so he went back to the easy slopes and called it a day early, at two.

He turned on Roy's television, wandered around restlessly, had a beer, turned the set off. It was too early to eat or hit the après-ski spots. Then he had a great idea: there was a communal Jacuzzi for the condominium complex.

He hadn't brought a bathing suit, but Roy had one in a dresser drawer. Grabbing a towel, he ran through the cold air in his shoes and shirt.

He turned on the air jets and lowered himself into the liquid heat gingerly. *Aahh.* There was a wooden bench under the water to sit on. He could feel his muscles relenting, thawing out. His knees forgave him for the day of skiing. He sat there, buoyed by the water, feeling the thrusts and spurts pummel his body pleasantly. He closed his eyes. *Aahh.*

"Hi, there!"

His eyes flew open. A woman stood on the redwood deck, wrapped in a long mink coat. "Oh, hi," he said, noticing that she was very blond and young and was wearing either false eyelashes or had extraordinarily long natural ones.

"Mind if I join you? My boyfriend is still up skiing." She made a face. "But I got tired of falling down."

"I don't mind a bit," Jeff said. "The water's great."

"Oh, goody!" she cooed. Then she took the coat off and stepped down into the water, and that was when Jeff saw that her eyelashes were real, but her blond hair definitely was not.

It wasn't long before Jeff fumbled for an excuse, climbed out of the churning pool of hot water and made his way swiftly back to Roy's condominium with his head ducked between his shoulders. And it wasn't until he was at the Eisenhower Tunnel on his way home that he stopped sweating.

CHAPTER FOURTEEN

FOR LUCY, the next few days were a round of catching up, opening mail, paying bills, going to the Hammond Foundation's office and writing her report about Yaxcaba. She spoke to Roy on the phone once and called her parents, promising to fill them in when she saw them.

Dinner at the Hammonds' was a formal affair. Thursday night was family night; whoever was in town was expected to be there, but Lucy's brother was away at school and her sister Betsy was in Florida, so it fell to Lucy to uphold the family tradition. Her parents jumped on her the minute she walked in. "You'd better tell me everything, Lucy," her father said sternly. "*Everything.*"

"I can't believe it, baby," her mother lamented. "I just can't believe it."

She told them the entire tale, skipping a few parts, such as how near she'd come to drowning, glossing over the danger but telling them all about Tom.

"That's what you get for flying all over in that plane of yours," her mother said. "I always knew it was dangerous."

"Tom McLaughlin dead," her father said bitterly. "And those murderers are running around loose. I'll tell you, it sticks in my craw."

"Poor Ethel," said Lucy's mother. "And the funeral's tomorrow. Oh, how I hate it."

"I can't believe it," her father repeated, shaking his head.

"But you're all right, baby," her mother said, "and Roy's friend really deserves our thanks. He sounds like a nice man. Should we have him over to dinner, Lucy, to show our appreciation?"

"Oh, no, I don't think so, Mom. He'd just be embarrassed." She could see Jeff sitting at the long dining room table, being polite, being miserable. No, it wouldn't work.

"He's that fellow who made the winning goal for the Gents in the Stanley Cup, isn't he?" her father asked, surprising her. "Sure, I remember the name. 'Zany', they called him."

"I didn't know you were a hockey fan, Dad."

"I follow the sports page. That was a big deal for Denver, you know." Her father sipped his coffee. "And this year the Gents seem to be coming along again. Last year they didn't do very well. There was some talk of a scandal, some games thrown. Athletes these days." He shook his head.

She couldn't sit there and listen to her father hash over the scandal again, or tell him that Jeff was the one who'd been blamed. It hurt even to think about him. Why couldn't she just *forget*?

"Isn't he the cute one who posed for the underwear ads?" her mother asked.

Did *everyone* know Jeff Zanicek? "Yes," Lucy said.

"Adorable young man. And you say he's an old friend of Roy's?"

"Yes."

"Well, I really feel we owe him something, baby. Maybe Roy could bring him over some evening."

"I don't think so, Mom, really," Lucy said carefully.

She escaped from her parents' house as soon as she could, but Jeff was everywhere, and she couldn't seem to evade him no matter what she did. He stayed in her mind, in her heart. It was as if a perverse destiny would not allow her to forget.

Except for Tom's funeral, Friday was one of those heaven-sent days that Denver had occasionally in the winter, the kind of day that restored a person's faith in his city—warm, sunny, tennis weather or golf, as soon as the snow melted on the fairways. After the services, Lucy went for a brisk walk on the bike path along Cherry Creek, having decided to sort things out in her mind, to get a grip on herself and stop moping around. It wasn't like her to be depressed and edgy like this. Or lonely or dissatisfied with her life.

Jeff. Roy. She strode along, hands in the pockets of her windbreaker, thinking, searching her feelings. Joggers were out in force, and a group of white-haired ladies marched along, swinging their arms. There were people on bicycles in shiny stretch pants and bright jerseys, mothers pushing strollers and walking dogs.

Did these people have problems like the one she was wrestling with?

She turned and headed back, walking fast, enjoying the sun despite herself, forgetting her problems for a short time. It came to her then, when her guard was down, with simple clarity. Her relationship with Roy would never work because she'd picked him as a perfect mate, deliberately and logically. She'd chosen him because he didn't need her money or her emotional support—or *her*. Therefore, she wouldn't be completely committed, and neither would Roy, and if the relationship failed, then she couldn't be hurt too badly.

But now, suddenly, she knew the fallacy of choosing a man with logic. It didn't work that way. Love and commitment came with loose ends and all sorts of strings attached, with need and pain and the imperfection of differing goals and life-styles and backgrounds, with compromise and quarrels. And the joy of fulfillment and sharing.

It could be that way with Jeff. Total giving. He was a man who allowed all of his emotions to come to the fore, who allowed the world to see how he felt, without a facade. *What courage,* she marveled. Could she face such a risk?

Lucy walked on with renewed confidence in herself. She'd learned something today, something very valuable. Thank God it wasn't too late. The hard part was telling Roy. He wasn't going to like this. Roy was not going to like losing control one bit.

He called her at the Hammond Foundation office that afternoon. "Hi, honey, working hard?"

"Umm, yes." Her heart beat slowly, heavily. He'd want to see her tonight, and she'd have to tell him what she'd discovered about herself, about love, about life. "And you?"

"The usual. I'll have to read some proposals over the weekend."

"No skiing, then." He had a condo at Cooper Mountain, but he never had time to use it.

"No. Say, honey, I've got a great idea for tonight. It's a surprise. Can I pick you up at seven?"

"Wait a minute. Should I dress up or not? And should I eat?" she asked, laughing.

"Jeans and popcorn. We'll eat later, if you're still hungry. I'd take you out first, but I've got a late meeting..."

"I know, I know. Okay, seven o'clock."

"See you."

She didn't care where he took her. It didn't matter. She just wanted some time alone with him to explain why their relationship would never work. Not that she'd mention Jeff. He'd only been a catalyst. No, it was her problem—and Roy's. She'd get that private time, and one day Roy would thank her for ending things.

The surprise Roy had in store for her became crystal clear when he turned his black BMW into the parking lot of the McNichols Sports Arena.

Lucy turned in her seat and looked at him, speechless.

He smiled widely. "A hockey game, of course. Jeff gave me some free tickets a while back. Second row, center ice. Right behind the bench. Now that you know Zany, I thought this would be a great idea. What do you say?"

"Sure, Roy, it'll be fun," she said, trying to smile.

"The seats are super. What a pal old Jeff is, isn't he?"

She swallowed. "Sure is."

He wouldn't be there, she thought, as she followed Roy across the parking lot. If she and Roy had his tickets, how could he be? Nevertheless, her hands were damp by the time they got inside the huge round building, and she kept glancing around nervously.

They found their seats, which were indeed right behind the benches where the two teams and their coaches and trainers sat.

Roy had bought bags of popcorn and Cokes. "Great seats, huh?" he asked proudly.

Lucy nodded. The crowd was waiting, with that barely suppressed impatience of sports fans, for the game to begin. The referees skated out onto the ice and the crowd booed with fervor.

"Everyone hates the refs," Roy explained.

Then the opposing team, the Toronto Maple Leafs, was introduced. More boos. But when the Gents skated out the arena filled with the sounds of cheers and air horns and whistles. Roy shouted and clapped. Lucy looked around uneasily. Jeff wasn't there. Why should he be?

Music came from the loudspeakers, burlesque-style stuff with a heavy drumbeat. Everyone yelled "hey" and punched fists up in the air on a certain beat of the music. They all knew what to do. Hockey fans. Seemingly fanatic. Even Roy.

The game began. The couple sitting in front of Lucy obviously attended every home competition. The man shouted remarks, rude personal ones, at the visiting team members. "Smith!" he screamed at the goalie. "Yer small and yer ugly!"

Roy chuckled. Lucy smiled tentatively.

"Check yer head, ref, it's empty!" the man cried.

Five men from each team faced each other on the ice. Big men, with heavy padding that made them look even bigger. Their skating skill was incredible, Lucy thought. They stopped short, spraying ice chips, changed direction, spun in tight circles so fast they were nearly parallel to the ice. When they hit the sides of the arena, the boards, the whole structure shook from the impact. The puck, flying free off a stick, struck the boards with the force of a gunshot. Two players crashed together in center ice with a thud Lucy heard clearly. She recoiled inadvertently.

What power, what speed. She could barely follow the puck with her eyes. "What's that, Bo, yer number or yer IQ?" taunted the man in front of Lucy.

So *this* was hockey. This was the game Jeff loved so much. If she closed her eyes she'd be back on the beach in Cozumel, listening to Jeff tell her how good he felt when he played well. His eyes had lit up.

It was a savage sport. Fast and skilled, graceful and very physical. How could Jeff be so gentle off the ice, then face these huge men night after night? But she'd seen that hard green glint in his eyes upon occasion, so maybe he could change. Of course, he *had*. And they'd called him "Zany."

"You should see a Gents game some day," Jeff had told her. "You'd like it." Yes, she'd like it, if he was sitting next to her, explaining the plays, shouting, cheering, booing, jumping up at a bad call.

"Great, isn't it?" Roy asked.

She nodded.

The first period was over. The teams skated off and a machine came on to resurface the ice. People left their seats for beer or hot dogs or a smoke. The arena, half-empty, took on a echoing quality.

"Want something?" Roy asked.

"No, I'm fine here."

"Some game," he remarked. "The Maple Leafs are favored to win, but there's no score yet, so who knows."

Slowly the throng trickled back in, filling seats. The second period would start shortly. The teams filed in, the Leafs to jeers, the Gents to cheers. The bench just in front of Lucy filled with the huge, hulking brutes in helmets and padding who were men underneath, men like Jeff. A whiff of locker-room aroma wafted up to Lucy, and she could hear the coach telling one of the players to "watch that flaming center before he scores. Kill the bugger."

She turned to Roy and smiled; he'd heard the remark, too. The buzzer went off for the period, and she looked toward the ice. Someone new stood near the Gents' bench in front of her, a man with longish light brown hair and a strong neck, a beige windbreaker, his hands in his pockets. A man who leaned over and said something to one of the players, then threw his head back and laughed.

Oh, Lord . . .

Her heart stopped in her breast. He was there, only a few yards away. She stared at him, feeling her insides melt and run together and tingle with utter delight. Abruptly she felt complete again, her fabric mended, smooth and strong. He looked as if he belonged there, talking to his teammates, hands in pockets, head cocked in that familiar way, and she belonged there, watching him.

How long could she stare at him, drink in his beauty, his rightness? Would he turn and see her? Did he know she was there?

His shoulders were broad, his hips narrow. In her mind's eye she could see his legs, strong thigh muscles, strong calves, tapering down to his ankles. The sunburn he'd gotten that day in Cozumel, the feel of his skin, hot satin under her hands as she smoothed lotion on his back.

"What d'you know, there's Zany," Roy said, pointing.

"Um," Lucy replied.

"We'll go say hi at the end of the period."

"Sure."

Jeff turned then, scanning the crowd, his eyes squinting into the lights. He must have recognized somebody, because he waved, a jolly grin on his lips. Then his eyes roved over the crowd, moved down, and he was just about to turn away, when his glance touched Lucy, continued, then stopped and backed up.

The grin faded from his face as their eyes met and held. Lucy felt as if all the air had gone out of her lungs. His look was eloquent, silent, but so full of unspoken words, and she understood each one of them.

"Yer mother sucks eggs, Caulfield!" screamed the man in front of her, but it was as if he were far, far away.

I love you, Jeff's gaze said, *and it hurts me that you're with Roy, but I love him, too.*

I'm sorry, Lucy's eyes said in return. *I'm going to tell him tonight. It will be over between Roy and me. I'm sorry it had to be this way.*

She was aware of Roy next to her, waving. "Zany!" he called out. "How are you, buddy?"

Jeff raised a hand to Roy, gave a smile and a nod and turned back to the action.

She breathed again, filled with an odd, remarkable lightness, an unfamiliar happiness and a corresponding sadness. Lucy wondered how she could feel all these things at the same time.

The Gents scored and the crowd screamed, whistled, rose to cheer their team. The man who'd scored threw his arms up in absolute triumph, a hero, and his teammates pounded him on the back.

"Give 'em hell!" shrieked the man in front of Lucy.

In the eye of the storm Lucy sat thinking, wondering, hoping, open to myriad feelings that blew hot and cold through her. And all the while she could see Jeff's back, and she knew he felt her eyes on him, but he didn't turn around again. He didn't have to.

At the end of the second period the teams filed out, Jeff with them. He turned briefly and looked up, waved to Roy, then disappeared into the locker room. Lucy felt drained, empty. She couldn't bear another period of seeing him there, so close, of knowing he was ill at ease because she was present. And yet she didn't want to leave.

But Jeff was not there when the Gents came back in for the third and last period.

The Maple Leafs won the game by one goal, and Roy was subdued as they left the arena, jostled by the disappointed, muttering crowd. "Oh, well," he said. "They played a good game. They're looking much better this year. Not like two years ago, but they're getting there. Last year was a disaster."

"Oh," Lucy said, wondering if Roy noticed how quiet she was. She'd been rehearsing in her mind what she was going to say to him.

"Zany'd better do something about that problem of his," Roy remarked. "It looks bad when the team plays so well without him."

"Do you think he can really prove anything?"

"If he wants to, if he really tries. Sometimes—" he shook his head "—he's too mellow, you know what I mean? And he just lets things slide."

Yes, she thought, *he could do that. He isn't perfect like you.*

They found Roy's car in the huge parking lot and waited patiently in line while thousands of cars exited onto Federal Boulevard. Lucy knew she should begin the speech she'd been rehearsing; this was as good a time as any. It was going to be hard—and unpleasant.

"Roy," she began, staring out the window, "I'd like to talk something over with you."

He looked at her, bemused. "This sounds serious."

"It is." Lucy took a deep breath. There was no point pussyfooting around. "I've been thinking a lot lately," she said in a level voice that amazingly did not falter. "I think we should date around, see other people."

He stopped the car abruptly, causing a horn to blast at them from behind. "What?"

"This is hard for me," she said, and gazed down at her hands. "I don't want to hurt you, Roy, but I can't go on like this."

"It's because I didn't meet you in Cozumel. I knew it," Roy said.

"No... well, in a way maybe it is."

He banged his hand on the steering wheel. "I knew it! When you didn't call me, I knew it. Damn! I should have passed on Telluride."

"No, it didn't matter. I mean, we aren't right for each other, and it's just as well we find out now."

"Of course we're right for each other! We're perfect, Lucy. I'm crazy about you. Please, honey, don't let that one incident ruin everything we have together."

"What do we have?" she asked quietly.

"A relationship. Caring, sharing, love—" he stopped short, looking at her. "Is it another man?"

She felt herself flush, and looked down again. She answered carefully. "No, it's not. Truly. It's me, Roy. I've been using you because I'm afraid to let myself really love anybody," she blurted out.

The horn honked behind them, and Roy jerked his car forward, following the line. He said nothing, though, and silence filled the car, pressing against the tinted windows and leather seats.

"Roy, I'm sorry. I like you so much. I'll always be—"

"Don't say it, Lucy," he muttered truculently. "My *friend*. I don't want you for my friend. I want you for my *wife*, damn it."

"No, you don't, Roy, not really. You want someone who would depend on you completely and *need* you. We don't need each other. We're only convenient. That's the problem."

"I do need you."

"Only for your ego."

He turned out of the lot onto the boulevard. She could see his profile against a streetlight. Her heart pounded slowly, heavily, painfully.

"Lucy," Roy began. Then he hesitated, sighed and started again. "Maybe you're right. I can't think now." He whistled. "You really threw me a curve."

"I'm sorry," she whispered.

"I had my eye on a house," he said sadly. "Overlooking the golf course."

"Oh, Roy." She took a deep breath. "It wouldn't work. One morning we'd wake up and look at each other and wonder why, and there wouldn't be an answer."

"I don't know."

"I do. Maybe, maybe it was being so close to death a couple of times. And Tom. Maybe those things changed my priorities," she said softly.

"I never should have let you go to Mexico," he said.

"You couldn't have stopped me."

"I guess not." He shook his head. "I don't know, Lucy. Maybe you're right. I know I'm busy and, well, women, a wife, seems like so much trouble. What I mean is, you weren't *trouble*. You took things easily and didn't depend on me and I thought . . ."

"I'm afraid love is a lot of trouble, Roy."

"Yes," he said slowly.

"Are you mad at me?"

"I'm not thrilled about this, you know."

"Me, neither."

"You'll keep in touch?" he asked. "My mother adores you. She'll be upset."

"Sure, you tell her I adore her, too."

"Damn, Lucy, I hate this!" He pounded the steering wheel again. "Why can't I take things easier? Why can't I be more like Zany? He'd just laugh it off."

Lucy glanced at Roy, considering telling him that she knew for a fact that Jeff would not just laugh it off. No, not any more than she would.

CHAPTER FIFTEEN

IT FIGURED, Jeff thought. Just as he'd managed to put Lucy out of his head for a few days, she'd been at that damn game Friday night and it started all over again. He was tired of thinking about her, of remembering; he was sick to death of going around and around on the same miserable endless treadmill.

He kicked an empty beer can across his living room floor and wished he could kick himself in the rear in the same way.

Honor. What good was his honor doing him right now? It had caused him nothing but trouble. First he was accused of throwing games and couldn't bring himself to confront the ones he thought were guilty, and then he lost the woman he loved. *Good guys come in last,* he told himself, brooding.

He stalked the length of his living room, treading on old newspapers and a pair of gym shorts. He was getting mad. It took a lot to get Jeff mad outside of the hockey rink, but he was starting to percolate. He was tired of seeing his life go down the drain and not lifting a finger.

Well, he couldn't do anything about Lucy Hammond, but he darn well could do something about his reputation. He'd talked about it for months, and it was time to get off his butt and make a move.

The videotapes. He had to get hold of the coach's tapes for the last half-dozen games they'd played before he'd been "retired." The assistant coach kept them under lock and key in the Gents office because a couple of years back the Barbeau twins had switched tapes on the head coach—the game videos for triple-X-rated films.

The assistant coach was an old friend of Jeff's, but would he lend the tapes out? The head coach wouldn't, that was for sure; he still thought Jeff had thrown those games. The bum.

The assistant coach lived in Aurora. Jeff looked up his phone number: Mel Carlucci, yeah, that was him. He dialed and got one of Mel's kids. "Daddy's at work. He'll be home—Mom! When will Daddy be home? Five-thirty, Mom says."

Okay, he'd wait. He didn't dare phone him at the rink.

At 5:45 he was dialing Mel's number again. "Hey, Mel, it's Zany."

"Zany, say, how are you?" Mel's voice was just a touch wary.

"Fine. I need a favor, Mel. I need the videotapes of six games last January. The tenth through the twentieth of the month."

"Now, Zany, you know I can't do that. Vic would have a fit," Mel said.

"Sure you can. He'll never know, Mel. It's important. I think I know who threw those games last year, but I need to see those tapes. Hey, it's my last chance, Mel. You know I'm trying to get that job at D.U." God, he hated to beg.

"I can't do it."

"You couldn't make it to Boston once, either, because you were too hung over, Mel, old pal, but I saved your butt and lied for you."

"Zany, I . . ."

"Six tapes. No one'll ever notice. I'll have them back before you know it."

"It'll mean my job if Vic finds out."

"Hey, Mel, it's already meant *my* job."

He picked up the bag of videotapes at Mel's house the next day and sped back to his place in his red Corvette, whistling all the way. Things were looking up; he was *doing* something at last. Maybe he'd needed Roy to bug him, yes, and Lucy, too. It just took Jeff a little longer to get around to things; he didn't like to rush into anything. But once he moved, it was gangbusters.

He drank a six-pack of Cherry Coke and ate a bag of potato chips while he watched the tapes over and over on his high-tech VCR, the kind that played in super slow motion and even stop-frame action. He studied every move made by three guys, the three he suspected: Todd McClosky, Scooter Hansen and Larry Defoe.

He'd sure hate to find out it was Scooter, an old teammate of his, but the other two were young and hot and full of themselves. Rookies last year. And rookies were forgiven all sorts of mistakes, were forgiven spells of being "off." Well, Jeff wasn't about to forgive the one who'd thrown those games.

Who'd gotten to him? A betting syndicate out of Las Vegas, an individual bookie, or just a fan, one rich enough to bribe a player and greedy enough to want to clean up? The Gents had been favored to win last season, after their Stanley Cup triumph the previous year, and the odds would have been just right.

A face popped into Jeff's head, the face of one of those megabuck fans who continually hung out at the arena, even traveled to away games. Rich Plassman, that was the guy. He was always around, and he had a reputation for gambling, high stakes bets in Las Vegas and New York and *always* in Denver.

Rich Plassman. Tall, lanky, formerly a Wyoming cattle rancher gone city slicker. He was just the type of creep to pull a stunt like that, to get to one of the young players and make an offer the kid couldn't refuse. Then good old Rich would be a very wealthy gambling man, and the hockey player would have a nice fat bank account. Forget the guilt, Jeff thought. Money had a way of soothing a lot of bad feelings—for some people.

And how much had the crook been paid?

Jeff sat there, hunched over a warm Cherry Coke, the screen flickering in his darkened living room, as he watched the moves, judging. Scooter was a solid player, uninspired but steady. He looked sluggish and tired in the tapes. But hadn't his little girl been sick or something? It could have affected his play. He wasn't doing anything wrong, just moving slowly.

Todd McClosky was a hotshot, no doubt about it. Fast and tough, but inexperienced. He tended to get out of position and leave holes in his line—deliberate or just overenthusiastic? McClosky wasn't a team player yet; he was still the college star he'd been at the University of Minnesota.

Larry Defoe. Another college star. A quiet kid, not as flashy as Todd. Jeff liked him. He was a competent player with a wicked and accurate slap shot. Jeff chewed on a knuckle and stared at the screen.

Slap shots were notoriously chancy, but Larry had always been amazingly accurate. Could those missed shots on goal have been deliberate? But, then, in the last game Larry made a perfect score in the third period, the winning goal. No, it couldn't have been him.

Todd again. Jeff studied every play, every frame, slowing the action so each move was isolated. He saw himself on the screen passing to Todd, who fumbled and missed the puck, letting the opposing team pick it up. And he saw Todd lose passes several more times. *That happens,* he thought, *when you're off your game.*

Was Todd off or purposely losing the puck?

Then he saw Todd in front of the goal, wide open, and he *had* to shoot, but it went high, and Todd looked around surreptitiously, as if wondering if anyone had seen him. Jeff stopped the tape, rewound, played it again, frowning. He watched the rest of the game and the next, too, and the one after that.

Yes, it sure looked like Todd. Now that he saw it he wondered how anyone could have overlooked the mistakes Todd had made consistently. But, then, Jeff had been the one on the hot seat.

Wearily Jeff rubbed his eyes and turned the VCR off. He leaned back on his couch and stuck his bottom lip out, thinking.

Todd McClosky. Twenty-one years old. First time away from the Minnesota farm that had been his home. Jeff tapped his lip with a finger. Hadn't Todd driven to work last year in a brand-new white Mustang convertible? A pricey item. He'd said it was a Christmas present from his family. Sure. And hadn't he sported a gold Rolex watch? Yeah. Hockey players got paid pretty darn well, but rookies didn't make *that* kind of dough.

It had to be Todd. Jeff turned on the VCR again and pushed a tape into it. He had to be certain, to see once again that move Todd had made in the first game, the one in which he hadn't yet been very good at covering up his errors.

There it was. Todd was skating backward as the other team made a rush for the goal. He was the only Gents player in front of the net. Suddenly he tripped and fell, leaving an opening for the opposition player to score. Jeff stopped the tape and rewound it, then studied it frame by frame. Todd fell again in super slow motion, but Jeff could see that it was deliberate. He hadn't fallen; he had thrown himself down on the ice.

Now, Jeff thought, *what do I do about it?*

He phoned Todd McClosky, finally, not enjoying one second of it, but angry enough to make himself do it. As he dialed, he kept hearing Roy telling him to do something about his problem, and he kept seeing Lucy watching him with troubled eyes verging on pity. *Pity.* He gripped the receiver more tightly and set his jaw.

Todd answered finally. It sounded as if he'd been laughing, talking to someone in the background.

"Zany, here."

"Hey, my man, how's it going?"

"Fair. Say, Todd, I think there's something you'd better see."

"Yeah, what?"

"I think you better *see* it. I'd rather not talk about it on the phone."

" 'I'd rather not talk about it on the phone,' " Todd jeered.

"Listen, punk, I've got your rotten little scheme all figured out, and I think we'd better talk," Jeff said, as hard and dangerous as steel.

Silence met his ear, then Todd laughed. "What in hell are you talking about? You gone off the deep end, Zany?"

"Like I said, we'd better talk. You know where I live? Good. I'll expect you here in an hour."

"You're nuts. What would I want to go to your place for?"

"Let's just say it's in your best interests," Jeff said coldly, then hung up.

But would Todd show?

Jeff paced. If the dumb kid didn't show up, then what in hell was Jeff supposed to do? He picked up some of the newspapers and empty beer cans and stuffed them in the trash, then nudged some socks and shorts into a corner with a toe. His laundry bag was getting full again; he'd better do some wash and make a run to the dry cleaners.

He looked out his living room window at the familiar street, the familiar houses across the street, the quiet suburban neighborhood he and Nance had chosen because it seemed so middle class, all-American clean and wholesome. He remembered with utter clarity their excitement when they'd signed the papers with both their names placed carefully on the mortgage and the deed. What had happened? Had it been *him*? Or had Nance not been able to take the bad with the good?

Could Lucy take it? Was she the kind of person who ran when things got nasty? Jeff yanked the drapes shut in irritation. He'd never find out.

Pretty Lucy with her big blue nearsighted eyes and soft skin. She was so unlikely in the role of fearless female pilot. And the way she'd thrown that money around and stopped the traffic! There was so much more to her than appearances, and he wondered somewhere deep inside if Roy Letterman, with all his terrific attributes, really *knew* Lucy, knew her the way Jeff did.

Again he wondered if Todd would show up. He looked at his watch; it was 6:45, only twenty minutes since he'd called the kid. *Cool it,* he told himself.

He wished he could talk over the situation with Lucy. She was so levelheaded and full of common sense; she'd know what was right to do and how to handle Todd. He wished, damn it all, he had Lucy to talk to the rest of his life whenever he needed advice. But Roy had her, and Roy never asked anyone's advice. What a waste.

Boy, you could have knocked Jeff over with a feather when he'd turned around at the game Friday night and seen Lucy. And he couldn't help staring the way he had, because all of his defenses had been down, and she'd stared back. Had he imagined it, or had her eyes held a wordless entreaty, a message? He could have sworn she'd been trying to tell him something, that her eyes had mirrored the swirling emotions he'd felt.

Had Roy noticed?

Wandering into the kitchen, Jeff winced at the mess and started putting dirty glasses into the dishwasher. It was, however, already full of plates and coffee mugs and silverware with caked-on food from days before. Disgusted, he turned it on. What a slob he'd become.

The hour was almost up. Would McClosky show? And what would Jeff do if he did? He meandered from room to room in his house. It was too big for him—three bedrooms. He ought to sell it and buy a small condo somewhere. He could use the money.

The third bedroom contained no furniture, only his big, bulging Koho bag of hockey gear: pads, helmet, gloves, pants. He stood and looked at it sorrowfully. The coach had kept his red-and-blue jersey, number thirteen, his number since he'd been a kid. No one else had ever wanted it, but thirteen had been Zany's lucky number. Or maybe, he suddenly realized, it hadn't.

He turned the light off and started out of the room just as a pair of headlights swung across the window, illuminating him, then sliding on. He froze; someone was turning into his driveway. Todd McClosky. The hotshot had decided to come, after all.

"So, Zany, what's up?" Todd inquired flippantly when Jeff opened the front door. "What's the big deal?"

With narrowed eyes, Jeff stared at the kid, gauging him. He was tough and plenty sure of himself, but he was young and untried and a little bit nervous. "Come on in, Todd. Want a beer?"

"Sure, why not? But I gotta tell you, pal, I can't stay all night."

"Hey, settle down. This won't take long." Jeff got a beer from the refrigerator, popped the top and handed it to Todd. Going over to his TV set, he turned on the VCR and fed a tape into it.

"What in hell... I'm not in the mood for home movies," Todd said.

"Sit down, relax, kid." Jeff ran the tape at fast forward until he got to the right spot, then punched slow motion. "Watch this."

Todd rose as if to leave. "What the... Come on, Zany."

"*Sit*," Jeff said, shooting him a look.

Todd sat.

The hockey game came on, every player's moves exaggerated in agonizing detail. Todd was skating backward in front of the goal, blocking the opposition from taking a shot; he fell, leaving the net wide open; the goalie couldn't stop the puck and there was a score, the player who'd made it throwing his arms up in the air in victory.

Jeff watched the kid sitting in his living room carefully; he made a face as he fell on screen, then took a long swig from the beer can, crossed his legs, uncrossed them. "So?" he said rudely. "What's the point?"

"Remember the game?"

"Sure, it was last year. We lost. And you played lousy," Todd said insolently.

"My knees hurt," Jeff said benignly.

"You old guys and your knees. Big deal."

"You didn't play so well yourself." Jeff fast-forwarded the tape and ran a few other episodes in which McClosky had made errors.

"Hey, I was a rookie. It was my first year," Todd said with false bravado.

"You want to see it again?"

"No, I gotta go."

"You want to know what I think, Todd? I think you deliberately fell. No, I take it back. I *know* you deliberately fell. You missed two easy goals. You lost passes and passed wide. You looked like a beginner. And there were other games, too. You want to watch them?"

"I'm getting out of here. You're nuts." Todd said.

"You're going nowhere. Just sit there and listen to me, you punk. You threw those games. I know it and you know it. And I got blamed. Now that's not fair, and you're going to see to it that my name gets cleared."

"You're crazy," Todd said, rising, his eyes darting anxiously.

But Jeff took a step right in front of the kid, put a hand on the middle of his chest and pushed him back down onto the couch. Todd stared at him, mouth open, gulping air. Jeff stood over him, hands on hips, chin thrust forward. "You go to the coach and tell him what you did."

"The hell I will," Todd sneered. "You have no proof!"

"There's proof in those tapes and you know it. I'll show them to the team. I'll show them to the coach and the hockey commissioner and every sportscaster on TV. You'll never play hockey again," Jeff said in an implacable voice.

"You're bluffing."

"Try me." Jeff kept eye contact and went on. "If you go to the coach and admit what you did, he'll cover for you. I'm letting you off easy, kid. No one wants a scandal in the league. He'll take you off the active roster for a while, fine you, maybe suspend you. A slap on the wrist. But my name'll be cleared, and you'll stay on the team."

"You're a has-been, Zany. No one'll ever believe you," Todd said nastily.

Fury exploded in Jeff's head. He grabbed the kid by the shirt, dragged him up off the couch, whirled him around and jacked him up against the wall hard. A picture frame crashed to the floor.

"You dirty little punk! I put my life into the game! And you're going to clear my name, you hear? You're going to go and tell the truth for once in your lousy life and say you're real sorry. And you're never *ever* going to throw a game again! You play your guts out from now on, because I'll be watching you. The rest of your life I'll be there watching. You make a false move, just one, and you're finished!" Jeff said, panting with the force of his temper.

McClosky was like a rag doll, his eyes wide, scared. His mouth worked, but nothing came out. Jeff held him like that for a moment, then pulled his hands away, feeling the anger subside. "Aw, you're not worth it, you dumb kid," he growled.

Todd straightened his shirt, but didn't move, afraid.

Jeff thrust his head forward again. "Go on, get out of here. And I want to hear from the coach soon. Don't disappoint me, Todd."

The kid sidled out of Jeff's reach without saying a word, scampered to the door and slammed it shut behind him. Feeling numb, Jeff stood in the middle of the room and heard McClosky's car start and his tires squeal as he made a hasty getaway. He wondered whether Todd would do what he'd told him to, and if he didn't, what he, Jeff, would do. Did he have the guts to show those tapes to everyone?

He sure hoped McClosky thought so.

THE NEXT DAY, Sunday, a storm blew down out of the foothills that stood guard to the west of Denver, and the glowering sky didn't make Jeff feel any better. He was edgy, not able to forget the ugly scene of the evening before, or to stop wondering what McClosky would do. Damn! His whole life depended on that green kid's whim! Maybe he should have knocked a couple of Todd's teeth down his throat, so that the guy looked like a *real* hockey player, even if he didn't act like one.

Well, he'd done something about his fix, at least. He should feel good. But he didn't.

He caught up on paying a pile of long neglected bills and desultorily vacuumed a corner of the living room. Another long day stretched ahead of him with nothing to do and no one to talk to. He phoned and ordered a pizza, but when it arrived he had no appetite.

He should call the athletic director at Denver University, he thought fleetingly, then decided not to. There wasn't a heck of a lot he could say until that damn kid made his move. Besides, it was Sunday.

Ah, stop feeling sorry for yourself, he thought. He'd get out of the house. Go down to Molly's Sports Center, where the beer flowed freely and the pool tables waited, green and inviting. Yeah, where good cheer filled the smoky atmosphere on a snowy Sunday and Molly made funny, sarcastic remarks and the guys hung out. Maybe Scooter would be there, or Marty, or old Uri, if he was still in town.

Sure, that's what he'd do. He pulled on his parka, couldn't find his gloves and went out through the garage to his Corvette, which was parked in the driveway because the garage was filled with junk. He had to brush three inches of snow off the windshield. Maybe he should move farther south, to Phoenix or Los Angeles. But what would a hockey coach do in those places?

The music in the Sports Center was loud, good old rock and roll; the joint reeked of stale beer, cigars and cheap perfume. Hey, there was Sal Tikonen over in the corner, playing a game of pool with Molly's husband. And Marty was at the bar. Jeff felt instantly renewed; Molly's was almost as good a place to be in as a locker room. He sure was glad he'd come. This was where he belonged, with the guys, not traipsing around Mexico with some rich lady, feeling guilty and miserable all the time. That was all in the past.

"Hey, you guys," he called, grinning, and Sal looked up from a shot and waved. Marty patted the bar stool next to his and told Molly to pour another brew.

"So, Zany, how's it going? You hear about that coaching job yet?" Marty asked.

"No, but it'll be coming soon. I'm working on it." He punched Marty in the arm. "You looked like a dog Friday night. I told you to shoot high at their goalie."

"Give me a break, Zany," Marty said, undisturbed.

They laughed together, sharing that good feeling a man got from working closely with others on a team.

"Want to play a game or two?" Jeff asked. "Five bucks is the limit."

"Nah, I gotta go soon." He rolled his eyes. "Sunday dinner with the in-laws."

But Sal was ready to shoot a few. "Ah, I always beat you," he said.

"Only when I feel sorry and let you."

"Sure, pal, keep believing that."

He shot a dozen games of nine ball with Sal, playing brilliantly, calling and sinking balls he had no right to sink, until the other guys came around and watched the match. Coolly, deliberately, he chalked the soft tip of his stick and moved around the table, gently elbowing a few of the guys aside, studying his options. With the right English—spin—on that shot, he thought, and good position, he could really be a hero. Did he dare?

Jeff pointed with his stick to a side pocket. "Six in the side," he said, then added recklessly but with surety, "and seven in the corner." He was going for the whole ball of wax.

Murmurs rose from the onlookers, but Jeff paid them no attention. He sighted along his cue and saw the angle, the perfect angle. He shot and the six ball plunked into the side pocket, then the deflected cue ball careered off the side, responding to the English just the way he'd seen it in his mind's eye, and nudged the seven into the corner pocket.

"Goddamn," Sal said. "You win again, you no good bum."

Jeff grinned and pocketed sixty dollars, his total winnings from the games. "I'm enjoying this," he said, "and I don't feel guilty."

"Just luck," Sal replied. "I'll get you next time."

Jeff faked a punch to Sal's midsection. "And, hey, watch that left-handed pass on the ice, buddy. Your grandmother could do better."

"Okay, coach," Sal said with overdone sarcasm.

Whistling, Jeff emptied his mug of beer, winked at Molly and, ostentatiously patting the pocket that held his winnings, he walked out into the snowy Sunday afternoon. Talent had its good side. In fact, things were definitely looking up. McClosky would own up, Jeff's reputation would be cleared, he'd get the job at D.U. Sure, as soon as that crooked kid confessed, and the word got out, he'd call D.U. about that job. They'd hire him, sure they would. All modesty aside, he was one of the best hockey players south of Canada, and if it wasn't for his knees he'd still be playing.

He started his car, and while it warmed up he scraped the ice off the windshield. He wished he had his gloves, but what the hay, he was tough. He whistled, lifting a wiper blade to get at the crusted snow. Yeah, life was fine, getting better every day. Suddenly he stopped whistling, held the blade up in his freezing hand, feeling the snowflakes sift down onto the back of his neck.

There was a terrible pang in his heart, as if he'd been checked by the Boston Bruins's biggest defenseman.

Who was he kidding? Without Lucy life was rotten.

CHAPTER SIXTEEN

LUCY STARED at the slim princess telephone as if it were a two-headed monster. She felt something akin to terror; it seemed that her whole life hung in suspense over this one call.

She took a deep breath and crossed the living room, her feet making soft imprints on the thick pile rug, her arms hugging her chest. If she called him and he said he wasn't interested, she'd curl up and die. On the other hand, he might just say he wanted to be with her, and then it meant total, steadfast commitment. Both prospects were daunting.

Two days, she thought, for two endless days she'd been staring at that phone as if it might bite her. Why hadn't *he* called? Lucy wondered. But of course, Jeff couldn't have known about her talk with Roy. And that was another thing; even if Lucy were free now, it was likely he still felt a loyalty to Roy, one that would keep them apart. Could she explain to Jeff that her breaking with his best friend had nothing to do with her feelings for him? There was no guarantee he would believe her.

Outside her window big snowflakes swirled—a return to winter after that brief respite. The dull grainy sky suited her mood exactly; she felt edgy and depressed, afraid, like a kid in the dark.

She glanced down at the phone and screwed up her courage. The worst he could say was no. It would be better to have some kind of answer than to sit around agonizing.

Of course she knew Jeff's number. She'd looked it up ten times in the past two days and knew it as well as her own by now.

Rehearsing her words, Lucy picked up the receiver. It felt cool and impersonal. Was that an omen? She dialed, realizing that her breath was coming in short little pants and that her fingers were trembling. Several times she almost hung up. *You're not ready for this, Lucy. You barely know the man,* she warned herself.

When it finally rang in her ear, Lucy thought the sound was different from the usual ring somehow, as if she'd never heard a phone before. Nothing would be quite the same again, she thought in a sudden rush of panic.

Ring . . . ring.

What was she doing? If he cared one little iota about her he'd have called—Roy or no Roy. If she didn't hang up this instant, she was going to make a whopping big fool of herself.

Ring.

Hang up, her mind commanded. *Stop this before it's too late.*

Ring.

Lucy had no idea how many times she let Jeff's phone ring before she realized that he actually wasn't home. And when she put the receiver back in its cradle she felt numb, blank.

It was easy, at last, to go about her daily routine. She put a load of laundry into the washer and wrote a few thank-you notes to foundation members who'd contributed generously at the Christmas fund-raiser this year. She thought about driving over to the Colfax Children's Home, the Hammond Foundation's first orphanage. It would be good to see the kids, especially the teenage boys who were in the middle of a winning basketball season. She could take them pizzas, a dozen of them, and Cokes—even if the cook, a die-hard nutritionist, would have Lucy's head. Yes, it had been over three weeks since she'd been there.

She put on a heavy Irish knit sweater over her green turtleneck and jeans, boots and a gray wool coat and matching knit hat. Outside the temperature was dropping, it was snowing heavily, and the wind had kicked up. She climbed into her Volvo and revved the engine, shoving the temperature control all the way over to hot.

I'm glad he wasn't home, Lucy decided. *I'm not ready for a lifelong commitment.*

Colfax Avenue, once the main east-west thoroughfare in Denver, was already jammed with traffic, workers leaving their jobs early to avoid the worst of the storm. She sat at a light and drummed her fingers on the steering wheel, idly recalling Jeff's street address in Lakewood. Colfax Avenue ran right through the downtown area and clear out to Lakewood and beyond....

Forget it, kiddo.

The orphanage, properly called a children's home now, was situation in a run-down neighborhood near downtown Denver, in the Capitol Hill area. The building was a tall old graystone that had been purchased by the foundation and totally gutted and refurbished. In truth, most of the kids living there were not really orphans, but rather children whose parents either didn't want them, or abused them, or were in prison; some of the kids had simply been deserted. Lucy could see the building up ahead now, some four blocks; the snow blew across its five-story roof like a sheet of gauze. Maybe there was even a basketball game later tonight. She really didn't have anything else to do.

She was thinking about where she'd get the pizzas nearby, when she looked up and saw the intersection. Good Lord! She'd driven too far, right past the home, and was now sitting at a downtown corner next to the State Capitol Building!

What was wrong with her?

But Lucy knew. She knew in her heart she wasn't going to turn around. All along she'd been heading to Lakewood. She'd find Jeff's address and cruise by slowly, praying that he wasn't home to see her car pass by, praying that he was. How juvenile could she get?

It was as if the Volvo steered itself through the storm. It was as if someone else stopped and checked the city map in Lucy's glove compartment, then drove on to locate 621 Evergreen Circle. It couldn't have been sensible, thirty-two-year-old Lucy Hammond doing it.

She slowed the car and squinted out her side window. A middle-class neighborhood in the suburbs, tidy front lawns all covered in snow now, trim fences, split-level homes, some brick and wood, some stone. Painted mailboxes. *This* was where Jeff lived? She could see him in one of those bachelor, singles-only complexes with tennis courts and spas. But, then, he had mentioned a girlfriend, a split-up, and obviously this was the resulting drain on his finances—a home mortgage.

In Jeff's driveway sat a partially covered dune buggy and a Windsurfer, but no car. Lucy breathed easier.

She'd just drive on down to the circle ahead and turn around, get out of there before he came home. What a stupid idea this had been.

She did turn around. And she did pass by his house again, but suddenly she hit the brake and ground the gears into reverse.

Don't do it, part of her begged; *ah, go ahead,* the rest of her taunted. She felt like laughing, and felt like crying—but, then, hadn't she been pulled apart like this for days?

It occurred to Lucy, while she sat in her car in his driveway, that Jeff might have gone out of town. Her car would probably run out of gas, and she'd freeze to death before he came home. But what if he did get back soon, and he had a date with him? Oh, God. Well, she'd better prepare her lines. But what was she planning on saying to him?

Four o'clock came and went. Four-fifteen slipped by. At times it seemed as if the minutes flew, while strangely the seconds dragged. Boy, was she a wreck.

"Look, Jeff," she'd say to him, "I broke up with Roy. Now it doesn't have anything to do with us, so you aren't to feel guilty, 'cause I don't... The point is, I love you, Jeffrey Zanicek, I love every muscle and bone and nerve ending. I love your green eyes and that crooked smile. I love the way you laugh hardest at your own jokes and tilt your head when you're listening to me. I love it when you're shy. I thought it was a cute act at first, but you really are bashful. God, how I love that in you. And I love your big, capable hands and your smooth skin, your back and your legs and even your feet. I especially love your lips, Zany. Oh, when you kissed me, I've never known—"

"Lucy?"

She almost went through that sturdy Volvo roof, she was to think later, and she definitely did bang her knee on the steering wheel.

"Luce? What on earth?" He was opening her door, and all she felt was an overpowering panic that sent adrenaline racing through every inch of her body like a strong electrical shock. "My God, are you all right? Has something happened?"

But no words came. She could only let him pull her from the car and prop her up against it as if she were a mannequin. Vaguely, in a corner of her mind, she was aware of his fire-engine-red Corvette behind her sedate Volvo, and of a motorcycle beneath a tarp next to the garage. And on his lawn was one of those spindly, pink flamingos with a bright red scarf around its scrawny neck.

"I'll bet your teammates gave you that," she remarked, and then she hadn't the least idea why she'd said it.

"You drove over here through a storm to tell me that?" Jeff asked as he stood back, bewildered.

"Well, no." Lucy looked over his shoulder at his house, glanced up at the sky until she had to blink away the snowflakes. Still he said nothing; he only stood there, his hands on his hips over the puffy parka he wore, his brow creased, as if in suspicion. She took a deep breath. "I came to tell you... Well, that Roy and I...we broke up." She gazed down at her boots and clutched her purse until her knuckles grew white.

The silence that followed was unbearable. Why didn't he say something, *anything*? Oh, God, what a hideous mistake she'd made! He hated her! "It wasn't over you," she whispered, her throat closing. "It was because I came to a realization..." She braved a glance at his face. His expression was unyielding, hard, disbelieving. "I found out," Lucy went on, swallowing several times, "that I was only using Roy because I was afraid of getting hurt again by... by..."

"A guy like me?"

"Yes," she said, shivering. "But you're not what I thought. I mean..."

"You're sure about that?"

"Yes, I've very sure, Jeff."

"So you told Roy about us?"

She shook her head. "I told you, it had nothing to do with our... our feelings. I was going to marry Roy because he fit my idea... my *logical* idea of what I thought I needed. And I guess I figured that if it didn't work, well, then we'd part and no one would be too badly hurt."

Jeff shifted and folded his arms across his chest. "What did Roy say to all this?"

"He understood, I think. Not at first, but he finally saw that we'd been using each other."

"Okay," he said slowly, still wary, "so why this? Why are you here, Lucy, in my driveway in the middle of a snowstorm?"

Oh, Lord. Oh, sweet Lord. He sure wasn't making this easy. She recalled her thought that the worst he could say was no. But she knew now that if he really said it, the word would kill her. "I..." she began, then faltered.

Jeff did a wonderful thing then; he took a step toward her and put his hands on either side of her cold cheeks. "I shouldn't have asked you that," he said quietly.

"Oh, God," she said, meeting his eyes, hers filling with tears, "it's so scary, Jeff. Are you scared, too?"

"Yes," he murmured, wiping the melted snow from her cold nose and cheeks. "Nothing like this has ever happened to me."

"Me, neither."

"So, what do we do about it?"

"I guess," she said hesitantly, "that we...well, would you kiss me, Jeff? Would you kiss me the way you did in Houston?" It was as if a lifetime of burying her needs and desires drained from her, pooling at her feet; Lucy closed her eyes and let sensation sweep her away. His lips touched hers and she felt free, as if she could soar with the birds—free at last to love, to cherish, to belong.

How long she stood leaning against him, tasting his lips on hers, clinging, she didn't know. Nothing mattered. Why had she waited, half killing herself these past days; how could she have wasted those precious moments?

When Jeff finally held her at arm's length he was smiling all the way to his eyes, those down-tilted, green eyes that roved her face as if he couldn't get enough of her. Lucy's heart flip-flopped in joy. No man had ever looked at her like that, with open need, with caring, with love.

"Will you come inside?" he asked.

Lucy nodded and followed him, her cold hand in his warm one, her breath caught deliciously in her lungs as he unlocked the door by his garage and pushed it inward for her. But then suddenly she felt his fingers on her coat sleeve, tugging, stopping her.

"Hey, Luce," he said timidly, "ah...how about you wait here a sec and I'll, uh, straighten up a bit."

"Oh, Jeff, you don't have to."

"Oh, yes, I do."

He left her in the narrow mud room, but she could peek around a corner into the living area. And oh, brother, was it lived in! There were pizza boxes and beer cans strewn around, a cigar that had fallen out of an ashtray onto a dusty tabletop, magazines scattered on the floor, and clothes. Didn't Jeff hang anything up?

"I should buy one of those cans of Lysol," he called from the depths of the clutter. "It probably smells like beer in here. The guys, you know."

Lucy put her hand to her mouth to keep from laughing. Jeff did present quite a spectacle. He was flying around the room, snatching up armfuls of debris and flinging it into an open closet.

"Almost done," he called. "Sorry about this."

She saw him swoop up a sweatshirt and a pair of mustard-colored jockey shorts, then cast about desperately for a safe hiding place. How about the oven? she thought in female amusement.

"Okay," Jeff said, dashing back to her side, panting, "you can get in the door now, at least."

"You really didn't have to."

"Wanna bet? The last cleaning lady I conned into coming over took one look and said, 'Forget it, buster, no way.'"

"Um," Lucy said, walking in behind him, still hiding her mirth.

"You want a beer? Wine? I think I have some white, a Chablis."

"A glass of wine, if it's no trouble."

Jeff grinned shyly. "The wine's a cinch, but a glass... Everything's in the dishwasher."

Lucy had to admit that for all the clutter and the faint locker-room odor, Jeff's place was warm and inviting. Someone—Nance?—had done a fair job of decorating once. Oh, it was a sportsman's haven for sure, surfing and skiing pictures, a great black-and-white blown-up photo of a hockey skate spraying ice chips, lots of trophies on bookshelves, *Sports' Illustrated* magazines stacked high. The furniture was upholstered, comfortable, done in light stripes, and the tables were solid oak, attractive despite the layers of dust and white beer can rings.

"You certainly are the sporty type," she commented. "And all those toys out in the drive."

"Yeah, well, you get what you see," Jeff said with a smile as he sat down beside her on the couch and handed her the wine—in a jelly jar.

It did feel like a real home, she thought; Jeff's home, of course, but she felt a part of it as she curled her stockinged feet beneath her and sat back with the jelly jar. There was no pretense with Jeff. She felt at ease, even though they'd known each other only a short time.

Lucy took a sip of her wine while he went to throw a few logs and some kindling in the fireplace. There was plenty of paper around, mountains of it, to get the fire going. Another man, Lucy thought, would have dragged her straight into the bedroom, especially after that flare-up of passion out in the driveway. But not Jeff. And she'd known that about him somehow, just as she sensed that their eventual lovemaking would be remarkable.

"You know," he was saying, sitting back down, "I like this. I mean, I really like having you here, Luce, a lot."

"More than the guys?"

"Even more than the guys," he said solemnly.

"You don't want to turn on the TV and watch a game? Is hockey on tonight?"

Jeff looked shocked and wounded. "Lucy, I'd *never* do that to you. I know how much women hate sports on TV."

"Really," she said, staring at him, wondering. "Are you telling me that if a good game was on right now you wouldn't want to be watching it?"

"You're pulling my leg, Luce. And you just might make a liar out of me, too."

"I thought so." She smiled, loving him, loving his gallantry and that boyish chagrined look on his face that told her it was a toss-up: her or the game. "You know," she said, picking up the remote control of the TV set, "my dad spends half his life in front of the tube. If it isn't college basketball, it's football. Then, of course, there's golf and tennis and wrestling. But none of us ever minded."

Jeff looked at her sheepishly. "We *could* check the score. It's the Gents and the Islanders tonight. Channel two," he added, his voice trailing away.

Watching the game with Jeff, and listening to his rather colorful commentary, Lucy couldn't remember having so much fun in a long time. She got to cheering along with him, "Go, go, go!" And putting her face in her hands when the Gents' goalie let one through. There was microwave popcorn and beer for dinner, and Jeff's arm around her shoulder when they propped their feet up on his coffee table. There were kisses on her cheek, and intimate caresses on her neck, and his fingers entwined with hers. There was the crackling fire in the fireplace, and the snow whipping against the windowpanes. But there was never a mention of sex. Lucy knew it would come in its own time; for now they had this special closeness, the laughter and whispers and the meaningful meetings of their eyes. They were getting to know each other, slowly, with patience.

The Gents won. The TV clicked into blank silence. And Jeff turned to her. "I have to tell you something," he began, his solemn tone belying the excitement in his gaze. "I talked to the guy who threw those games."

"Oh, Jeff..."

"I'm afraid I did a little more than *talk* to him, but what the hay? The point is," Jeff said, "I think he's scared. He's young, and I think I've got him believing that if he admits what he did and soon, he can save his career."

"But what if he doesn't?"

Jeff frowned. "I'll have to take what I've got to the commissioner myself, maybe even the newspapers. There'll be quite a ruckus."

"I hate to see you go through this," she said softly. "All the publicity."

"Me, too. But I've run out of options. I only hope this kid sees the light and turns himself in."

"Will the press know? I mean, will you be cleared with the public?"

He shrugged. "I don't know how it'll come down. The way I look at it, the commissioner can always give the coaching staff at Denver University a call on my behalf. It's gotta help."

"Oh, it will," she said, her voice encouraging and hopeful as he reached over and touched her cheek with a finger. She felt a warmth spread in her belly, and half closed her eyes, sighing. "I wonder," she said after a time.

"What do you wonder, Miss Lucy Hammond?"

"Oh, who got to that kid, you know, with money to throw those games."

"Could have been any number of people," Jeff remarked. "A betting syndicate out of Las Vegas, somebody from Los Angeles." He shrugged. "Could have been a local bettor. A wealthy guy who wanted to line his pockets some more. There're several who hang around the Gents."

"But will the man, or men," she asked, "be exposed, too?"

"If this kid comes clean, probably. I've even been thinking of one guy in particular, this guy, Plassman."

"Rich Plassman, the cattleman? I know him," Lucy said. "He buys a lot of art around town for charity auctions, that kind of stuff. Throws his money around. He's on a real power trip."

"Like I said," Jeff put in, "it could be any number of people."

"I wouldn't put it past him, though," she said, and they snuggled up against each other contentedly. She listened to the beating of his heart through his shirt for a time, happy, relaxed, warm inside.

"Lucy," he began, "you don't know what it did to me seeing you here today. I was so afraid that you'd only come to tell me something about the money or the D.A. . . . I never dreamed . . ."

"I know," she whispered.

"Is it really . . . okay with Roy? I mean, he knows it's not another man . . . me?"

She nodded. "But I can't promise he won't be hurt," she said softly, "when he finds out."

"He won't like it," Jeff said to himself.

"Jeff," she asked hesitantly, "can we...can we be together and not feel bad about Roy?" She knew his reply was going to mean a lot, possibly their future. She held her breath.

But Jeff said nothing. Instead he answered her by moving closer, by pulling her to him gently. "We'll make it work," he murmured against her lips as his tongue traced a path across her teeth, forcing her mouth open until he was kissing her harder, searching, probing, pressing her to him with urgent need.

He felt so good, so *right*. She shivered in anticipation when he pulled her big sweater over her head and tossed it aside, his hand returning to slip up beneath her turtleneck and cup a breast warmly.

"I feel like a kid let out of school," he said, breathing against the heavy pulse at her throat. "I can't believe I'm this lucky. Pinch me, will you, Lucy?" His head lowered to kiss her breasts as he fiddled with the snap on her blue jeans. "Come on," he said, giving up and pulling her to her feet, "my bed's already unmade," he teased softly.

They moved into his room silently, savoring the moments, then stood apart and took off their clothes, with only the glow from the living room illuminating them. Then Jeff stepped toward her and took a deep breath as his hands touched her shoulders and moved down her arms to brush her hips. He took her buttocks in his hands tenderly, and brought her up against him until she could feel his hardness pressed to her belly.

"Oh, Jeff," she whispered as her breath caught in her throat. "Oh, God, Jeff, you feel so good to me."

They slid beneath the sheets, and he ran his hands over her naked flesh while he kissed her, plunging his tongue deep into her mouth. She felt her body ready-ing itself, moving against his hands, her pulse begin-ning to quicken as physical need took hold of her.

He kissed her long and deep, then trailed his warm lips across the bridge of her nose, her forehead, her earlobes. The sensation of his tongue at her ear sent rippling shock waves down her side and into her hip that tingled until she giggled against his chest, nuz-zling him, half-delirious with her need.

Lucy gripped his shoulders when he lowered his head and kissed her breasts, each in turn, circling the nip-ples with his tongue, savoring the stiff peaks until she twisted beneath him, a red-hot flush spreading and throbbing deep inside her. "Oh, wow," she whis-pered, her breathing ragged, "oh, Jeff... you're driv-ing me crazy."

"Good," he answered, drawing his mouth across the flesh of her belly, "I want to do this to you all night. Can I love you all night?"

"Yes," she breathed as he positioned himself be-tween her thighs and that beautiful, long male part moved against her, searching, pressing, sliding in and upward until she was blissfully filled with him, rising to meet his movements, his gentle and persistent thrusts.

Lucy felt every nerve ending in her body respond-ing, twitching, yearning. She released herself to the moment, riding the sensations, climbing, reaching out as if to grasp the unattainable, falling back, then reaching out harder, straining with her body.

She began to feel her belly, of its own accord, em-bracing him, sending forth its own cry, begging for release. Meeting him thrust for thrust, she arched her back and moaned against his mouth, turning her head, gasping for air as her need mounted to an unbearable pitch before she cried out suddenly, her eyes meeting his at the moment of climax. Above her Jeff, too, was shuddering, his hands gripping her hips, digging into her until finally they collapsed together, panting and perspiring, holding each other close, laughing gently, happily, into the darkness.

Later they talked about Lucy's work and about Jeff's new hopes for the future. She felt wholly content, joyous. Before tonight, she wouldn't have thought such peace in her heart and mind was possible. Jeff had done this for her, and she felt a love so deep for him at that moment it was actually a physical pain.

"I'll talk to Roy," he was saying against her shoulder as his fingers moved lovingly through her hair. "He's got to know. And I think, Luce," he said, "that in time Roy will be as happy for us as I am."

"In time," she said, and knew a small ache that she guessed would be there for a while. Roy had been special, she thought; he always would be.

"What are you thinking?"

She smiled and turned her face to him. "I'm thinking about us. I'm thinking that for the first time in my life love isn't so fragile."

"What is it, then?"

"It's as sturdy as a rock," she replied.

He kissed her softly, then lay back. "It is for me, too. I can't believe this, Lucy. I can't believe how happy I am."

They slept, and they awakened, and Jeff made love to her again, slowly and patiently. They had all the time in the world now.

CHAPTER SEVENTEEN

LUCY LOOKED AT THE DIGITAL CLOCK in her room through drowsy eyes. Three o'clock. In the afternoon. She couldn't remember the last time she'd slept half the day away.

She rolled over dreamily, contentedly, and thought about last night and about sneaking into her apartment building just as the morning papers were being delivered. She hugged her quilt to her chin and giggled.

How many times, she wondered, blushing, had she and Jeff made love? Three, she thought, not counting all the caresses and teasing touches. Amazing. She'd thought those nights were only for the movies or books; no one could make love all night.

Oh, how they'd talked, too, whispering into the darkness, sharing their dreams, their hopes, admitting their fears.

"You don't think I'm after your money, do you, Luce?" he'd asked, dead serious.

And she'd been able to tell him truthfully that for the first time in her life she knew in her heart that someone loved her for herself. "It's the best feeling I've ever had," she'd told him.

He'd been firm, insisting that he never wanted to feel kept by her and that he was always going to foot the bills. Lucy would just have to live his life-style, and if he made it big coaching, then so be it. If he flopped, she'd have to go along for that ride, too.

"In case you didn't notice," she said, "I don't live extravagantly. The foundation pays for my plane, but it's work related, and as much as I travel, it's cheaper than commercial airlines. All my money has allowed me to do is choose my own career."

Yes, they'd talked, she remembered, and laughed and touched and loved. And Jeff had been so forthright, so unrestrained; he'd even asked her for one small favor, and if the Hammond Foundation couldn't do it, then he'd find funding elsewhere.

"I've always dreamed of starting a city-wide hockey league for kids who can't afford the equipment and ice time," he'd said. "Of course, I'd coach for free, and so will some of the other guys who play with the Gents. But starting up... Luce, do you think the foundation could help?"

She'd kissed him and laughed and remembered the other requests she'd had from men in the past for money: the speedboats, the race car, the condo on Nassau. Never had she been asked for something totally unselfish.

"What's so funny?"

Shyly she told him, and Jeff had been astounded that she'd even dated the creeps. "Maybe," he'd said, *"I'm* asking too much."

Recalling his openness, his caring, his warmth, Lucy knew that she'd never love this way again—there was only Jeff, for now and for always.

She showered and dressed and looked out her window toward the Rockies, where the storm was finally breaking up. Long shafts of pale winter sunlight lay on the mountainsides and white peaks to the west. She fixed tea and drank some, but her stomach was ridiculously unsettled, churning with butterflies. What a wonderful feeling, Lucy thought, being hopelessly, madly in love.

I wonder what Jeff's doing? She decided to call him, to say good morning, no, good afternoon.

Lucy dialed his number as she settled back with her cup of tea. She felt silly and girlish, unable to wipe the smile off her lips. If her parents could see her, they'd think she'd gone crazy. *Ain't love grand?*

Jeff answered on the third ring.

"Hi," Lucy said, "did I wake you?"

"No way. I've been up since noon."

"You sound, well, strange. Is everything . . . ?"

"Things are perfect," he said, "in fact, I can't believe it, Lucy, I had a call this afternoon . . . from the hockey commissioner."

"Oh, Jeff!" she cried, sitting up straight. "Did the kid turn himself in?"

"Right you are. I can't believe it. I guess he's going to have to go through some heavy stuff. A suspension, a closed hearing. Anyway, that's his tough luck. Hell, he just about destroyed me. The point is," he said excitedly, "they're going to do everything possible to clear my name."

"With the press and everything?"

"Yes. And I bet I'll have that coaching job sewn up before the semester is out."

"I'm so happy for you, Jeff," she said, her heart filling with love.

"I am, too," he admitted. "I feel kind of sorry for McClosky, though, but he's an ace player. He'll spring back."

"I'm glad. But I'm happiest for you."

"There's another thing," Jeff said. "I hate to always be right, but apparently Plassman is the one who got to him."

"How did you know? Amazing!"

"Instinct, pilgrim," he said, affecting a John Wayne drawl.

"Oh, stop it, Jeff. What will happen to Plassman?"

"I suppose there'll be a grand jury investigation here in Denver, and maybe he'll get charged with a crime if the authorities can prove he paid off McClosky."

"Well, I'm sure he didn't write the kid a personal check."

"You'd be surprised. I think they'll nail him."

"I *hope* they do."

"Say," Jeff said, his voice deep and tender, "want to come over?"

"Now?"

"No time like the present. And dress up, Lucy. I'll take you out to celebrate."

"I've got a better idea," she said. "The basketball team at our Colfax house has a big game tonight. Let me take you. I'll even buy the hot dogs."

"You really want to spend your evening at a game? No lamb or steak or chateaubriand for two?" he teased.

"There's nothing I'd rather do."

"Okay. Should I come and get you?"

She thought a minute. "No, I'll pick you up. I've got to stop by my folks' for a bit anyway, and you're not far from them. Say an hour?"

"An hour it is. And Lucy... I love you. God, how I love you."

All the way over to her parents' house she drove the slushy streets of Denver with Jeff's words singing in her head. What an utter, blind fool she'd been to think that what she'd had with Roy was love. How could she have calculatingly made a decision about something that had to come naturally, that was actually a gift? But that was over—thank heavens—and a bright future awaited her.

She wanted to tell her parents about Jeff; in fact, she was bursting with the news, but she thought she'd wait, let them see how happy she was first, get used to the idea. She was hardly used to it herself!

Her father was in his study, going over railroad stock quarterlies and dividend disbursements. "Hi, kid," he said, looking up. "Well, don't you look cheery today."

"It's a great day, Dad," she said, handing him some paperwork on the new orphanage in Yaxcaba. "Can you look this over for me sometime soon? I want to make sure I'm not missing anything."

"Sure."

"Where's Mom?"

"Out spending my money," he commented, then took off his glasses and gazed at her. "Lucy," he said after a moment, "you really *do* look ready to pop. What's going on?"

She laughed, picking up her purse and heading out. "My secret, Dad. I'll tell you all in a day or so, maybe at dinner."

"I'll be waiting with bated breath," he said dryly and went back to his work.

They'd love Jeff, Lucy knew, once they got used to the idea. Oh, at first her folks would say it was too sudden. But how could they fail to come around?

She crossed town using the Sixth Avenue Freeway and turned off at Lakewood. The snowplows were out, making it slow going, but the late afternoon sun sat on her shoulder warmly, and somehow even the traffic delays didn't bother her. Amazing how rosy the world was when you were in love.

Jeff's flashy red Corvette was in the driveway when she pulled in. And of course there was his Windsurfer and motorcycle, the snow melting off the tarp and falling to the ground in big, wet clumps. Maybe now, Lucy thought, he'd get that job and be able to afford his toys. But when they had kids, Jeff would have to tighten his belt. Kids. Marriage and a home—this house?—and tricycles on the lawn. A swing set. It promised to be a busy life with Jeff, but a beautifully full one. She wondered idly when they'd set the date— It would be a big wedding. She wanted all her friends and all her parents' friends to see how lucky she was. Jeff would just have to live through the rigamarole— men hated it, but too bad.

Of course, he hadn't asked her yet, but that would come. Lucy stepped through the slush, stamping her boots on his doormat, then rang the bell. It *was* a nice house, a good neighborhood. She wouldn't mind living here at all.

She rang the bell once more, shifting impatiently from foot to foot, anxious to be swept up into those arms and kissed.

Finally she tried the knob. He wouldn't mind. Surprisingly it turned and the door cracked open. Jeff was probably showering. Should she scare him? No, that was too mean. But she *could* take another shower.

"Jeff," Lucy called, pushing the door open. "Jeff."

But there was no answer. He must be in the shower. She closed the door behind her and took off her wet boots, putting them in a corner of the mud room, hanging up her coat on a peg. She was longing to see him again, her stomach leaping about madly. If she hadn't been so love-crazy blind, Lucy would think later, she might have noticed the red smear on the white wall right next to her hand.

"Jeff," she called one last time. It really was kind of rude to walk right in.

At first she chalked up the disarray in the living room to good old Zany's bachelor habits. She even smiled to herself, half listening for the sound of running water in the bathroom while she picked up a stack of scattered magazines.

"What a mess," Lucy muttered, shaking her head, and that was when the overturned lamp caught her eye. She stared at it for a moment, her head cocked curiously. And the curtain behind the television set... Had it been pulled off a bunch of hooks like that last night?

Lucy stood in the middle of the floor, a magazine still held in her hand, and she realized simultaneously that the house was dead silent and that at her feet were dark spots, as if someone had dripped paint from a brush.

She saw everything that was out of kilter all at once, and her breathing became hollow as an alarm sounded in her brain. The trophies were knocked over; the coffee table sat askew; the ashtray was upside down on the floor. Coupled with the overturned lamp and torn curtain—and God, those drops on the floor...

"Jeff!" she cried, breaking into a run, banging open his bedroom door, frantically looking into the bathroom. "Jeff!" She spun around, circling in one spot helplessly, panic coiling in her breast like a serpent ready to strike.

It took her long minutes to get a grip on herself, to try to sort out in her mind the possibilities. *Be logical,* she told herself, *don't go jumping to any conclusions.* But panic crouched inside her.

What *were* the possibilities? She sat in his living room, stiff backed and trembling, and tried desperately to think.

The hockey player who'd taken money to throw those games. McClosky, that was his name. Perhaps he'd come over, furious, scared, and he and Jeff had fought. Where was Jeff now? The police station? Of course, Lucy told herself, there were always those men in dark suits who'd followed them across Mexico...

They'd murdered Tom, she thought abruptly, a hand going to her throat. Could they have followed them all the way to Denver? Did they still think Jeff had that money?

Dear God.

Lucy gazed around at the clutter again, not wanting to believe it was real. She wished she could blink and it would all go away. She found herself staring at those drying, red droplets on the beige carpet, and the panic welled up inside her with ferocity.

A half hour later she felt no better. She'd called the local police, carefully not mentioning anything about the Mexican episode, but they'd had no reports of a disturbance at Jeffrey Zanicek's home. They'd send a car if she needed one. But she didn't know what they could do.

She'd tried the local hospitals, too. But there had been no emergency check-ins fitting Jeff's description that afternoon. She hated the feeling that there wasn't anything she could do. Surely if Jeff was okay, he would call her. But he might be trying to get her at home. Of course! He wouldn't think she'd just walk into his house.

Lucy drove back across town like an Indy 500 driver, never even stopping to worry about getting a speeding ticket. She could almost hear her phone, ringing off the hook, Jeff trying and trying to reach her to tell her everything was fine. He'd explain; it would all be so logical, and later they'd laugh at her ridiculous suspicions. She almost felt relieved.

But eight o'clock rolled around with agonizing slowness, and nine. Nine-thirty. She wanted desperately to call a few more hospitals, but each time she reached for the phone she stopped. Jeff might be trying to reach her.

Nine forty-five. Ten o'clock.

She was frantic.

At 10:07, when the shrill ringing began, she nearly leaped out of her skin. Jeff!

"Hello," Lucy said breathlessly, "Jeff..."

"Listen carefully" came a strange male voice, muffled and sounding far away.

"What...?"

"Just shut up and listen, Miss Hammond, and your boyfriend won't get hurt." Lucy gripped the receiver as all the blood drained from her face. "You're to bring that half a million to Houston," the voice said. "Fly it there yourself, lady, first thing in the morning. Now get a pencil and write down this number." She did, her hands trembling, her voice lost. "Outside the main terminal at the airport is a row of pay phones. Look for the number 555-0100, you got that?"

"Yes," she whispered in a strangled voice.

"Be there at six p.m., lady, with the money."

"But I don't have it!" Lucy managed to stammer.

"Oh, Miss Hammond, don't try to jerk us around. You can get it. You'd *better* get it, lady, or your pal here—"

"Jeff! Oh, God, is he all right? Let me speak to him! Please!"

"Forget it" came the gruff reply.

"You have to," she managed to say. "How do I know you haven't . . . already . . . hurt him?"

There was a pause, a clinking, as if the phone had been put down onto something metal. Then a voice. "Luce?" *Was that Jeff?* "Luce . . . I don't feel so good . . ." The voice faded.

"Jeff, what have they done to you?"

"Don't come here," he said, but suddenly the other man was back on the line.

"Six o'clock, lady, and have the money. If you contact anyone, *anyone*, your lover here is dead." She heard the abrupt click of the phone as it was hung up, and then there was only the endless drone of the dial tone.

For the next few hours, time ceased to have any meaning for Lucy. A distant part of her knew she was in a state of shock, and the rest of her was unable to function. She had to pull out of this; she had to gather her wits and do everything humanly possible to save Jeff.

Houston, the man on the phone had said. *Dr. Dover's clinic is in Houston,* was all she could think. And the man's voice—pure Texas, totally American, no Mexican accent. The responsibility for getting the money back must have been transferred to Dover.

Should she call Harry Fields? Oh, Lord, no, she couldn't. They'd find out because he'd send the police, and they'd kill Jeff, just as they'd killed Tom without a qualm. She'd have to handle this herself.

The money, she thought, as she paced her floor like a restive cat; she had to get the money and quickly. She'd call her broker first thing in the morning and sell everything she owned. It could be done. It *had* to be done. There were enough railroad shares.

The FBI. Shouldn't she contact them? Wasn't this situation something they handled every day? But, then, people were so often killed, anyway.

God, what she wouldn't do to unload this ghastly burden onto someone—someone in authority. But that man had said she was to tell no one. If he found out somehow...

At three in the morning, she finally broke down and made one call. She telephoned Roy, because she was unable to bear the stress alone another minute. And Roy, she knew, would do nothing that could cause Jeff harm.

He was at her place by three-thirty. "Lucy," he said, coming straight in and tossing aside his coat, "what in God's name is going on?"

At least then she could cry. Through her sobs and tears she managed to tell him as much as she knew, while Roy held her and listened with a grim expression. It hadn't occurred to Lucy before, though, that by bringing Roy into this, she would have to tell him everything. She looked into his eyes for a moment, sniffed, then glanced down at her hands.

"Roy," she began, her tears spent, "there's something you have to know. This whole thing is more than just the money and...well, Jeff and I being the ones who were chased."

Roy sighed and moved away from her. "I have a feeling," he said, sitting down on her couch, "that I don't want to hear this."

"I'm sorry... I'm so sorry you have to find out like this...but Jeff and I, well..."

"Don't say it. Just don't say it."

"All right," she replied, softly, miserably, "but you have to know that there wasn't anything...nothing happened until after I talked to you."

"Shut up, Lucy, will you?"

But she couldn't. She couldn't let him believe a lie. "You have to listen," she said, her voice fierce, desperate. "I left you because we were wrong together, Roy! We were both using each other so calculatingly that—"

"My best friend," he said to himself. He laughed bitterly. "You two must have had a good chuckle in Houston when I got there."

"No. You're so wrong! Jeff never said a word . . . he never touched me. He cared about you too much."

"Drop it, will you?" Roy said, getting to his feet and going over to her window. He pulled the curtain aside and stared out across the lights of the city.

Somehow, exhausted, Lucy dozed on the couch until he shook her awake at seven. And then it was all business; she called her broker and arranged to pick up the cash in a briefcase at ten sharp in front of her bank, and Roy telephoned the airstrip to make sure Lucy's plane was serviced and fueled and ready to go by ten-thirty. They never spoke again about Jeff or even the fact that Roy was going with her; it was understood— but she could see the wounded look in his eyes, the pain, the betrayal. How could she have thought, even for a minute, that Roy would understand?

In time, Lucy hoped, *perhaps in time.*

CHAPTER EIGHTEEN

IT TOOK EVERY OUNCE OF COURAGE Lucy possessed to make that flight to Houston. She even marveled at herself for being able to fly at all, likening it in her head to a woman whose child was pinned under a car and who somehow, by some miracle, was able to lift that car.

Roy was preoccupied. He spoke little, only helping Lucy with her map and flight plans. She longed to talk about Jeff, to voice her worst fears, but Roy was gone somewhere from her, caught up in his own dark troubles.

He did say once, as they skirted the Dallas area, that he honestly believed they should contact the FBI the minute they touched down in Houston.

"No," Lucy said adamantly. "They said I'm not to tell *anyone*."

"You told me."

She looked over at him for a long moment. "I couldn't stand it, feeling so alone, so terrified."

"Okay," Roy said, "I can understand your reluctance, but it's Jeff's life we're dealing with here, and I'm betting the minute you hand over that briefcase both Jeff and you...." He hesitated. "They'll kill you, Lucy. They'll have to."

She took a deep breath. "I've been thinking of nothing else since we took off, Roy, but I've got to risk it."

He swore. "Look," he said, "there's something else we haven't considered. You told me the man on the phone had an American accent."

"That's right."

"So there's really only one possible assumption," Roy went on. "That it's either this doctor, whatever his name is—"

"Dover."

"That's right, or a henchman of his, who's got Jeff. Why else Houston, Lucy?"

"I already know that," she said.

"And this Dover character has to assume that you're going to figure it out."

"Probably."

"So, Lucy, do you think he can afford to just let the two of you go?"

Of course Roy was right. She'd been thinking of nothing else, in fact. But there had to be a way, *some* way, to get them both out of this safe and sound.

They landed in Houston at five-thirty, with just enough time to park the plane and rush to the main terminal. Roy carried the briefcase, keeping pace with Lucy, still trying to convince her to call in the authorities.

"No," she kept saying, "don't you read about how the FBI botch up kidnappings whenever they're involved?"

"That's in the movies, Lucy."

"It's *real*," she insisted, hurrying through the doors to the terminal.

"God, you make me mad" was all Roy said.

They found the phone booth with minutes to spare, then had to stand there keeping it open, ticking off the time, silent in their anxiety.

"I'd better make sure I tell that man I want to see Jeff before he gets this briefcase," Lucy said, half to herself, her heart beating uncomfortably against her ribs.

"I think I'd better go along with you," Roy said.

"No. If they see you... I'll take a cab."

"Insist that you make the exchange in an open place with people around. Promise you'll do that much, at least."

"Okay, sure," she said, feeling sweat pop out on her brow as she stared at the ominous black phone.

At exactly six o'clock it rang. Taking a deep breath, Lucy stepped into the enclosure and picked up the receiver.

"Good" came the same voice. "You're doing fine. You got the money?"

"Yes," Lucy answered unsteadily. "Is Jeff... is he all right?"

"So far he is, lady. Now I want you to take a cab to the corner of—"

"Wait," Lucy said, trying to overcome her fear. "I'll only do this exchange in a place that's got people around. A big, open place."

"No."

"*Yes*," she insisted. "You want this briefcase or not?"

Silence.

"I don't trust you," she went on, controlling the shaking in her voice. "And I want to get Jeff back *before* I leave the money."

There was nothing on the other end of the line for too long. Finally, mercifully, he gave her the name of a shopping mall at the west end of Houston. "Be at the north entrance," he instructed, "at eight. There's a fountain and a fast-food place. Be there, lady, or your pal's history. And no cops. If I even *think* you're not alone, that's it.''

"How do we make the exchange?" Lucy asked, pressing, afraid he already had a trick up his sleeve.

"Just be there" was all she heard before the line went dead. Slowly wiping the perspiration from her hairline, she turned to Roy.

"Well?"

"It's at a mall. At eight," she said.

"*Which* mall?"

"It's called the Westend Shopping Center. There's a fast-food place, a fountain."

"And how," Roy said, a stern look on his face, "is the exchange to be made?"

Lucy shrugged, afraid. "He wouldn't tell me."

"Hell. You know why, don't you? It's because they'll grab you before you even get near the entrance. It'll be dark. Lucy, you can't do this!"

She listened, disbelieving, yet the panic mounted as his words sank in. "Oh, God," she whispered, "Jeff."

"He'll be nowhere around," Roy said in a careful voice. "You told me he sounded drugged. My bet is that he's being held at this Dover's clinic or something, drugged, whatever. Lucy," Roy went on, "you have to call the FBI. It's the only way."

The words caught in her throat. "No," she finally got out, "I can't—" But before she was even finished, before a single idea of how they were going to save Jeff even occurred to her, Roy was snatching up the telephone book.

"If you won't call them, I will!" he said roughly.

Lucy knew in a sudden flash what she had to do. It came to her with shocking clarity. She looked at Roy's back, which was turned to her, and at her watch. Carefully picking up the briefcase, she stole silently away, the night shadows beckoning and, finally, mercifully, swallowing her.

THE CABDRIVER turned in his seat and eyed Lucy. "So, where to, lady?"

Good Lord. "I don't know the address," she said, her nerves so raw they felt like pins pricking her from the inside out. "It's a clinic, Malcolm Dover's clinic. It's very famous."

"Swell. Tell you what, lady," he said, "Houston's a big place. Maybe we oughta stop and look in a phone book."

"Fine, anything, just drive, please." She glanced out the back window automatically, even though she was sure Roy hadn't seen her get into this cab. No Roy, only the long airport terminal, growing smaller by the second now.

Lucy was positive the driver could find the clinic, but she wasn't sure what she'd do once they got there. What if Jeff wasn't being held there? What would happen if that man on the phone really did bring Jeff to the Westend Mall and she wasn't there?

But Jeff had to be at Dover's clinic. He'd definitely sounded drugged when she'd spoken to him for that brief minute. And the man, most likely *men*, holding Jeff had been Americans. It had to be Dover. And where better to hide a kidnap victim than in a clinic, where private rooms and drugs were readily available?

She looked at her watch. It was already well past six. When that man on the phone got to the shopping mall and realized Lucy had double-crossed him, he would telephone the clinic immediately, warn someone, maybe even get rid of the evidence—Jeff? Oh, dear God! But worse, Roy was really calling in the FBI.

Surely a team would rush to the mall, as well, and if the kidnapper saw them . . .

Renewed panic welled up in her breast as the cabbie pulled into a gas station and went to a phone booth to look up the address of Dover's clinic.

Hurry, Lucy thought, *hurry!*

"It's clear on the other side of the city," the cabbie told her. "Gonna cost you plenty, lady."

"You get me there quick and I'll double whatever the meter says," she said, leaning forward in her seat urgently.

Houston was perhaps the most sprawling city in America. It ran in all directions for thirty or forty miles, a huge metropolitan expanse. Unfortunately, Dover's clinic was in the opposite direction from where she had landed.

It was dark now, the lights of the city flashing by as they sped from one freeway to another and yet another. To Lucy's right ran a frontage highway that was lined for miles and miles with fast-food joints and used-car dealerships, with giant furniture outlets and motels. Mile after mile of them.

She wondered what kind of security she'd find at the clinic. It wasn't as if it were a prison, but she had a feeling it was a very private place just from the things Andy Martin had told her. And what was Malcolm Dover like? An egomaniac? A madman who thought he was going to save the world from a dreaded disease, and who had chosen to ignore the law?

It *had* to be Dover holding Jeff. He wanted his five hundred thousand back, the money his caretaker on Cozumel had been planning on stealing. It all made sense. Dover had probably received his drugs from that man, Morales, who worked for the drug company in Mexico City, but Dover still owed him the half million. In Mexico, she thought, it had been Morales's men who had chased them and murdered Tom. But now Dover had obviously taken over.

"Couple of more miles," the driver told her, and Lucy's stomach lurched. What *was* she planning on doing? Storming the place like a one-woman SWAT team? Casing the grounds or something? Calling in the police? Had Roy been right all along? Oh, God . . .

It crossed Lucy's mind that she might not be doing this at all if the person involved was anyone other than Jeff. Would she rush into this dangerous situation on Roy's behalf? She hoped she had enough guts to do this for Roy or someone else, but she wondered.

They left the main highway and were immediately enfolded by dark, uninhabited marshland. Only occasionally did they pass a house or farm as the driver made his way deeper into the countryside. Finally he turned off the narrow road, past a long stand of bare trees, onto a curving dirt tract that had a small sign reading Old Bay Road.

Lucy leaned forward anxiously. "Are you sure this is the place?" she asked. They seemed to be a hundred miles from civilization—was the driver lost? And it was getting late. That man would be waiting at the Westend Mall . . .

"I think this is it, lady. I used to know these parts, had a brother out here on a farm back in the sixties."

"How far up do you think this clinic is?" she asked.

"Road's not real long. Half mile up is a reservoir, as I recall."

"Stop then. Right here," she said suddenly.

"Here? You nuts, lady? It's pitch-black out."

"Just stop. Please."

He did. And she paid him, as promised, twice what the meter read. "Listen," he said, "you in some kind of trouble or something?"

"Oh, no. I want to surprise someone," she said.

The fear that had been lurking just at the edge of her consciousness began to seep through Lucy as she started to walk down the narrow, rutted country road. It was so dark out, not even a star showing, that several times she stumbled, landing on her knees once. What if the cabdriver was wrong? She could be miles from the clinic. The man on the phone would be getting to that mall any second now. And maybe the clinic wasn't even on this road at all!

Tall trees, their bare limbs twisting into the black sky, rose on either side of the road like silent guards, as she made her way. There was a system of one-lane wooden bridges spanning a swampy waterway that Lucy had to cross, but up ahead she could see the glow of lights. Yes, around the next bend there was a luminescence that brightened as she hurried on.

Oh, yes, thank heavens, it was the clinic! Dover's establishment was a two-story structure reminiscent of the Old South, and it was surrounded by a tall fence. She wondered why. To keep the patients in; to keep intruders out? And how was *she* going to sneak in?

Using tree trunks as cover, ducking behind the fat pines that ran nearly to the metal fence, Lucy surveyed the place. She could see no guard, but surely there was a night watchman, or orderlies somewhere, who sat around a lounge, smoking and watching late-night TV. Were there dogs? Security cameras around the fence? She had to think of all the possibilities. And somehow she had to get over that eight-foot fence, get inside and find Jeff.

There was an awful notion, as well, beating at her head: he might not even be there at all. If he was, Lucy guessed, certainly he was being drugged or even guarded constantly—but she'd worry about that when she got inside. *If* she got inside.

She edged around the fenced perimeter until she found a tree that had low limbs and was within a few feet of the barrier. If she could get up to that branch...

Climbing the tree was easy. She'd taken off her coat, left her purse at the base of the trunk and pulled herself up. But from eight feet high, the ground suddenly looked awfully far down, and the limb wasn't nearly as close to the fence as she'd first thought. God, if she missed or jumped short, she'd impale herself! And even if she made it over, she'd probably break a leg or knock herself out.

She stood on the twisted limb, held on to a branch above her and felt her knees shake. One, two, three! She leaped with everything in her, feeling herself fly, her pant leg catching on the top of a fence post; then she was tumbling, falling, *thump*, hitting hard and rolling like a ball. For several minutes she lay on the cold, hard ground in a heap, mentally feeling her body parts, gauging the damage, hearing her breath whistle in her chest.

You're okay. Calm down. Get your wind. Her right leg hurt a little bit, though, and she guessed her thigh had absorbed most of the impact. But she'd be fine. It was Jeff she had to concentrate on.

Lucy wasn't sure when she first heard the sound of pads on the wooden porch of the clinic—shuffling, scratching feet. A dog. Two of them. Dobermans? German shepherds? Had someone heard her, or was this normal procedure, time to let the pooch out? She lay there, invisible in the shadows, her chest feeling hollow. But invisibility wasn't going to do her a darn bit of good around a dog.

There was lawn between the fence and the clinic. And a couple of trees, too, but reaching them meant exposing herself to the lights from the porch. Suddenly it seemed as bright out as day. And how long would it be before the dogs caught her scent?

She made it to the first tree and crouched there, breathing hard, straining her eyes through the darkness, her heart pounding. How was she going to get closer? And if she did manage to, how was she going to get in?

Don't panic, she told herself, *think of Jeff.*

A stirring in the night caught her eye then. Her head swiveled; her heart leaped. There, in the shrubs at the side of the building. A white shadow, like a ghost, and it was moving.

Simultaneously she heard the scrape of paws on the porch and a growl. A door opened, and a man's voice said, "Will you mutts shut up? Hey, Fred, go see what those dogs are up to." Another man's voice. "Come here, you useless mutts, come!" The man's footsteps sounded on the porch, then came the whine of a dog, the rattle of a chain.

The next few seconds were chaos.

She saw the white wraith move, swaying, and the dogs threw themselves against their chains and began to bark furiously.

"Turn on the floodlights!" one of the men called, and abruptly the area was bathed in blinding light, illuminating a figure.

The ghost was a man, yes, a man in a white hospital gown, and he was stumbling, lurching. Something was wrong with him—he couldn't seem to run. The figure staggered out into the dazzling light, and Lucy gasped. It was Jeff! Oh, God, it was Jeff!

The dogs were snarling; the men were shouting. Doors banged. Lucy broke cover like a deer darting from the woods and raced toward Jeff. She reached him just as he fell, his hospital gown flapping.

"Jeff!" she cried, frantic, pulling at him, trying to drag him to his feet, breathless. "Jeff! We have to run! Hurry!"

"Luce," he mumbled, clinging to her, swaying. "They drugged me, Luce."

"Run, Jeff, run!"

The gate was closed, and it looked as if it were miles away across the wide open, floodlit lawn. Two orderlies were rounding the corner of the building, shouting, "Stop! Hold it there!" And in front of them, straining at their leashes, were the snarling dogs.

Jeff began to sag again. "Luce, I don't thing we're going to..." he said, slurring, and she was afraid, desperately afraid, that he was right.

CHAPTER NINETEEN

LUCY FELT JEFF'S HAND, and his fingers moved in between hers, warm and firm, secure. There was strong sun on her eyelids, and hot sand beneath her. She could hear the little wavelets lapping at the shore with contented gurgles as she drowsed. This was heaven, she thought, paradise.

"Want some suntan lotion on your shoulders?" she heard him ask. "Well? Hey, sleepy, wake up."

"I'm awake," she murmured, smiling but not opening her eyes. Lazily Lucy rolled over and felt his hand move to the small of her back in a loving caress.

"You're cooking," he said softly, and began to rub the lotion on her. She lay on the beach in front of the Cozumel Caribe Hotel like a purring feline resting in the sun. How good it felt to be there with Jeff, alone at last. She opened her eyes and squinted at the diamond on her finger—the unpretentious diamond Jeff had bought with his first paycheck from Denver University. It glittered with all the dazzling splendor of a rainbow in the tropical sun.

"You know, Roy was great at the wedding," she said, twisting her hand to catch the spectrum of color.

"He's a real pal." Jeff moved his hand to the back of her leg, rubbing the cream in, stroking her skin softly.

"Do you think it was terribly hard for him, being your best man, I mean?"

"Yes...and no. We had a good long talk over a few beers a couple of weeks after that mess at Dover's."

For a moment Lucy was going to ask the details of their discussion, but then she thought better of it. She herself had spoken to Roy only a few days before the wedding, and he'd been a dear. He'd also shown up at the affair with a date, she remembered.

"A friend's a friend," Jeff was saying, "through thick and thin."

"He was a lifesaver," Lucy replied. "I'll never forget hearing those sirens that night, and there was Roy with the FBI."

"*You'll* never forget it."

She smiled and stifled a giggle. "You looked so funny in that hospital gown."

"Oh, yeah? And would you have been any happier if I'd stayed in that room and let them drug me some more?"

"Of course not. But did you really think you were going to get away after climbing through that storeroom window?"

"As far as you were going to get by climbing in," he quipped. "Lucy, the white knight."

"Knightress."

"There's no such word."

"There should be."

Jeff pushed aside the hair at the back of her neck and massaged the tender white skin with the cream. "I don't know, Luce," he said after a while. "If I were Roy, I'd have been so jealous of you I might not have called in the feds that night. I might have taken my chances that you'd be safe and let old Dover do what he wanted."

"Roy would never have done that. He...he loves us, *both* of us."

"He's a better man than I am then. Not that I don't love him. I do, you know. But you..." He kissed her sun-warmed shoulder. "You, I really love. I never knew, Luce, I never even dreamed."

"Me, neither." She rolled over finally and shaded her eyes with a hand. "I just wish we could stay here forever."

"*I* could stay," he said, propping his head on a hand as he stretched out beside her. "I don't have to be back in Denver until the start of next hockey season at D.U."

"Ah, but you have to start organizing your city league, remember?"

He nodded, his eyes resting on her.

"Are you really going to have time for both next winter?"

"Sure, I'm a great organizer when I need to be."

"Except in your house."

"*Our* house."

"'Our house,'" Lucy repeated, liking the sound of it. And as soon as the honeymoon was over she would move in with him. "Mrs. Jeffrey Zanicek," she said, musing. "For two whole days now. In a way," Lucy said, "I'm glad I found that money. If I hadn't... Well, I'd have flown home."

"But the minute I saw you with Roy for the first time, I would have fallen in love with you, Luce. Honest."

"When did you know?" she asked. "I mean, when did you really *know* it was love?"

"Oh, about ten seconds after we met."

"Be serious, Jeff!"

"Well, I guess it must have been when I saw you in that black thing, that nightgown," he said, smiling lazily.

"Jeff!"

The afternoon slid by. They swam and sunned and kissed each other shamelessly on the crowded beach. Lucy felt at times as if none of it were real, as if she'd open her eyes and find herself in her apartment in Denver, alone, maybe just waking up from a nap and a girlish dream. But it was real. The sand beneath her fingers was real, the hot spring sun overhead and Jeff was beside her.

And that caretaker of Dover's had been real, too, so real that he'd been killed for trying to double-cross both Morales's henchmen here in Cozumel and Dover up in Houston. He'd hidden the money in his room, evidently planning on avoiding Dover's beach house just in case the dark men caught on to him before he'd gotten off the island. But it hadn't worked out that way.

"You're frowning," Jeff said, rousing her. "What is it, Luce?"

"Just thinking. Thinking about Houston and the trial in September. You know, Dover and all that."

"I don't think Fields will ask you too many questions," Jeff said reassuringly.

"He'll put it to you, though," Lucy said. "He'll want you to tell the jury every last detail of the kidnapping."

"I don't remember much after Dover's three goons stuck me with the hypodermic needle. But," he said with a glint in his eye, "I did get a few good licks in before I passed out. I barely even remember the flight. It was a charter job, I think."

"I wish," Lucy said, "that it was all over. The Mexicans sure worked fast."

"They don't fool around down there. As soon as they were given Morales's name they got him and his thugs and they're behind bars for life. Swift justice."

"I hope they throw away the key," Lucy said, "for Tom's sake."

"They will. And Dover's going to get the same. There's the kidnapping and fraud, and use of a controlled substance.... Your father even told me that Andy Martin, that friend of his who was at Dover's clinic, is going to testify."

"Do you think planifolia will ever be legalized in the States?"

Jeff shook his head. "Not a chance. Since Dover was busted that night, the Federal Drug Administration has come out with tons of test results from the past few years. It flat out doesn't work."

"What a hoax," she said pensively. "And Dover would have gotten that money back from us, paid his debt to Morales and gone right on treating all those poor, unsuspecting souls with the drug."

"Yeah, well," Jeff said, "we stopped him, Luce. You and I." He gave her a big thumbs-up and winked. "We even saw to it that the half million is going to go to cancer research. Hey, maybe we ought to name our first kid, Malcolm Dover Zanicek. I mean, after all, if it hadn't been for the good doctor..."

Lucy chased him all the way into the water, and he even let her hold him under until he came up gasping and reaching for her, spanning her waist with his hands and tossing her. They played, and they swam, and they stood with their toes dug into the sandy bottom and clung to each other, their lips tasting cool and smooth and salty, their hands gliding along thighs and buttocks beneath the rippling surface.

"Let's go," Jeff said, breathing hard against her mouth.

"Go?" Lucy drew her tongue across his upper lip.

"To our room, Mrs. Zanicek."

Towels draped over their arms, they hurried along the flower-lined, winding path, holding hands. Lucy felt sunburned and sandy, languid with the heat and desire for the man beside her, her husband, her best friend, her knight on a white horse. She gave him a meaningful glance and squeezed his hand.

Inside the door of the honeymoon suite, Jeff tugged her around to face him and studied her wordlessly for a time. "I'm a lucky guy," he whispered. Lowering his head, he kissed her slowly and lingeringly.

Lucy put her hand to his cheek, stroking his smooth skin, feeling his lips move on hers. Her heart began to beat in that slow, expectant rhythm. Then his arms went around her waist and pulled her against him. She leaned back in his embrace and smiled up at him. "Shameful, aren't we?"

"Absolutely."

She cupped his face in her hands and drew his mouth down to hers again. "Um," she murmured against his lips.

He kissed her thoroughly, then shifted his attention to her neck, to the soft place above her breasts. Her hands roamed over his bare back, feeling the muscles move under his skin, adoring the sensations of their bodies touching, gliding together. He pushed one of her bathing-suit straps aside and put his lips to the white skin that had been under it. He did the same with the other strap. Lucy's hands moved aside the waistband of his bathing trunks and wiggled beneath the fabric, caressing the muscular roundness of his buttocks, digging into his flesh and drawing him closer.

"Savage," he whispered into her ear, tickling her, and she felt goose bumps rise all along her side down to her toes.

Her bathing suit slid off; he stepped out of his. She kneaded his back and felt the whole warm, strong length of him against her, crushing her breasts. There were few words between them. It was all murmurs and swift intakes of breath and hands stroking sun-fevered skin. She kissed his chest and strong back and breathed in his scent, deeply, sensuously. She felt his thighs, powerful and rough with curling blond hair, push against her legs. She moaned, wanting him right then, yet wanting to hold off the exquisite pleasure forever until neither of them could stand to wait another endless, panting moment.

They lay on the bed, locked together. His body lifted, smoothly, hotly, over hers, and she quivered with anticipation. They joined forcefully, and Lucy gasped with the eternal surprise of its glory. Her man, so different, so alien from her own femaleness, and yet he was the other half of her, the part that made her complete.

He filled her and withdrew and filled her again. She arched up, moaning unashamedly, her belly aching with pleasure and need. She held him to her, hard, breathing fast, her heartbeat quickening until she gasped. He was powerful above her; throbbing, she lost all sense of time and space, conscious only of being filled with his beauty and strength.

Jeff whispered in her ear, lifted her buttocks with his hands, and she almost screamed with the instant, piercing pleasure of it. "Hurry," she panted, and their rhythm became faster, uncontrolled.

She felt it coming and cried out, and he drove into her, abandoned, groaning with his own need. They shook together in a quivering intensity of sensation, as if they were one.

"Oh!" Lucy collapsed under him, damp with sweat, still breathing hard. He held her lightly with his strong hands, his chest heaving. "Oh, Jeff."

He rested on his elbows and bent his head to her lips once more. "'Oh,' yourself," he said, licking her neck, tasting the saltiness of her skin.

She took a deep breath and closed her eyes. She felt his finger trace the curve of her eyebrow and heard his voice murmur in her ear, "That was, my dear wife, like a tough shift against the Oilers."

Her eyes flew open. "Jeff!"

"Only kidding, Luce."

"The heck you are," she said.

He embraced her then and buried his face in her neck, laughing.

They lay like that for a long time, fingers entwined, as they dozed on and off, talked, touched each other.

"In the middle of the afternoon," Lucy said. "We're awful."

"Um, terrible." His hand cupped her breast, then moved on, tickling.

They got up at dusk, showered together and dressed.

"Maybe we should stay here," Jeff suggested, zipping up his pants.

"We have to eat."

"I guess so."

They had gulf shrimp and dark, tasty Mexican beer and held hands across the table. "This is perfect," Lucy breathed. "Here in paradise with my big, strong husband, my brilliant husband."

"Brilliant?"

She laughed. "Sure. Remember when you told me about that cattleman, Plassman, maybe paying McClosky off? Giving him a check?"

"Yeah, I said that."

"Well, I saw in the papers that Plassman's being indicted for *just* that. He actually wrote the kid a thirty thousand dollar check."

"Really? You know, I like that. Brilliant, you said. It's got a nice ring to it."

Dessert was skipped. They went back to their bungalow and closed the door behind them. They were safe and together, in the first bloom of love, without a care in the world.

Jeff yawned. "I'm sleepy," he announced. "Getting old, I guess."

He went into the bathroom, and Lucy could hear him turn the water on and begin brushing his teeth. He always hummed through the bubbles and gargled. She smiled to herself as she undressed, thinking she would hear him doing that for the rest of their lives.

Pulling on the T-shirt Jeff had given her, the extra large Denver Gents T-shirt in red and blue, she lay down on the bed, put her glasses on and idly picked up the magazine on the nightstand that advertised the activities available in Cozumel. She heard water splashing and Jeff gargling, and looked up from the page, smiling, loving him.

It caught her eye then, the crumpled brown paper bag underneath the dresser. She froze, her heart leaping in panic. *No, not again,* she thought. Then she lay back, laughing to herself. Jeff had put it there to tease her. Of course. It was just the sort of thing he'd do. She was dying to get up and look inside. There was probably something comical in it, something hilarious, knowing him, like an old jock strap or something.

"Very funny," she called out to Jeff.

"What?" He came out of the bathroom dressed only in a pair of jockey shorts, a yellow-and-green striped pair.

"Very funny, Zany," she repeated, pointing.

He bent over and looked. "What's that?" He sounded utterly innocent.

"A paper bag," she said calmly, not wanting to give him the pleasure of a reaction.

But he was already pulling the bag out from under the dresser and opening it, looking inside, looking at her.

"What is it?" she whispered, wide-eyed.

"Oh, Luce," he said, dead serious, his face frozen, "Oh, no...."

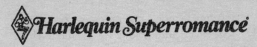
Harlequin Superromance

The elemental passions of *Spring Thunder*
come alive once again in the sequel. . . .

SUMMER LIGHTNING

by

SANDRA JAMES

You enjoyed Maggie Howard's strong fiery nature
in *Spring Thunder*. Now she's back in *Summer
Lightning*, determined to fight against the resump-
tion of logging in her small Oregon town. McBride
Lumber has caused nothing but grief for her in the
past. But when Jared McBride returns to head the
operation, Maggie finds that her greatest struggle is
with her heart.

Summer Lightning is Maggie Howard's story of
love. Coming in April.

SR335-1

COMING IN MARCH FROM

Harlequin
Superromance

**Book Two of the
Merriman County Trilogy
AFTER ALL THESE YEARS
the sizzle of Eve Gladstone's
One Hot Summer continues!**

Sarah Crewes is at it again, throwing Merriman County
into a tailspin with her archival diggings. In *One Hot
Summer* (September 1988) she discovered that the town
of Ramsey Falls was celebrating its tricentennial one
year too early.

Now she's found that Riveredge, the Creweses'
ancestral home and property, does not rightfully belong
to her family. Worse, the legitimate heir to Riveredge
may be none other than the disquieting Australian,
Tyler Lassiter.

Sarah's not sure why Tyler's in town, but she suspects
he is out to right some old wrongs—and some new
ones!

The unforgettable characters of *One Hot Summer* and
After All These Years will continue to delight you in
book three of the trilogy. Watch for *Wouldn't It Be
Lovely* in November 1989.

SR349-1

You'll flip . . . your pages won't!
Read paperbacks *hands-free* with

Book Mate • I

The perfect "mate" for all your romance paperbacks

Traveling • Vacationing • At Work • In Bed • Studying • Cooking • Eating

Perfect size for all standard paperbacks, this wonderful invention makes reading a pure pleasure! Ingenious design holds paperback books OPEN and FLAT so even wind can't ruffle pages – leaves your hands free to do other things. Reinforced, wipe-clean vinyl-covered holder flexes to let you turn pages without undoing the strap . . . supports paperbacks so well, they have the strength of hardcovers!

Pages turn WITHOUT opening the strap.

SEE-THROUGH STRAP

Reinforced back stays flat.

Built in bookmark

BOOK MARK

BACK COVER HOLDING STRIP

10˝ x 7¼˝, opened.
Snaps closed for easy carrying, too